Unlawful Games

Adam Klein

Baby Blue Publishing—Edison, NJ
Paperback ISBN: 979-8-9871604-0-4
Hardcover ISBN: 979-8-9871604-2-8
Library of Congress Control Number: 2022919400
Title: Unlawful Games
Author: Adam Klein
Digital distribution | 2022
Paperback | 2022
Hardcover | 2022

Cover design by David Ter-Avanesyan

This is a work of fiction. The characters, names, incidents, places, and dialogue are products of the author's imagination, and are not to be construed as real.

To my beautiful and loving wife, Jennifer. You are my rock and inspiration.

Part I

Chapter 1

*O*bjection! That is a word I had used so frequently, I often did not think of when and where I used it. The confused look on the innocent face of my six-year-old daughter told me I was not in the courtroom, but rather in the family room of my newly purchased home. I had never owned a home before, so it was understandable that I would object to my daughter's request of building an extension for a playroom.

"But Daddy, it would make me so happy, and I will never ask for anything ever again!" my daughter said enthusiastically.

"I know, angel, but—" I began to say, then stopped as I heard a loud scream from the other room.

"Honey, honey, come quick! You are on the news!" my wife said frantically.

As I ran into the living room where my hysterical wife was pressing the record button on the DVR, I heard the newscaster say, "It was a banner day yesterday for defense attorney Salvatore Amici as he worked his courtroom magic once more and was able to deliver an acquittal for his client, David Flores, today in Mid-Town Manhattan Community Court."

"Deliver an acquittal? More like came through in the clutch, or performed on an all-star level," I said jokingly.

"Oh, honey, just be proud of what you accomplished and forget what anyone else says or thinks," my wife said.

Danielle Amici was as loving, caring, and inspirational a woman as one will ever meet. We met by chance at a New York Yankees game in 2007 when she was just eighteen years old. She had attended the game with two of her best friends and was sitting in the row in front of me when a foul ball came hurtling toward her head. Before she could react, a brave, devastatingly handsome (I might add) man reached over her head and caught the ball with his bare hand. The sound the ball made crashing into my palm made her realize I had broken a finger or two, but she was so much in awe of my reaction that it took her a minute to say something to me. It was in that moment that she fell in love. Not so much by my bravery or willingness to break my fingers for her, but in the way I looked at and spoke to her. Fourteen years and two children later, I think Danielle is more in love with me now than ever before, if that's even possible.

"I am, but it was a bit more than just delivering an acquittal. David Flores was charged with two counts of assault and battery and destruction of property. To be able to acquit of all charges was a miracle!" I expressed.

"Daddy, what does bludgeon mean?" my daughter, Angela, asked innocently. I turned to look at Angela and wondered where she could have heard that word and realized the newscast was still on. I quickly grabbed the remote and changed the channel to Nickelodeon where SpongeBob SquarePants was frying up some Krabby Patties.

"It's an adult word, angel. Watch SpongeBob." At that moment, for some reason unbeknownst to me, I began to reflect on my family and how lucky I was to have them all in my life. Not only is my wife beautiful and devoted; she is an excellent mother and supporter of my career. My eleven-year-old son, Giovanni, is an energetic, curious little boy who has unlimited potential. He loves sports, especially baseball, which helps create our unbreakable father-son bond.

Angela is the sunshine of my life. She can cheer me up when I am down or bring me up even higher when I'm having a good day. She means everything to me, and I would do anything for her, which is why I felt so bad not answering her question like I always had.

"I'm sorry, Angela, but there are some things you are too young for, and this is one of them. I promise when you get older, I will explain that word to you, okay?"

"Okay, Daddy, I guess," Angela responded sadly.

Now that I felt better about not answering my daughter, my attention turned to how I was going to handle the newfound fame I would have at the firm. The guys and gals at the office are jokesters and would no doubt not let me live this down. What would it be? Toilet paper streamers around my desk? A photoshopped picture of me with the president? Or a request for an autograph as soon as I arrived at the office later in the morning? I contemplated taking a personal day to let things settle down first, but that is not my style. I have always been the hardest working person in the office, and I needed to push myself to maintain that title.

Once I decided to head into the office, I went to the kitchen to devour the delicious food Danielle was cooking. She was a fantastic cook and could take any ingredient and turn it into a gourmet meal. On this morning, she was making turkey bacon, scrambled eggs, French toast, and home fries. It sounds so simple, yet she prepared it in a way that still amazes me to this day. She set my plate down in front of me and began pouring my coffee while screaming for Giovanni to come downstairs.

"Gio, wake up! Come down for breakfast. Gio!" Giovanni could sleep through a thunderstorm that makes the house shake. He gets that from Danielle because I am the world's lightest sleeper. I could be deep in REM sleep and be touched on the shoulder in the slightest way, and I would wake up almost every time.

"Gio!" Danielle yelled again.

"I'll go get him. Just keep my breakfast warm."

When I stood to walk upstairs and wake my deep-sleeping son, the doorbell rang. Danielle said she would get it, so I continued up the stairs. Once I reached the top, I heard Danielle call me back downstairs, but something was off in her tone. I turned around and saw two gentlemen in designer suits standing on my front porch with very concerned looks on their faces. What they were about to tell me would change my life forever.

Chapter 2

As I approached the front door, I did not know what to expect. I knew it could not be good because they definitely looked like cops with an agenda. I approached the front door with both trepidation and fear.

"Good morning, gentlemen. What can I do for you?"

"Are you Salvatore Amici?" one of the suited men asked.

"Yes, I am. Who are you?"

"Detectives Blake and Rodriguez, sir," one of the men retorted.

"What is this in reference to?"

"May we come in for a moment, please?"

"First, tell me what this is in reference to," I said hastily.

"Sir, it is a delicate matter that would best be discussed in private," Detective Blake answered.

I was reluctant to let them in because I had no idea what could possibly have happened to have two NYPD detectives at my front door at seven thirty in the morning. However, I also knew that my interest was piqued, and they would not leave until they came into my house.

"I understand. Please, follow me."

Both detectives entered the house and immediately began to look around as if they were searching for something specific. It made me uneasy and highly suspicious if they were indeed detectives. In my line of work, I am always aware of being a target for just about anyone. I have been a defense attorney for six years and have defended both small-time and hard criminals. Some of my clients have been connected with some dangerous people, which always scared Danielle. She'd urge, "Don't let those people in our lives. Turn them down." I would have to remind her that "those people" are the ones who pay the bills, and the risk is worth the reward. Most of the cases I take on are petty theft or assault charges, with a few racketeering cases sprinkled in, but nothing more serious than that.

Once my paranoia subsided, I was able to refocus and concentrate on my unexpected guests.

"Can I see your identifications, please?" I asked.

"Sure thing, Mr. Amici," Detective Blake replied.

Both detectives took out their badges and handed them to me. I know what a NYPD detective badge looks like, and these badges were either impeccable replicas or they were the real thing.

"Thank you. You never can be too careful."

"We completely understand, Mr. Amici."

"Please, call me Sal. Now, what is this about?"

"Sal, you recently defended David Flores, is that correct?" Detective Blake asked.

Suddenly a knot formed in my stomach. I began to feel nauseated and dizzy. I had a feeling what was coming next, yet I did not want to hear it.

"Yes, why?"

"I'm sorry to have to tell you this, Sal, but David Flores was just arrested for the first-degree murders of both his wife and son."

I did not know what to think. How could this happen? David Flores was a violent person, yes, but murder? He was not capable of that. At least I thought he was not.

"What evidence do you have against him?" I asked quietly.

"Well, we are not at liberty to discuss that at the moment but—"

"Wait, wait, wait a minute. You come to my home at seven thirty in the morning to tell me that the man I helped set free eighteen hours ago just killed his wife and son, and then you have the nerve to tell me you can't discuss what evidence you have on him? What kind of bullshit is that?" I yelled.

"Please, Sal, calm down. I understand your frustration, but you of all people should understand that if I tell you, I am potentially jeopardizing the case we have to build against Mr. Flores," Detective Rodriguez answered calmly.

I knew he was right. I have used this same reasoning to defend clients in the past. Whether it was a matter of chain of custody, evidence tampering, or neglect to file paperwork, I was always looking for the procedure that was not followed. If Detectives Blake and Rodriguez told me the evidence they had on David Flores and something happened to that evidence or something similar, their case would be dead in the water, and I would be in heap of trouble as well.

"Very well. I do understand. Is he asking for me?"

"I do not know if he has asked for a lawyer yet. All he has said so far is, 'It's about fucking time.'"

I thanked the detectives for coming to tell me personally and showed them to the door. They both gave me their card and asked that I contact them if I had any further information or if I went to visit David Flores in jail. When I closed the door, I went into a daze and lost all sense of where I was and what was going on. I must not have hidden it well because Danielle came up to me asking what was wrong. She had a concerned look on her face, one that should have prompted me to tell her what happened and reassure her that our family is okay. Instead, I just stood there, motionless. I did not know what to do. I tried to talk, but nothing came out. I tried to take a step, but my legs didn't move. I tried to blink, but my eyes remained wide open. I began to feel like Richard Gere's character at the end of *Primal Fear* when he realized that he had been conned by his client and wondered if he was really as good as he thought he was. As I began to ponder that thought, everything became blurry and began to turn dark.

Chapter 3

When I came to, there must have been at least ten people surrounding me. I had no idea what was going on or what had happened. All I knew is that all the attention was on me, and it made me feel very uncomfortable.

"Sir! Sir, are you okay? Do you know your name?" asked one of EMTs.

"Huh? Wuh-wuh... What's going on? Who are you?"

"Sir, you passed out. Your wife called 911. Are you okay? Can you sit up for me?"

"I'll try."

As I began to sit up, I felt the dizziest I have ever felt in my life. The room was spinning so fast, it was like I had just drank a fifth of vodka. I heard the EMT say to his partner, "BP is 90/74. Pulse 110. Pulse ox reading is 94."

Normally, I am aware of what those numbers meant; however, in this case, I didn't know if they meant I would live or die. Danielle came running over to me and gave me a monster bear hug. It almost knocked the wind out of me, but I managed to give her a little squeeze back. She looked so concerned, yet I still did not know why.

"Danielle, what happened?"

"You collapsed after those two detectives left."

Now it was coming back to me. David Flores! That son of a bitch. I can't believe he played me. What makes matters worse is that I fell for it. I believed him when he told me he hit his wife in self-defense. I believed him when he told me she threw the lamp at the TV and tore open the couch. It was then I realized that Danielle had no idea what the detectives and I talked about, which led to my syncope episode.

"Sir, we need you to see if you can stand up because you're going to have to hop on the stretcher," an EMT instructed.

"Oh no, you're not. I do not need to go to the hospital. Maybe just rest a little, but there is no need for me to go to the hospital. I will be okay."

"Sir, your blood pressure it on the low side, and you passed out. We strongly urge you to get yourself checked out in the hospital."

"I understand that, but there's no need for me to go. I will sign whatever forms I have to."

The EMT handed me a waiver to sign stating I was refusing hospital treatment, then they packed up and left. Once they were gone, I was able to sit with Danielle on the couch and tell her what was going on.

When I told her that David Flores had murdered his wife and son and showed no remorse at all, tears came streaming down her face. I was not sure if she was upset for the murders, for me, or both. It really did not matter because there is no worse feeling in the world than seeing the woman you love and care for more than anything in the world cry. I did all I could do in that moment, holding her tight and letting her sob as hard as she needed to.

When she calmed down enough to talk, her first question was why.

"I will be wondering that for the rest of my life. What did I miss? Is it really my fault?"

Danielle looked at me with a puzzled look on her face, as if she was shocked I would ask that.

"What do you mean, *Is it your fault?* How can this be your fault?"

"I don't know. I feel responsible for what happened because if I hadn't defended him or won his case, his wife and son would still be alive."

"I get that, but wise up," Danielle said angrily. "This is not your fault. You did your job. If that asshole killed someone, that is on him, not you."

I appreciated what she was trying to do, and in lighter situations it may have worked, but not in this case. The guilt that was coursing through me was so thick, you could make a milkshake out of it. I knew I should not be feeling this way. I did my job, and I did it well. I was also paid handsomely for it. Besides, are defense attorneys really supposed to have a conscience?

"You are right, but you know how I am."

Danielle gave me a kiss on the forehead and went to wash her face in bathroom. Just as she closed the door, my son finally came downstairs, asking where his breakfast was. For an eleven-year-old, Gio can be pretty demanding. I explained that he could have my plate because I was not hungry anymore, and he pounced at the opportunity.

"Are you going to work today, Dad?" Gio asked.

"Yes, in a little bit. Why do you ask?"

"Because you are usually gone by now."

"I had to handle something earlier, but I'm good now," I said hoping to end the inquisition.

"Everything okay?" Gio went on.

"Yup, all good."

I went upstairs to take a shower and get ready for work. I had done this routine for six years without even thinking, yet today I had to concentrate on what to do next. Danielle walked into the room as I was struggling to put my tie on; thankfully, she took over. It always amazed me how she was able to do everything with such grace and elegance.

"Don't let the partners see you like this," she teased. "They will never let you live it down."

"I wonder if they know or if I will have to be the one to tell them."

"I am sure they know, but don't let them see how much it is affecting you."

With those words of encouragement, I kissed Danielle goodbye and headed out to my car, not knowing what the day would bring.

Chapter 4

One of the many advantages of living in New York City is the public transportation. Most days, I take the three line to Forty-Second Street and walk the four blocks to our office on Forty-Eighth Street, while watching the occasional street performer or impromptu flash mob. Sometimes, I'll enjoy a dirty water dog, which sounds disgusting but is, in fact, heaven on earth; however, today, I needed time to myself, so I decided to drive in. I do not often drive in NYC, even though I live here, because it is very similar to a death wish. All traffic laws seem to be abandoned here, which leads to drivers weaving in and out of lanes and running red lights. It can be very scary and intimidating at times, but on this day, it allowed me to gather myself and my thoughts before heading into the office.

Usually, I arrive at my office around eight o'clock in the morning. I am a very punctual person; something that drives Danielle crazy. She is as casual as it gets and often forgets that I operate on Tom Coughlin time: arrive five minutes early or you are late. So when I walked into the office at 8:45, I got so many disturbing looks. I was not sure if the stares were because I arrived later than I usually do or if everyone knew what had happened. I said hello to everyone and went right to my office.

I was lucky when I joined Lowery, Hill, and Greenwood, because one of their long-time attorneys was retiring and had a nice office with a breathtaking view of Midtown Manhattan. I was given that office out of necessity until they could find an alternate location for me. Six years later, I am still here. I set my bag down and sat in my chair, already feeling like I had gone fifteen rounds with Mike Tyson.

As I unpacked my bag, I glanced at the phone on my desk. The handset was lit up red, which meant I had voicemails to retrieve. I had thirty-four missed calls since yesterday, an alarming number considering I usually only have three or four. I knew that most of those calls had to be about David Flores, which only heightened my anxiety. I began to feel the same way I did before I passed out earlier in the day but was thankfully brought out of it by a familiar voice.

"You look like shit. What happened?" said Jill, my assistant.

"You mean to tell me you don't know?" I asked, hoping she did not.

"Know what?'

"Uh, nothing. Don't worry about it."

Jill Lawson has been my assistant for four years and is my rock in the office. She knows all of my moods, mannerisms, needs, and pet peeves. She graduated from NYU in 2019 with a 3.8 GPA and is studying to be a paralegal. Sometimes I think she is too qualified to be making copies and bringing me coffee, but if someone has to do it, I'm glad it is her. She is also highly intuitive, so when I told her there was nothing to worry about, she knew I was lying.

"Don't give me that shit. What's going on? You know I will find out sooner or later." It didn't hurt that her uncle was Steven Hill of Lowery, *Hill*, and Greenwood.

"Okay, but you can't tell anyone, especially your uncle. I need to be the one to tell the team," I said quietly. I told her what happened with David Flores, and she could not believe it. She asked me if I had any suspicions that he would do this and, of course, I said no. I truly was shocked at what happened because David Flores had always told me he was the one who was abused in that relationship. I might have continued to believe him to this day if his son had not been murdered as well. Innocent until proven guilty, I guess.

I could tell by the look on her face that she knew I was flustered and not acting like myself. I try not to let anything bother me emotionally in the office. It is not so much a macho thing as it is a proper leadership technique. I like to convey a calm and collected persona in the office so others will look up to me and think of me as a leader. I have been able to do that up to this point; however, the gravity of the situation began to overwhelm me, and I could no longer hide it, as much I tried to.

"Wow, I cannot believe this. What are you going to do?" asked Jill.

"I have no idea. I guess first thing I have to do is find out if the partners know and, if they do, what their thoughts are," I answered with uncertainty.

"Well, you'd better decide quick, because the three of them are coming right now."

Chapter 5

Alan Lowery, Steven Hill, and Thomas Greenwood founded the law firm of Lowery, Hill, and Greenwood in 1985. They had been roommates at Cornell Law School and shared the same dream of one day running a law firm in New York City. They each brought a different characteristic to the firm, which, when meshed together, created as perfect a leadership team as one can hope for.

Alan Lowery is a mellow, even-keeled man in his early sixties. He has never been one to embrace a confrontation or argument but can certainly hold his own in a courtroom. He has a reputation with the judges as someone who has a level head and can be reasoned with at any time. Alan has often had to put out a few fires in the boardroom, which is why I tend to go to him whenever I have an issue that I need help resolving.

Steven Hill is certainly the hothead of the trio. Even at the ripe age of sixty-three, he has not learned to keep his emotions in check. He has blown up in the office and courtroom on more than one occasion and has gotten into trouble because of it numerous times. Every firm needs that person who is not afraid to ruffle feathers or push buttons because it shows toughness and grit. Steven Hill can argue with the best of them. I once saw him have an argument with his brother at a birthday party about socks. *Socks*. I did not pay close attention, but I do know that his brother ended up apologizing out of fear, not guilt.

The man who brings it all together is Thomas Greenwood. It was Thomas's idea to create a criminal defense law firm and open it in the heart of Manhattan. It was Thomas's vision that helped mold the early years, in which the firm struggled to attract clients. In the 1980s, New York City was littered with crime. Murder rates were at an all-time high, and muggings on the subway trains were an almost daily occurrence. Thomas Greenwood envisioned a law firm that could help those who could not afford a lawyer so the client would not be stuck with the $50,000 per year public defender. Thomas would spend most of his days in the courthouse lobbies promoting his firm's services and promises. In the first few years, those efforts did not pay off; however, his persistence and presence in those lobbies eventually landed his firm an opportunity to represent a multimillionaire accused of domestic abuse in 1988. Thomas and Steven won that case and, in effect, put Lowery, Hill, and Greenwood on the map.

"Sal, what's the latest?" questioned Thomas. I could not tell if he knew about Flores and was testing me or if he genuinely wanted to know what the latest developments were. There are a few moments in one's life that can be classified as a turning point. For me, this was one of them. It was a simple question, yet I agonized over how I should answer it a lot longer than I should have. If I brought up Flores and the partners did not know about it, then I would look like a fool for not going to them sooner. If I kept quiet about Flores and the partners knew, then it would be like I was admitting defeat, something I had never done before. I was truly between a rock and hard place.

"Hello? Earth to Sal? You there, buddy?"

"Yeah, sorry, Thomas. I was... Well, I don't know where I was."

I knew that I had dug myself a hole, but I was not able to utter any other words. It was like everything was in slow motion and I could not speed it up. For the first time in my six years at the firm, I froze in front of the senior partners.

"Sal, what's wrong? You look like something is really bothering you," Thomas said, worried.

"A lot, Thomas. Do you have a few minutes so we can speak?" Before I got an answer, I walked into my office and hoped they would follow me without reservation.

My office is larger than most of the other attorneys who are at Lowery, Hill, and Greenwood. I have the benefit of not only having an antique mahogany desk, but a solid oak round table in the corner as well. I have plastered pictures of Danielle, Giovanni, and Angela all over my office to the point of nauseum for some people in the office. I am proud of my family and the life we have built and enjoy showing them off.

Thomas motioned for Steven and Alan to join him in my office with a quick wave of his hand. It was obvious to everyone that

Thomas is the head senior partner and that he has the final say on mostly everything. One of the mysteries of the office is: How did it get to be that way? Because if it was this way from the beginning, then Thomas's last name would be first, not last. One of the popular theories is that Thomas does not like the spotlight and wants to remain the wizard behind the curtain. Another theory is that he strong-armed his way to this position by way of bribery. A more outrageous theory is that Steven Hill and Alan Lowery are no longer partners yet the firm still uses their names to save face. I personally believe that Thomas is just that humble and does not care about accolades or having his name first. He is content with having himself heard and his ideas implemented.

Whichever it was, humble or ruthless, Thomas wanted to know what was wrong with me—and fast. He is a no-nonsense guy, so I knew I would have to come clean. But for some reason I was shaking. Was this really my fault? Would I lose my job over this? Would the firm question my moral judgement? Only one way to find out.

"Thank you for taking the time to speak to me," I said cautiously.

"Sal, I have never seen you like this. What the hell is going on?" asked Alan.

"Do you guys really not know what happened earlier today?

"If we did, I don't think we would be asking you what is wrong," answered Thomas.

"I see. So why are all three of you here at nine a.m.?

"Because we want to share some exciting news with you!" exclaimed Steven.

I wasn't sure what was going on at this point. The senior partners were not here to scold me or fire me. They had good news, which would do wonders for me because of the morning I had up to that point. Still, I was reluctant to ask them what the news was because once they found out about David Flores, they may not be in such a jovial mood anymore.

"That's great to hear. What is this exciting news?"

"We just landed a major case that will be very lucrative for this firm, should we win it. We would like you to take on this case."

"Wow, thank you for the confidence. Who is the client and what did he do?"

"You know who Sean Lancaster is, right?" asked Thomas.

"Of course. He made his fortune off the invention of the touchless payment pads that every taxi in NYC uses. He is also one of New York City's biggest philanthropists. What is he being accused of?"

"First degree murder of his entire family," said Steven solemnly.

"What the fuck? How can a man like Sean Lancaster do something like that?"

"Naturally, he said he didn't do it. We were hired not to prove who did it, only to prove that he did not. Oh, by the way, I forgot to mention that if you win this case, let's just say your road to partner becomes wide open," Thomas said with a sly smirk.

"Well then, let's get to work, but first I have to tell you what happened this morning."

Chapter 6

I have taken the New York State bar exam, asked the love of my life to marry me, and defended the most vial of criminals in a courtroom. I have even gone bungee jumping and sky diving, yet I have never been as nervous and scared as I was in that moment. I felt as though my career was on the line and that the confidence the partners had just exuded in me would be short-lived. I began to think of the time when I received the email that my bar exam results were ready. I remember logging into my account, thinking, *If I don't pass, what am I going to I do?* I did not want to be one of those people who needs four attempts to pass the bar exam. What alternative career would I choose, and how would I get there? Fortunately, an education from Columbia Law School does wonders, and I passed on my first attempt. Reflecting on that moment had me pondering if I would need to resign or if I would be fired. What would I do? What would I tell Danielle and the kids right away?

"Thomas, Alan, Steven, have you heard about David Flores yet?" I asked with unease.

"Of course, we have," Thomas said. "Do you honestly think that being the second biggest law firm in New York City we would not have been told what he did?"

"I wasn't sure because no one has said anything to me."

"That's because there is nothing to say other than the guy is a piece of shit," Steven added emphatically.

"You mean you are not upset with me?"

"Um . . .?" Alan asked with a puzzled look on his face.

"I have been dreading coming to work today because I thought you all would blame me for what happened because I defended him and got him acquitted."

Even before I got a response, I knew that I would be okay. All that worrying. All that pondering what I was going to do. All the fear I had conjured up in my mind that I was going to lose my job. It was all gone in an instant. I felt a peace come over me that I had not felt in quite some time. All the tension released from my head to my toes, and I suddenly felt like I was floating on a cloud. I got a warm feeling in my heart that I only get when I see Danielle for the first time each day.

"I don't know why," Alan said. "You did your job. It's not your fault David Flores is a murdering, vindictive asshole."

"That's true. Don't you for one second think you did something wrong. He played all of us, not just you!" Steven exclaimed.

"I can't tell you what a relief it is to hear you say that. I really thought I was going to be blamed for this and lose my job."

All three partners laughed at what I said and let me know that I was fine and had nothing to worry about. Thomas explained to me that it happens in this line of work, especially being a defense attorney. If he had a nickel for every time he was duped by a client, he would have been able to retire a decade ago.

"I do want to caution you though. He reached out to us to defend him again, but this time we were not so quick to oblige," Thomas told me as he tried to calm himself down from laughing.

"There is no way in hell I am defending him again. If someone else wants to do it, more power to them, but not me."

Thomas, Alan, and Steven got the message loud and clear. They told me they would never dream of asking me to defend him. Partly because they knew I would not want to, but more importantly, they had bigger plans for me. Sean Lancaster.

"How much do you know about Sean's case?" I asked, trying to change the topic.

"All we know is that he is in processing downtown and lawyered up already. He said he knows of the work we do here and wanted us to represent him. He specifically asked for you. Do you know why?" Thomas asked inquisitively.

"I have no idea," I said as I wondered how he knew who I was, let alone where I work. "Anyway, what's the plan? Where is he being held?"

"Central booking on Centre Street. We would like you to go see him first thing tomorrow morning. He is due to be arraigned tomorrow morning at ten a.m. in New York County Criminal Court."

"What are the charges?"

"Four counts of first-degree murder and two counts of sexual assault," Thomas told me while bowing his head in disgust.

"Who did he allegedly sexually abuse?"

"His wife and daughter," Thomas replied.

I felt a gut punch to my stomach. I know there are some bad crimes out there, and some cases will test my resolve, but this one had the making of being the worst case I have ever taken on. The thought of anyone sexually assaulting a child makes me sick and angry at the same time. As a defense attorney, one of the first things you are taught is to put emotion aside. One of the great rights we are given in the United States is to be presumed innocent until proven guilty. Unfortunately, most people have their mind made up before the trial begins. This case would surely reach the front page of the *Daily News* and *New York Post*, which would make my job much more difficult.

"What are we doing about the press?" I asked Thomas.

"We are working on a strategy for that right now, but as of this moment, nobody is allowed to speak to anyone from the press. Is that understood?" Thomas stated.

Thomas does not often get bothered by the cases we take on. He has an incredible ability to compartmentalize all of his thoughts and not let his true feelings show. However, with this case, it was very evident he was disturbed by the nature of the crime and how it would potentially affect the firm.

"Yes, Thomas, I understand," I said without even thinking.

"Good, because starting tomorrow morning, our lives as we know it are over."

Chapter 7

There are very few times during the day when I can forget everything that happened at work and just focus on the current moment; dinner with the family is one of those moments. The idea of having dinner with my family every evening is something I look forward to. I try my hardest to make sure I am home on time, and if I am running late, I call Danielle to tell her. She is a wonderful cook and is always trying something new. On this night, however, I was running late and forgot to call Danielle to let her know. My mind was racing all over the place, and it never dawned on me to let her know I was going to be at least an hour late.

When I walked in the door, the house smelled like a five-star steakhouse. I knew I missed dinner and would probably spend the rest of the evening apologizing to Danielle, but I deserved it. I have always been able to admit when I am wrong and take my licks. I am not one to hide from confrontation or consequence. As I set my keys down, I began to think of what to tell her. Should I tell her everything that went on in the office or just give her the CliffsNotes version. Before I had a chance to think about it more, Danielle was bringing a platter full of New York strip steaks to the dining room table.

"Perfect timing. I just took these out of the broiler," Danielle said without missing a beat.

"Did you wait for me? How did you know I would be late?"

"When I didn't hear from you, I called your office. Jill told me you had just left and that you were meeting with the partners all day. I figured I would wait to start dinner so I could time it perfectly," answered Danielle.

Danielle never ceases to amaze me. You would figure after ten years of marriage, I would know all of her tricks; however, she continues to either develop new ones or has more in the bag that I have not yet seen.

"Well, thank you. This is a nice surprise. Kids, come on! Dinner is ready!" I yelled.

"Daddy! I missed you!" Angela said in the sweetest voice I had heard all day.

"Hey, Dad," Gio said calmly.

Gio is eleven years old yet acts like a teenager. He is very smart for his age but does not understand that he is a child and should be enjoying these years and not rushing growing up. Whenever we go to the mall, he is always three or four steps in front or behind us because he does not want to be seen with "Mom and Dad." When his friends come over, he rushes them upstairs so I do not have a chance to talk to them. At first it was kind of amusing, but lately, it has become more consistent and worrisome.

"Hey yourself, buddy. How was your day?"

"Eh, nothing exciting."

"Come on, something must have happened," I prodded.

"I did finally finish *Breath of the Wild*. It took me forever," Gio said excitedly.

Gio has been into video games since he was three years old. He has a knack for understanding how a game works without reading the directions and somehow always knows exactly what to do. I am an avid gamer as well when I have time to play, so I understand the excitement of completing a game.

"How many hours did you put into it?" I questioned Gio.

"I'm not sure, like a million," Gio said with a straight face.

Both Danielle and I tried not to laugh but could not help ourselves. It is quite amusing to see how an eleven-year-old perceives time. What seems like a basic skill to us takes time for children to master.

"Well, I am glad you were able accomplish that," I said to reassure him.

"Video games are for dummies," Angela said as she took a plateful of green beans.

"We don't talk like that, missy," Danielle scolded her.

Angela has always spoken her mind whenever she wanted. She has no filter, but what six-year-old does? Even though she does not know she is doing something wrong half of the time, Danielle and I still try to let her know what is right and what is wrong. She does not always get it, but most of the time she will just accept it and not say another word.

"So, you gonna tell me what the meeting with the partners was about, or is it an adult conversation?" Danielle asked.

"Oh, it's an adult conversation, for sure," I said with wide-open eyes.

"That's not fair. Why do we never get to hear about Daddy's work?" Angela whined.

"Because you are not old enough to hear it. Someday you will be, and when that happens, we will be happy to share with you any details you want," Danielle told Angela.

"That's still not fair. I tell you about my day at school all the time, even when I don't want to."

"Well, I ask you to tell me because I am interested and want to know what is going on in my daughter's life. Plus, there are no adult conversations that happen in first grade," Danielle responded.

Angela folded her arms in disgust and let out a huge sigh. When Danielle or I did not respond, she let out a louder one. Then a louder one. Finally, I told her to stop and that we got the point. The next thing I heard was a ball of laughter coming from Gio.

"What is so funny, young man?"

"I love it when Angela gets in trouble," Gio said through his laughter.

"Alright, both of you, enough! We do not act like this at the dinner table. Your mother has spent all this time cooking this terrific meal, and we need to enjoy it!" I yelled like I was cross-examining a witness.

I had put fear into my children, which is something I did not enjoy doing, but understand that sometimes it is necessary. I also had clearly startled both of them because neither one knew what to say. Normally, I would apologize or make a joke to lighten the mood, but this time, I just dug into my steak and began to eat as fast as I could.

The rest of the dinner was in complete silence. I was not sure if it was because of my yelling or if my children were scared. Whatever the reason was, I had never seen them so timid. I knew I had to say something, especially since Danielle kept giving me those bug eyes that screamed, *You better make this right or you will have to deal with me!* For some reason, I kept quiet. I did not make a sound, other than the chewing of my food. I did not look at anyone. I did not pay attention to anything around me. I was in a sort of trance, something I had never experienced before. It scared me a little bit, and I could feel an emotion coming on that I was not sure how to handle. I finished my dinner, got out of my chair, and ran upstairs without looking at anyone.

When I got into the master bathroom, everything from that day came pouring out. Frustration, anger, regret, sadness. *Everything.* I was bawling so hard that I didn't hear Danielle come into the bedroom. She went to open the bathroom door, but I had locked it. She knocked ever so gently and asked me what was going on in her sweetest voice possible. I was sobbing so uncontrollably that I became hysterical and could not answer her. Eventually, after about fifteen minutes, I calmed down and emerged from the bathroom. Danielle was sitting on the bed with a box of tissues and a look of great concern on her face. I had never lost control like that in front of her before. It was not so much awkward as it was embarrassing when I eventually made eye contact with her. My eyes were bloodshot, and my nose was running pretty heavily. Danielle didn't say a word. She simply handed me a tissue and held me until I fell asleep.

Chapter 8

When I woke up, I was tucked under our Tommy Hilfiger comforter and nestled in our one-thousand-thread-count Hotel Collection bed sheets. I had no idea what time it was or if I was alone. I sat up and looked at the clock. It was eleven thirty-seven at night, and Jimmy Fallon was beginning his opening monologue.

"Hey, you," Danielle said as if she was falling in love with me all over again.

"Hey. How long was I out for?"

"A few hours. I told the kids you weren't feeling well and that you would see them in the morning."

I was still groggy but managed to utter a thank-you to Danielle. I knew that I had to explain what happened and that Danielle would have a million questions. How much would I tell her? How would I explain the way I had just acted? I was not even sure why I acted that way myself. I sat up and leaned over the edge of the bed with my head in my hands, collecting my thoughts.

"I don't even know where to begin to explain what happened," I mumbled.

"Shh. Don't worry about it, honey. Not now. When you are ready, you can tell me."

Sometimes, I wish Danielle was a bit more assertive. She is a wonderful wife and a fantastic mother, but she also tends to be a pushover. I try not to take advantage of that because I know how self-conscious she is about it, but I must admit, I do on occasion.

"No, I need to tell you what's going on. What my day at work was like and the immense pressure that was placed on me today. But for some reason, every time I try to say something, I get a knot in my throat and have to fight back tears."

"Sal, if you need to cry, then cry. It is okay. I understand, whatever it is, I know you'll tell me when the time is right," Danielle reassured me.

It is not that I can't cry in front of Danielle. I have on numerous occasions, but not like I did earlier in the evening. It may sound childish, but I felt as though I lost some sense of pride. I know I should not feel that way with her, but I have always been the stronger person. I was the one who was there for her when her parents were killed in a horrific automobile accident nine years ago. I was the one who helped her deal with her postpartum depression after Angela was born. Now I had turned into a blubbering fool right in front of her and felt I had let her down.

"Danielle, you don't get it. I can't just let go whenever I feel like it. I have to be strong. I have to maintain my composure and dignity. I know you don't get it, but that's the way it is." I stopped myself from whining before I started crying again. "Never mind. Let me tell you about what happened in the office today."

I spent the next twenty minutes explaining to Danielle that the partners were handing me the case for Sean Lancaster. I detailed what his charges were and what the expectations were of me. I also mentioned what was at stake if I won. After I was done telling Danielle all of the details of my day, I took a moment to reflect on the magnitude of what this all meant. Not only would I be front and center at perhaps the biggest trial in NYC since the Son of Sam, but I would also have the prospect of being a partner if I won. Making partner would change my whole life. It is what I have always wanted, and to be able to achieve that in my late thirties is something I never would have thought possible.

"Wow that is a lot to take in. Now I understand why you were the way you were earlier," Danielle said softly.

"Yeah, and throw in what happened with David Flores, I am surprised I'm still standing."

"What did the partners say about him?"

"They said it wasn't my fault and that I should not beat myself up over it," I told Danielle. I knew what was coming next.

"See, I told you not to worry. I told you that it wasn't your fault," Danielle responded with glee. She is not one to gloat, but she knew this was one time that an exception could be made.

"Yeah, yeah. I get it," I said, brushing her off. "I guess I can try to put it behind me now, but it will not be easy."

"No, it won't, but if anyone can do it, you can."

There it was again. Danielle's perfect timing. The ability she has to know what I need to hear and when I need to hear it is uncanny. Sometimes I think she doesn't believe what she is saying, but it doesn't matter. What matters is that she is always there for me, no matter what. She is always willing to take the hits with me and never questions anything. She always will try her best to lighten my load with the kids and house chores. I don't thank her enough, which I feel guilty about sometimes; however, this time, I made sure she knew how I felt.

"Thank you, honey. Not just for tonight but for everything you do for me and the kids. I know it is a lot, and you always put us first. It is not unnoticed or unappreciated, even if I don't tell you as often or as much as I should. I love you, baby!" I told Danielle with as much emotion as I could muster in that moment.

She did not say anything to me in response. All she did was tear up, lean in, and kiss me in the most passionate way she ever has. I knew it was her way of saying thank you, so I just went with it. We spent the next thirty minutes making love to each other in a way that we had not done in a long time. I wasn't about desire or lust. It was about the love and appreciation we feel for each other. We were both so into the moment emotionally, it was as if we were connecting for the first time. It was the perfect ending to an otherwise shitty day.

Once we finished, we were lying in bed in silence. It was not an awkward moment, but it was certainly strange. Finally, Danielle asked the question I was waiting for her to ask all night.

"So, what are you going to do now?"

"Well, I guess I am going to start preparing for the biggest trial of my life. But first, I have to get to know Sean Lancaster."

Chapter 9

Sean Lancaster stared out of the bars in central booking and pondered what the hell just happened. His entire family had just been savagely murdered, and he was being accused of committing the crime. He was not sure what to be more upset about: the fact his family was gone or that he was about to be formally charged with their murders. What evidence did they have on him to arrest him so quickly? Was he set up?

Born in 1978, Sean Lancaster was an only child and had as normal a childhood as one can have. His father was a college professor and taught economics. His mother was a sixth-grade schoolteacher. They lived in a 2400 square foot colonial that was the envy of the town. The lawn was always immaculate, and there was never a speck of dust anywhere in the house. As a hobby, Sean would often help his father restore the 1964 Mustang his father had bought when he was six. He was close with his parents, had a lot of friends, was captain of his high school football team, and volunteered at the local clinic, which is why he was so miffed as to how anyone could think he could do such a horrible thing.

As he rested his hands in between the bars, he heard a deep voice behind him come to life. "What did you do, homie?"

"Excuse me? You talking to me?" Sean asked.

"Yeah, what you do to get in here, dude? You look like you don't know what a crime is," said the fellow prisoner.

"Why do you care? You writing a book?" Sean retorted with an attitude that surprised him.

"Damn, dude, chill out. I'm just asking," the man said, annoyed.

"Yeah, well don't ask, because it isn't any of your business."

The man stood up, and right away Sean knew he'd made a mistake. The guy must have been at least six foot six and weighed close to three hundred pounds. Sean was six foot himself but had a slender body that used to be much more toned. Sean began to back himself into a corner, hoping that the man would retreat to where he once sat; however, to his horror, the man kept walking toward him.

"I can tell you are new to this, so let me tell how it works. I ask a question and you answer. There is no other option. Now, I will ask you again. What did you do?"

Sean felt a lump in his throat that he tried to swallow away, but it was not going anywhere. His heart began to beat rapidly and sweat was now dripping down the left side of his forehead. His legs got weak, and he was afraid that he would soon topple over. He recognized he was having a panic attack and quickly decided the best way to mitigate the attack was to comply with the man. Naturally, he did the opposite.

"Fuck you, asshole. I don't have to tell you shit. Now go back to your corner and shut up!" demanded Sean.

The pain hit Sean like a tidal wave and seemingly came out of nowhere. He heard a loud ringing in his ear and his clothes were suddenly wet. He tried to move but was only able to scoot his feet a few inches. It was then that Sean realized what had happened to him: he'd gotten his ass handed to him by the man with whom he was defiant with.

When Sean got all of his bearings and was able to get up, the man stood next to him with a smirk on his face that struck a nerve Sean didn't know he had. He felt a rage go through him that he knew he would not be able to control if he let it out. On the other hand, if he let this guy win and backed down, he may be setting himself up for future beatings. Without thinking, Sean charged the man, picked him up, and body-slammed him to the ground. Sean was able to land two solid cross punches to the jaw before the guards pulled him off.

"That's right, you piece of shit! You can't tell me what to do!" Sean yelled.

"I'll be seeing you later, bitch," the guy retorted.

Sean was surprised by his reaction, but he paid it no thought; he'd enjoyed every minute of it. He couldn't help but think he had set the precedent that he was not to be messed with and that he would stand up to any challenge. He knew that this would not help his case because, after all, he was arrested for murder. However, he knew that fighting back was something he needed to do. And besides the throbbing pain in his head and the soreness of his hands, he was glad he did.

Once order was restored, Sean was escorted to a private cell by one of the guards who broke up the fight. He was enjoying the silence between them, even smiling at what had happened, when the guard decided it was time to break that silence.

"You're one dumb man, son," the guard said.

"Why is that?"

"Cuz you don't know how things work around here. That man you fought, Titus Baxter, he runs this place. He even has influence over some of the guards."

"Are you one of them?" Sean asked, and immediately knew he made a mistake.

The guard turned around and looked at Sean like he wanted to pummel him into submission. Instead, he took his baton and whipped Sean in the gut. The attack was so sudden and so smooth, Sean did not have time to react, only to grunt and fall to the floor. While on the floor, Sean was aware that this was a test, so he started to smile and stand up.

"That all you got?" Sean teased.

The guard went to hit him again, but Sean did not flinch or blink. The guard, realizing he was not intimidating Sean, put his baton away and kept walking. At that moment, it seemed to click for Sean. If he could show he could take a beating, he would earn the respect of the guards and inmates. Now the question was, how would Titus Baxter react to getting blindsided by Sean earlier.

Chapter 10

When my alarm went off at six o'clock, I already felt like I'd had a long day. I had a lot of trouble sleeping the night before and did not fall asleep until three or four in the morning. With such little sleep, I was dreading the idea of having to attend the most important arraignment of my career. Philanthropist sweetheart Sean Lancaster was about to be indicted on four counts of first-degree murder and two counts of sexual assault. He asked specifically for me when my firm won the rights to defend him. After racking my brain for the past twenty-four hours on why he would ask for me, I came up with the same solution as I did when I first found out he wanted me to defend him: *nothing.*

I barely said anything to Danielle and the kids, grabbed my coffee to go, and bolted out of the door by seven fifteen. I was due in the courthouse by eight o'clock, but I wanted a few minutes to speak with Sean Lancaster first. As I pulled into the parking garage and into the same spot I have parked in for the past six years, I was greeted at my car by Thomas Greenwood. I was not expecting anyone to be there, so when I turned around and swung, I hit Thomas square in the nose.

"Oh my God! Thomas, I am so sorry. I had no idea you were there? Are you okay?"

"Yeah, yeah, I'm fine. I probably should not have snuck up on you like that. Do you have a few minutes before you head in?" Thomas asked.

"Yeah, what's up?" I said, staring at his bleeding nose.

"Well, as you know, this is a monster case for the firm. We have all the confidence in the world that you are more than capable of defending Mr. Lancaster. However, I want you to know that if you get yourself in a bind or are not sure of what direction you need to go, there are people at the firm who can help you," Thomas said with urgency. "Do not forget that. You have help."

I understood the message Thomas was relaying to me. I have a reputation of being stubborn when it comes to asking for help. There have been several cases in the past where the partners have offered me unsolicited advice, and I brushed them off. Most of those cases were either minor offenses or drug charges; however, this case is crucial to not only the firm's success, but to Sean Lancaster's well-being and his life.

"Thank you, Thomas, I appreciate that," I said in the most dignified manner I could. "I am sure I will need some guidance along the way. Any word on who the judge is?"

Thomas looked to the ground and began to kick a rock around. "DeSanto."

"Oh, that's just great. We might as well just go straight to trial and skip the arraignment."

Judge Nicholas DeSanto was known as one of the strictest and most arrogant judges in New York City. He has a no-nonsense reputation and a very short fuse. He rarely grants any type of bail on felony cases, and if he does, he always sets the maximum allowable amount. I had a feeling that he may be the preceding judge on this case because of the magnitude of it, but I was hoping he would have a full docket to deal with. So much for hope.

"We will deal with it the best way we can. Nick and I have a long history, and he tends to listen to me," Thomas said reassuringly.

"Okay," I said, taking a deep breath. "Let's do this."

Chapter 11

Sean Lancaster was taller than I thought he would be. He had long, thin legs that seemed to flow right into his midsection. He was not muscular at all, which right away made me wonder how he could commit these violent crimes. He had dusty brown hair that was buzzed all the way around and hazel eyes that radiated a look of innocence. At first glance, one could easily mistake him for a high school English teacher rather than a cold-blooded killer. I knew I only had a few minutes with him before the arraignment, so I wanted to find out why he asked for me above anyone else.

"Hello, Mr. Lancaster. I am Salvatore Amici, but I gather you already knew that," I said with an attitude. "My question is how you knew to hire me specifically?"

"It is a lovely day, isn't it?" Sean said, ignoring my question.

"What happened to your face? Let me guess. You bumped into wall."

"Yeah, hurt like a bitch too. I don't recommend it."

"Listen, if you want me to defend you, then you need to understand a few things. The first one being cooperation. I don't deal with bullshit. I have too much to do and not enough time to do it. So either tell me why you asked for me, or I walk."

"In due time, Sally baby. In due time," Sean answered arrogantly.

Even though I knew he was going to be a pain in the ass to work with and he had not answered my question, something about him was intriguing. I had to know how he knew me and why I could not place him. Reluctantly, I moved on.

"Whatever. We only have a few minutes. Tell me what happened and why you were arrested."

Sean looked at me with one of the most annoying smirks I have ever seen and began laughing. "Oh, we are going to need much more time than we have now to get into that. For now, I want you to be a good little servant and when the judge asks for a plea, you just say *not guilty*. Can you handle that Mr. 'I let a murderer walk free'?"

I lunged out of my seat about as quickly as I ever had and grabbed Sean by the collar of his shirt. I pushed him back to the wall and threw a jab right into his midsection. He doubled over but kept on laughing as he stood back up. His laugh was so evil, it reminded me of Jack Nicholson's portrayal of The Joker in *Batman.*

I was able to calm down before the cops pulled me off of him. When I looked over at Sean, he continued to smile and laugh just to taunt me.

"You're gonna have to do better than that, Counselor. You need much thicker skin if you are going to work for me."

"Who said I was taking your case?" I asked him, already knowing that he knew I was bluffing.

"Well, you wouldn't be here if you weren't, and I'm pretty sure the partners at Lowery, Hill, and Greenwood would fire you if you didn't."

I could tell Sean was much smarter than he looked, so I tried a different approach. I was hoping he would not see through the shift in strategy but doubted I would fool him.

"Okay, Mr. Lancaster, I—"

"I think it's about time you called me Sean."

"Okay, Sean. Tell me what you would like me to do today other than enter a plea of not guilty," I said, feeling like a dog with its tail between its legs.

"That's a good boy. See, you act like this, and we can become fast friends. Obviously, I am expecting the judge to deny bail. After all, Judge DeSanto grants bail about as often as the Mets win the World Series." I immediately asked myself how he knew DeSanto would be the judge. "When this happens, I want you to fight like hell to get bail. Show me what you are made of and if that reputation of yours is warranted."

I hated being in this position. I had no power or say in anything, and the arraignment hadn't even begun. I knew the partners were watching every move I made, even if they weren't present. I also knew that Sean Lancaster wanted to call the shots and at some point, our visions would collide. I had to begin to strategize how I would handle those situations when they came up immediately. I was used to being the one telling my clients what to say, what to wear, how to react to something if it didn't go our way. I was not used to being bullied, especially not by an asshole like Sean Lancaster. But if I wanted to keep my job, I would need to swallow my pride and play the game.

"Alright, listen. I will go along with what you want for now, but just know this. I am the lawyer. I know the law. I graduated at the top of my class at Columbia Law, and I am not going to be pushed around. These charges that are about to brought against you are as serious as they come, and if you want any hope of becoming a free man in the next few months, you will begin to listen to what *I* have to say and follow *my* lead. Got it, *Sean baby*?"

"Wow, now *that's* what I am talking about. Fight, grit, and no bullshit. I want to run through a wall for you, Counselor. Let's go tell this fucking court that I am *not guilty*!

Chapter 12

The courtroom was packed with family members of both Sean Lancaster and his wife's, along with curious spectators who lived in the area. I am not used to such a large crowd at an arraignment, mainly because it is such a short procedure. As I took out my legal pad with my notes, I happened to catch out of the corner of my eye Manhattan District Attorney Bryce Weatherford speaking to Sean Lancaster's mother-in-law. She was sobbing very heavily and looked like she was having a hard time breathing. Weatherford tried to comfort her, but she pushed him away and started screaming, "I want my baby girl back! Bring her back!" The entire courtroom froze and began staring at her, but she didn't care. She kept going on and on and eventually had to be removed by the bailiff. I had never seen such a scene at an arraignment before. It sure didn't take long to let me know this would be unlike anything I have ever been through.

"You got your hands full with this one, Sal," Bryce Weatherford said to me.

"Yup, sure seems like it," was all I could muster after what just happened.

"All rise. The Court of the Southern District Second Circuit of New York is now in session, the Honorable Judge Nicholas DeSanto presiding!" the bridge officer shouted.

At that moment, Sean Lancaster was brought into the courtroom in a white jumpsuit and shackles on both his hands and feet. It was out of the norm to have a defendant shackled for an arraignment; however, the DA's office wanted to make a statement from the beginning that Sean Lancaster would not receive any special treatment because of his stature with the city.

When Sean sat down next to me, he winked and reminded me of what we had talked about earlier in the morning. I did not need any reminders of that conversation, but I stroked his ego and told him I remembered and would do what he asked me to. The idea that I was even playing his game made me sick to my stomach, but I had to play this out if I was going to earn his trust and respect.

"Docket number 21 CR. 7812 (ND), State versus Sean Lancaster. Mr. Amici, do you wish to waive the reading?" the bridge officer stated.

"No, I wish to have the charges read."

Proper NYC courtroom etiquette is for a defense attorney to agree to waiving the charges being read and keep the arraignment moving forward. In this case, however, I wanted the charges read to establish that I will go off book if I have to and am willing to stop at nothing to defend my client. I knew this was a bad move because it would anger Judge DeSanto, but I also wanted him to know I was not afraid of him. I had never been in his courtroom before, and I doubted he had ever heard of me. I didn't care. If he didn't know me before, he would know me now.

"Very well, Counselor," Judge DeSanto said with tempered anger.

"Mr. Lancaster, you are charged with the first-degree murders of Denise Lancaster, James Lancaster, Paul Lancaster, and Samantha Lancaster. You are also charged with the sexual assault in the first degree of Samantha Lancaster and sexual assault in the third degree of Denise Lancaster. How do you plead?"

I had been through this part so many times before and knew the procedure like the back of my hand; however, after hearing the charges read out loud, I didn't react when Judge DeSanto asked how my client pleaded. Instead, I stood next to my client with my mouth slightly open in shock. The reality of the gruesomeness of these crimes was settling in. Suddenly, flashes of David Flores ran through my head. I began to wonder if I could really do this. If I could defend another person who may be guilty. I was doubting myself and had not even looked at one piece of evidence yet.

As I stood in complete shock, Sean Lancaster began to answer the judge when I put my hand on his arm to silence him. It is not customary for the defendant to speak to the judge at an arraignment, but since I was almost comatose, Sean felt he had no other choice. Once I grabbed his arm, it was like I was jolted with a steady stream of electricity because I snapped out of my funk and returned to the courtroom.

"Not guilty, Your Honor."

"Very well. Bridge Officer, please record a plea of not guilty for Mr. Lancaster," ordered Judge DeSanto.

The next minute felt like an eternity. The judge was reviewing the charges and notices given to him by the prosecution to determine bail. We all knew what he was going to say, which is why it was so frustrating that he was taking his time. I felt as though he was putting on a show for me as a way to get back at me for having him read the charges. The cat and mouse game had begun.

"Mr. Lancaster, in light of the seriousness of the charges brought against you and your seemingly unlimited resources, I am denying bail. You will be remanded to Rikers Island pending a grand jury hearing," Judge DeSanto said calmly as though he were dealing cards at a poker game.

"Your Honor, please. My client does not have a criminal record and has been one of the biggest philanthropists in this city over the past twenty years. He poses no flight risk or danger to anyone. I motion the court to please reconsider," I said, knowing that it was pointless to argue.

"Mr. Amici, your client is accused of four counts of first-degree murder and two counts of sexual assault. If that isn't a reason to think he is a danger to the public, then I don't know what is. Motion denied."

"Your Honor, please," I begged.

"Mr. Amici. Your motion was heard and denied!" Judge DeSanto yelled.

I know I could have pressed the issue a little harder, but I did not want the judge to say anything more than he already had. Sean had told me he expected me to fight the judge when he denied bail, and I did that. I just hoped it would satisfy Sean to the point he would not bring it up again.

After the arraignment, Sean was immediately brought back to the jail in the courthouse. I would see him again at Rikers Island; however, I did not know when that would be. As I began to pack up my stuff to head back to the office, Bryce Weatherford came over to me, gloating.

"Boy, you sure gave that the old college try, huh?" he said as he swung his right hand across his body. "For your sake, I hope you bring more than that to the trail. Mr. Lancaster is going to need it."

"You just worry about proving your case and leave the defending to me," I said back to him.

"Oh, after that I am not worried at all. As a matter of fact, I may need to ease off the gas a little to keep you in the game," Weatherford teased.

"Hey, Bryce, you ever hear of the phrase 'don't show your cards'?" I asked him.

"Of course I have, but don't tell me that's what you did here."

"Not only did I not show you my cards, but I also didn't even pull up to the table yet. See ya in a few weeks."

With that, I finished packing up my things, headed out of the courtroom, and left the building to go to my office. I knew it was going to be another long day, but at least the most difficult part of my day was over; however, I had no idea just how bad things would get in the days to come.

Chapter 13

Rikers Island is the hellhole of all hellholes. It is a place that even the vilest offenders want no part of. There are fights on a daily basis that involve both prisoners and guards. There are usually multiple stabbings per week. Most inmates have crafted a shiv that they hold by their side twenty-four seven. It takes a willingness to take or give a beating, to comply with the occasional sexual favor, and to bribe a guard just to survive. More often than not, the prisoners are the ones who rule the prison, not the guards. Given that his only interaction in a jail had resulted in a fight, Sean Lancaster knew he had to be on his toes and more aware than ever.

When he finally got to his cell, Sean immediately laid down on his cot and began to ponder what his next move was, not the next move in his case. For that, he knew he was in good shape. No, he was thinking of his next move in Rikers. How would he initiate himself to the wretched of the earth? He was not one to look for trouble, but he also knew that he needed to assert himself and let everyone know he was not to be fucked with.

Sean had been fast asleep when he was suddenly awoken by banging steel. He thought it was still a dream, so he didn't react right away, but quickly realized it wasn't when he heard a familiar voice.

"Found you, you little bitch," Titus Baxter said.

"Oh, Titus. How's my favorite punching bag doing?" Sean teased.

"Watch yourself now. You ain't in county lockup no mo."

"Yeah, neither are you, fuckhead."

For a moment, Sean thought Titus was going to burst through the steel bars and tear his head off. He knew that he was setting himself up for a beating at some point, but it was something he had to do to gain respect.

"You're a funny guy, you know that?" Titus said, laughing. "Aren't you wondering how it is that I am outside my cell at three in the morning?"

"Not really, because I was sound asleep until your punk ass woke me up," Sean retorted.

"I'm gonna let you go back to sleep because I'm a nice guy. I just wanted you to know that I am here and to always look behind your back, because you never know when I might appear," Titus warned.

"Yeah, yeah. I'm shaking uncontrollably. Good night, bitch," Sean said as he yawned and laid back down.

"Sweet dreams, sweetheart."

Within seconds of Titus leaving, Sean fell back asleep.

Chapter 14

Mostly everyone I know loves the fall. They love the leaves changing colors, the brisk morning air, pumpkin everything, and so much more. Me, I *hate* the fall. I am not a fan of waking up at six o'clock and it still being dark in the house. I do not like deciding what to wear because I will be cold in the morning, yet hot in the afternoon. I like my coffee with just a little milk and sugar and do not get the whole pumpkin spice craze. I was born and raised in New York City, so I am used to the seasons changing every few months, but I am a summer guy through and through. Nothing is better than a nice eighty-five-degree day and Yankees baseball. However, on this mid-October morning, my mind had been so occupied with Sean Lancaster, I did not have the energy to hate the fall. I also forgot that it was my turn to get the kids up and ready for school.

I went into Gio's room first. Right away, I was stepping on toys.

"Damnit, Gio. I told you to pick these up before you go to bed!" I yelled.

Giovanni was sound asleep still and didn't hear a word I said.

"Wake up, dude. Time to get ready for school," I said as I took his blankets off and opened the curtains.

"Five more minutes, please?" Gio groggily said.

"No, let's go."

"Dad, please just five more minutes?" pleaded Gio.

"I said no! Now get your ass up and get ready!" I yelled back at him.

Next, I went to wake up Angela, but she was already downstairs munching away at Danielle's chocolate chip pancakes.

"Rough morning?" Danielle said sarcastically.

"Danielle, not today. I don't need any lip."

I usually do not snap at Danielle, especially in front of the kids. We made an agreement when we decided to have kids that we would never fight in front of them. Whatever issues we needed to discuss, we were to do it behind closed doors.

"Excuse me? Jesus, I was just making a joke," Danielle said, surprised at my response.

"Well, there is a time and a place, and this isn't it."

"Daddy, what's wrong?" Angela asked with that innocent voice of hers.

"Nothing, sweetheart. Daddy is just a little stressed because of work," I answered, trying not to sound angry.

"Does this have anything to do with that Sean guy and his family?" Angela asked me.

The look on my face must have showed what I was feeling because Danielle immediately tried to change the topic.

"Sweetheart, why don't you eat your pancakes in the living room and watch TV," Danielle told her.

"Really? Okay!"

"Before you go, honey, how do you know about Sean?" I questioned Angela.

"I heard Mommy talking about it with Aunt Kate."

"Okay, go enjoy those delicious pancakes, and be sure to save me some!" I calmly said to Angela.

As soon as Angela was in the other room, my attention turned to Danielle. I hate fighting with Danielle. We have such a loving relationship that it makes me very uncomfortable; however, this time I did not care. I gave her such a scalding look, she could have easily thought I was a murderer.

"What the fuck, Danielle? Are you kidding me?" I yelled at her.

"What?"

"Are you serious? What? You let our six-year-old daughter hear about my case? What were you thinking?"

"Like I knew she was there. Come on, do you really think I would let her hear about it if I knew she was there?" Danielle said with apprehension.

"Well maybe you should have closed the door or went outside instead of talking out in the open. What did you say to Kate anyway?"

"Nothing crazy. Just that you landed this big case and Sean Lancaster is the defendant," Danielle said.

"And?"

"And what? That was it," Danielle tried to reassure me.

"Whatever. Just watch what you say because the last thing I need is false information going out."

Through all the arguing, I didn't even realize that Gio was still upstairs.

"Gio, get your ass down here! Now!" I yelled.

"Dad, I'm right here. What's wrong?" Gio asked while walking down the stairs.

"Nothing, I gotta go," I said as I grabbed my laptop bag and stormed out.

Just as I got to my car, Danielle came out to have a few choice words with me.

"Look, buddy. I know you are stressed with this case, and this is only the beginning, but don't you ever, *ever* speak to your son like that again. You want to yell at me, fine. You want to be mad at me, fine. Don't take it out on Gio. He did nothing wrong and did not deserve that. Grow the fuck up."

In our fourteen years together, I had never heard Danielle so angry. I knew I had touched a nerve with her that I had never known was there, but for some reason, I did not care. All I could think about was getting in my car and getting the hell out of there as fast as I could.

"Are you done?" I said with an attitude.

"You're a piece of shit, you know that?" Danielle said as she stormed off.

I finally was able to get into my car and drive to work. Again, I needed time to myself, and taking public transportation on this day was a recipe for disaster. When I pulled into my parking space at the office, I just stared out of the window. My mind was racing between everything that just happened and the amount of work I had in front of me with this case.

Finally, it all got to me.

"Fuuuuck!" I screamed, pounding the steering wheel.

When I was able to calm down a little, I noticed people staring at me. I didn't care though. In fact, I didn't care about anything. What was wrong with me? It was at that moment I made a decision that I knew I had to make. I was going to tell the partners at Lowery, Hill, and Greenwood that I wanted off the Sean Lancaster case.

Chapter 15

As soon as I got to my office, Jill stopped me before I entered. "I just want to warn you, it is a shit show in there," Jill said to me.

"What is? My office?"

"Yes. I tried to stop them, but they weren't listening to me."

"Stop who?" I asked.

"The partners," Jill answered with her head hanging down.

I knew exactly what she meant and needed to take a few deep breaths before I entered my office. Right away, I caught a glimpse of what I had expected, and that anger I tried so hard to suppress in the parking lot came roaring back like a lion on the loose.

"Jesus Christ, are you fucking kidding me?" I said as I looked around my office at the piles and piles of boxes scattered all over the place. "What the hell is this?"

"Thomas and Alan said they need you to look through these files and start building a defense for Sean Lancaster like... yesterday," Jill said with disgust.

"Did they say anything else?"

"Nope. They just said that, dropped off the files, and left."

"Okay, thank you, Jill. Can you shut the door on your way out, please?"

"Sal, you okay? You never close your door unless you are with a client," Jill inquired.

"Jill, shut the door, please," I said, trying to hold back my anger.

"Okay."

Jill was right. I never close my door unless I am with a client. I believe in the idea of an open-door policy, and what better way to express that than leaving my office door open. I like to hear the hustle and bustle of the office, the ringing of the telephones, and the occasional shouting match. However, today was not the day for me to let anyone walk in because I was ready to blow up at any moment.

I had no idea where to begin. There were files on Sean Lancaster that went back to his high school days. I have been through this process many times before and have always been able to strategize, no matter how many files I have to sift through. This time was different. This time I could not focus. I kept thinking of David Flores. How guilty I still felt about what happened after he was acquitted—even thought I knew I shouldn't feel this way. I was replaying the trial in my head, trying to think if there was anything I missed. Anything I would have done differently. Should I have taken the case to begin with? All the things that a defense attorney is not supposed to think, I was thinking. The only way I knew how to clear my head was to talk to Danielle, but we had a major fight earlier in the morning, so I was not sure she wanted to talk to me or if I wanted to talk to her.

Instead of calling Danielle, I decided to head up to Thomas's office. I knew that if I did not do this soon, I would relent and not say anything at all. Just as I got to the elevator, my cell phone buzzed. It was Danielle.

"Honey, listen, I'm sorry about what happened earlier. I know you are going through a lot right now, and I should be more understanding, but you also have to understand that you are at fault too," Danielle said.

"Are you really calling me now and passive aggressively saying this is my fault?"

"Well, no, but I need you to understand how I feel," Danielle answered.

"Danielle, I know how you feel. You do not need to tell me. I am having a really shitty day, and I don't need this right now." I was surprised at how I reacted to my wife's phone call. Almost any other time I would be receptive and reciprocated the apology. "Look, I know you mean well, but now is just not a good time."

"Goddamnit, Sal. What the hell is going on with you?" I could tell she was pissed now. "I was trying to be nice and tell you I'm sorry and am here for you, but you continue to shelter yourself against me," Danielle said almost in tears.

"You call, telling me that I need to realize I am wrong. Then, after you apologize, you tell me that you are here for me? Seriously?" I was even more angry at her now. "Tell you what, let's just not talk for the rest of the day and see it goes. Maybe it will do both of us some good." There was no turning back now.

"What does that mean?" Danielle asked as she began to cry.

I had not meant what I said. It was purely a heat-of-the-moment thing. Or did I? As a lawyer, I was trained to focus on subtle mistakes in language from both witnesses being deposed and questioned on the witness stand. The slightest slipup from a witness for the prosecution, and I was all over it like a cheap suit. I had taught Danielle this technique as well. It was about to backfire.

"Nothing, nothing at all," I said after taking a loud, audible deep breath.

"You obviously meant something. You know I picked up on that using what you taught me."

"It's nothing. Look, I have been doubting myself all day. I feel I am not good enough for you," I said, hoping to put this issue to bed.

"What a load of horse shit. Man up and tell me what's going on!" Danielle yelled at me, no longer crying.

"Where is this coming from? What is going on with *you*?"

"I don't know. Something hit me after we fought this morning. I began to realize that all you do is order me around and tell me what I can and cannot do. I go along with it for the kids and, frankly, because it never bothered me before. But this morning, this morning I felt different. And when you said that maybe it will do us both some good not to talk, I didn't get upset like I thought I would. I felt... relief," Danielle said with confidence.

"Well, I don't know how to take that. Is this a conversation we really should be having over the phone?"

"Take it however you want, and no, we should be having this conversation in person. I just don't want to right now. Make sure to stop off for dinner tonight because I am taking the kids out. Don't wait up."

With that, Danielle hung up. I was in complete shock at what had just happened. How long had she felt this way, and why did the bubble finally burst? I looked at my watch and it read 10:12 a.m. My day had just begun, and it was already one of the worst I have ever had. It was then that I thought to myself that maybe I ought to keep quiet about the Lancaster case for now and see how things played out with Danielle. I could barely handle one catastrophe, but two? I might go into full self-destruct mode. I decided I wasn't going to wait. I got into the elevator and took what seemed to be the longest elevator ride I have ever taken and got off on the fifth floor. I headed straight for Thomas Greenwood's office, took a deep breath, wiped away the sweat from my brow, and knocked on his door.

Chapter 16

Yard time is sacred time for most inmates, especially on beautiful fall mornings. It is beyond refreshing for inmates to feel the sun beat down on them and smell the crisp, cool autumn air. There are three different yard times that an inmate can take advantage of: nine thirty a.m., eleven o'clock a.m., and two o'clock p.m. Sean Lancaster always chose the nine thirty time slot because there were less people and less of a chance of something bad happening.

As Sean made his way to the 1/7-mile track, he spotted out of the corner of his eye Titus Baxter. This made Sean very uneasy because Titus was a late riser and was never in the yard this early. He hoped that Titus did not spot him and kept making his way toward the track. Once he hit the track, he started a slow jog and began to be at peace. It didn't take long for things to go south.

"Surprised I'm here, punk?" Titus asked Sean.

"A little, yes. To what do I owe the pleasure?" Sean said calmly.

"Ha-ha, you are a funny dude. You know why I am here."

"Actually, no, I don't. We don't have any business together, unless you want to start one," Sean responded.

"Like what?" Titus seemed genuinely curious. "Drug pushing or weapon sales?"

"No, no, nothing like that," Sean said as he began to laugh. "No, I meant protection."

"Protection for who, you?"

"Precisely," Sean said as he pointed his finger at Titus to let him know he was correct.

"What's in it for me?"

"Look, Titus, I know you are big dog around here, and I don't want to get into it with you anymore. I know there is not much I can offer you that you don't already have, but there is something."

Looking really intrigued now, Titus leaned in closer to Sean.

"What's that, homie?"

"A full commissary account."

"I got that already, dog," Titus said dismissingly.

"Not like I can provide. Do you know who I am? How much money I have? Name your price and it is yours. No amount is too big.

After some thought, Titus let Sean know exactly who was king.

"I don't think so. I don't need another gang member," Titus said as he shook his head back and forth.

"Just think about it, Titus," Sean said as he began to walk away. But before he left, he added one final piece of intrigue. "We can make a lot of money together."

Chapter 17

As Sean was chowing down his food, he caught a glimpse of another inmate that he could swear he knew. He didn't quite know how he knew this person, but he knew he did. Even though Sean was only in jail for a little bit, he knew it was a no-no to stare. Staring would cause an inmate to act like a wild dog and go on the offensive without even thinking. It was often a sign that one wants to start trouble and the prey has been picked. Despite knowing this, Sean continued to stare. Eventually, the inmate got up and walked over to Sean with every intention of finding out what was going on,

"Something I can help you with?" the inmate asked.

"Not really, but I swear I know you from somewhere," Sean answered the inmate.

"Oh, yeah? From where, cuz I sure as hell don't know you," the inmate said as he looked Sean up and down.

Sean continued to stare, not knowing to say next.

"What are you in for?"

"Excuse me?" the guy asked, very annoyed. "Who the hell do you think you are asking someone that question without even know him?"

"What are you in for?" Sean asked again, knowing this was going to cause a problem.

The inmate grabbed Sean by his collar and stood him up with one hand. Immediately, Sean knew he made a mistake, but it was a mistake well worth it. He finally recognized the inmate. Not from his jet-black hair, his scruffy face, or his voice, but from the brute strength the guy just exhibited.

"Johnny?" Sean asked.

All of a sudden, the inmate had a look on his face like he had seen a ghost.

"Uh, how... how do you know my name?" Johnny asked nervously.

"OMG, Johnny, how the hell have you been?" Sean yelled, stepping forward to give him a hug.

"Whoa, what the hell are you doing, man?" Johnny said and pushed Sean away. "I don't know you, man. You must have me confused with someone else."

"What are you talking about? It's me, Sean."

"Yeah, I know who you are, mister philanthropy."

Sean was confused as to why Johnny was pretending not to know him. There was no way on earth that Johnny would not remember him. Not after what they had been through.

"Johnny, I don't get it. What going on?"

"Why don't you just go back to eating your grub and we will forget this ever happened," Johnny said as he jerked his head to the right.

Sean knew what that meant, so he apologized for the mistake and assured it would not happen again. He was also wondering what was with all the secrecy. What they had been involved in happened decades ago, and surely nobody knew anything about it.

After he finished his meal, Sean headed over to the corner of the cafeteria where there was a small hallway just beyond the entrance.

"What the hell, man? What was that about?" Sean asked Johnny once he saw him in the shadows.

"Are you fucking stupid, you asshole?" Johnny said angrily.

"Well, obviously I am because I have no fucking idea what's going on."

"Nobody knows about my past, especially what you and I did together. And it needs to stay that way, you got it?" Johnny demanded.

"I get that, but jeez, you don't have to go all ape shit on me. If you are not in here for that, then what are you in here for?"

"Assault and battery. I beat the shit out a store clerk who pissed me off," Johnny said nonchalantly.

"You are deeply disturbed. I am glad to see nothing has changed."

"Come here, you prick," Johnny said as he gave Sean a monster bear hug. "What the hell are you in here for? Obviously not that thing we did, so what then?"

"Someone murdered my family and pinned it on me."

"Oh, damn! I am sorry, man. I always liked your family. Denise is, was, a sweetheart," Johnny said with a clear sense of sadness in his voice.

"Thanks. I have no idea what happened. All I know is it wasn't me."

"You don't need to plead your case to me, man. I'm not the one who can sentence you to life at Sing Sing."

"I know, but I felt you should know it. I'm not sure why."

After a few more minutes of catching up, Johnny left to go back to his cell and let Sean know where he could find him the next day. Sean was left pondering how much Johnny had told people about their past together. What they did. How it went down. Who was involved? He wouldn't have much time to think about it because Titus Baxter came walking up almost immediately after Johnny left.

"Alright, man. I've thought about what you said. Let's talk."

Chapter 18

"Sal, come on in," said Thomas Greenwood as he opened his office door.

"Thanks, Thomas. I need to talk to you about something rather important. Do you have a few minutes?" Sal asked politely.

"Sure. Do you want me to get Alan and Steve as well?"

"No, I would like to keep this between you and me, if that is okay with you," I asked as if I was asking for permission to use the restroom.

"No problem. What's on your mind, Sal?"

My heart was racing a mile a minute. I could feel the sweat forming on my forehead and beginning to drip down the side of my face. I was also getting lightheaded and dizzy at the same time. My face became very pale, and Thomas took notice.

"My god, Sal. Are you okay? You need some water?" asked a concerned Thomas.

"Please. Yes, that would be great. Thank you," I said with my hands shaking uncontrollably.

It was a chore just to hold the glass of water with two hands and take a small sip. I had experienced anxiety attacks before, but not in the office and especially nothing this severe. I understood that I was about to make a life-altering decision, which is why I began doubting if it was the right move since I was reacting like this.

"Sal, talk to me. What's going on?" Thomas asked as he put his hand on my shoulder.

"Thomas, you know when you have those moments in life where you know you are at a crossroad, and no matter which avenue you take, it will be the wrong one?" I asked, already knowing the answer."

"Yeah. Sal, just come out with it."

"Thomas, I want off the Sean Lancaster case," I stated ever so quietly.

Thomas Greenwood sat back in his black leather executive chair and did not say a word for a good minute or so. There was dead silence in his office. The kind of silence that is both uncomfortable and confusing at the same time. I didn't know whether I should say something, but then I kept remembering what my first manager in retail sales had told me back in 2001. *The first person who speaks loses.*

Finally, Thomas Greenwood broke the silence. "What do you mean you want off the case? It hasn't even started yet."

"Thomas, you have no idea what it is doing to me. I am arguing with my wife, something I *never* do. I am snapping at my kids for no good reason. I am not sleeping. Plus, I don't know why, but I think he is hiding something from me," I answered.

"Like what?"

"I don't know. But he asked for me personally. There has to be a reason for that. When I asked him about it, he completely changed the topic and acted like I never even asked him a question. Look, I know this is not what you want to hear, and I know how surprised you must be at this, but I truly believe it is in my and the firm's best interest if other counsel were assigned to this case," I pleaded.

"Sal, I completely understand your position and where you are coming from. Trust me, I do. But I can't take you off for two reasons. Number one is that I just don't have the manpower. And two, there is nobody else I can trust with this case. You proved yourself with David Flores and earned the right to represent Sean Lancaster. Now, you want to give that up because you've had a few bad days?"

"David Flores is a major reason why I don't feel right for the job. I know you and the partners said it is not my fault, but you do not know the guilt I live with every day. The guilt that his family is dead because I helped set him free. The fact that I should have seen through his facade and called him out on his bullshit. These are the things that have been eating at me, and now you want me to take that fear into a courtroom to defend a man accused of killing his family who just happens to be one of the wealthiest people in New York City?" I said with a bit of anger creeping in my tone.

"Watch your tone, Sal. I may be your friend, but I am still your boss and a partner at this firm. You got that?" Thomas rarely showed emotion, let alone anger. He, along with Alan Hill, are the calm ones in the office. On certain occasions, Thomas would let out a curse word or a "damn it" for a laugh from the staff. But he had never spoken to me like that before, and it caught me off guard.

"Sorry, Thomas, I didn't mean to get loud or offend you. I just want you to understand."

"You want a drink, Sal?" Thomas asked, changing the topic.

"Thomas, it's ten thirty in the morning," I answered, surprised.

"Eh, it's five o'clock in the afternoon somewhere, right? Scotch okay?"

"Um, yeah. I guess."

Thomas Greenwood poured two double shots of Glenfiddich 12 into Waterford scotch glasses and set one in front of me. I am not much of a scotch drinker, but in this case, I knew I didn't have a choice.

"Sal," Thomas began as he sipped his scotch ever so slightly like they do in the movies. "Listen, I want to be there for you, and I am. As a matter of fact, the partners will be too. But you have to understand that we need you on this case. We need your fire. We need your expertise. We need your knowledge. In case you are not getting the picture here, you are the best we have. You are our Mariano Rivera." Thomas spoke as if he were giving a pep talk to a high school football team.

Thomas knew that my love for the New York Yankees would be something I could relate to. Mariano Rivera is my favorite player of all time, and I have earned the nickname Sandman in the office because of my ability to close cases.

"I appreciate that, Thomas. And don't think I didn't notice you trying to soften me up with the Mariano reference," I said as I chuckled and took a sip of the scotch. "Yikes, how do you drink this shit?"

"You are too young to enjoy it. Trust me, you will drink it when you hit my age. Anyway, how about we make a deal," Thomas asked.

"Okay, I am listening."

"Let's see how the first few weeks play out. Start the discovery phase, question some witnesses, begin to refute evidence. You know, the usual. Meet with Sean a few times at Rikers, and if, at that point, before the grand jury trial begins, you still want off the case, we can revisit this then," Thomas said as he made his case, although I knew he wasn't asking.

"Okay, but let's agree on two weeks. I will give you two weeks of my best work, with an open mind." I said, using my best bargaining skills.

Thomas stood up and extended his hand. We shook hands to formalize the agreement, then he raised his glass to toast.

"Here is to the art of compromise. May it last for a long time," Thomas said, then downed the rest of his scotch.

I met his glass but put my glass down. "Sorry, Thomas, but I not drinking this shit anymore."

Chapter 19

Preparing for a defense is a tedious task. It involves digging through piles upon piles of files, photographs, and deposition testimony. It is grueling, boring, time consuming, and monotonous. There rarely is that aha moment seen in the movies, where the key piece of evidence is discovered at the last minute to exonerate the defendant. There is no secret witness that comes out of nowhere to save the day. All there is to rely on is reading and note taking. The occasional surprise will present itself, but for the most part, it is a bland process. I had no doubt that the grand jury would indict Sean in the next few weeks, so I wasted no time in starting my defense strategy. I should have prepared myself better because I had no idea what I was about to uncover.

I have defended many people who were accused of violent crimes. Some were guilty and some were not. It is not my job to prove their innocence, but rather to provide enough doubt in the prosecution's case for the jury to acquit. Violent crimes never bothered me before; in fact, I have always been able to block those details out and do my job without distraction. However, when I looked at the photos of the crime scene that took place at Sean Lancaster's home in the Upper East Side of Manhattan, I felt my stomach turn and nausea overtake my body.

Sean's wife and three children had been savagely murdered. His wife was not only stabbed over fifty times; she was also beaten so badly that she was unrecognizable. His children were also stabbed numerous times, and his daughter, Samantha, was beaten just as savagely as her mother. It is never a good feeling to see photos of a murder scene, but when the photos are of children, that just brings it to another level of disgust and anger.

The photos were so grotesque that I had to take a break from looking at them for the first time in my career. I don't know what it was that came over me so suddenly, but I was feeling a sense of doubt if I could defend someone accused of these heinous crimes. It was then I began to picture David Flores in my mind and what he had done. Why was that still getting to me? I should have been able to move on by now. I grabbed a bottle of Poland Spring water and took three big sips, followed by three deep breaths. I was able to calm down to the point that I became refocused on the task at hand.

I continued my preparation with the next file labeled Sean Lancaster Education. I had some idea of where he came from but did not know the full extent of his education until I opened the file jacket. Right there on top was a copy of his master's degree diploma from NYU in Business Management. That was followed by a copy of his bachelor's degree diploma from UCLA. That caught me off guard because Sean is a New Yorker, just like I am. He was born and raised in Staten Island, so why did he go to school in California, and why was this knowledge not publicly known? I would have to table that thought for the moment because the next file I opened explained where his money currently was and how much he had.

There must have been over one hundred bank statements that dated back five years. I knew Sean Lancaster had money, but nothing like this. According to his last statement from Fidelity, Sean had a portfolio valued at $25 million. He had another $6 million with TD Ameritrade, and $500,000 in his checking account at Chase. I had never seen numbers like this from a client before and quickly realized I had severely underestimated the gravity of the case. Not only was my task to put doubt in the fact that Sean killed his family, but I also was now facing the prospect of saying money was not a motive. When murder and numbers this large go together, it never ends well for the defendant. I would have to be the exception to the rule if Sean Lancaster was going to be set free. Once I digested the information from all the bank statements, I decided to take a break and call Danielle. I was not sure if she would talk to me, but I had to try. It was killing me the way we left things earlier, and I needed to apologize. To no surprise, I got her voicemail. I told her I needed to talk to her and to call me back as soon as she could. After I hung up the phone, I went back to the grueling task of digging through more files on Sean Lancaster.

Chapter 20

"I stock your commissary account with one hundred dollars every week, and you provide me protection from anyone and anything I need. Does that sound like a deal?" Sean asked Titus.

Titus Baxter thought about that for a few seconds. He had never been in a position like this before and knew that he had one chance to maximize his return. He usually spoke before he thought, but this time he knew he had to carefully think of what he wanted to say.

"Nah, that doesn't work for me. It's gonna cost you more," Titus replied.

"Okay, name your price. Money is no object for me, but then I think you know that."

"Five hundred dollars a week. Yeah, that will get it done," Titus blurted out without even thinking.

"And just how do you think you will explain the sudden fortune you have?"

"You really think the guards or warden will question me?" Titus responded with a smug look on his face. "They know better than that."

"Okay. Just don't mention my name at all. You got that?" Sean said with authority.

"Yeah, man, I got it. Just watch your tone."

"My tone will be whatever I want it to be because I am your personal bank and can close at any moment."

"Whatever. So how's this going to work?" Titus inquired.

"You tell me. You're the one who *runs* things in here, even though you have been here for less time than I have."

"I'll figure it out. Make sure my first deposit comes in two days. I need more soup," Titus demanded.

"You will have it. I promise," Sean assured Titus.

After his conversation with Titus, Sean went to use one of the free phones that were scattered throughout Rikers Island. The line for the phone was longer than usual, and Sean did not have the patience to wait an hour or more, so he began to think of what to do next. He had an extremely important call to make, and he knew he could not be late. He tracked down the nearest guard and asked if he could speak to him in private.

"What do you want, inmate?" the guard asked.

"I was wondering if you could do me a favor. Can you let me use your cell phone for just two minutes? I will give you any amount of money you want," Sean begged.

"What do you take me for, an asshole? Get back in line," the guard replied.

"No, not at all, boss. It's just I need to make an important call and am on sort of a time crunch. I know you don't care and have no reason to care, but I can pay you whatever you want. You know who I am and that I'm good for it."

"I said get back in line, inmate, or I'll give you a reason to visit the infirmary where there are no phones," the guard said with increasing anger.

"Fine, be that way, you asshole!" Sean yelled back.

Sean was hoping to get a reaction out of the guard so he could get a read on him, but the guard just stood there and ignored what Sean had called him.

"Okay, have it your way, boss. When it's my turn to make a call, I will be sure to call Hailey and let her know what a sweetheart you are at work," Sean said, knowing that would get the guard's attention.

"What did you say?" the guard said between his clenched teeth.

"Oh, stop the game. You know exactly what I said, you fuck."

"Who the hell are you?" the guard asked with a bit more fear than before.

"I'm the guy who can make you rich or a widower. Your choice," Sean answered.

"Okay, just don't hurt my family. Here, you have three minutes," the guard said as he handed Sean his phone.

"Why thank you, boss. So kind of you. Check your bank account tomorrow. You will find a nice surprise."

Once Sean had the guard's phone, he quickly went off to a secluded corner to make his phone call. He checked three times to make sure there was nobody hiding around the corner or in the ceiling or anywhere else he could think of. When he felt safe, he dialed the number he had memorized before he was sent to Rikers.

"It's me," Sean said.

"What took you so long? You are two minutes late," the voice on the other end said.

"I'm sorry. I hit a snag and it took me a while to work through it. How are you?" Sean asked gently.

"I miss you. I wish you were with me," the voice answered.

"So do I. In time, I promise we will be together again," Sean said, knowing that might not be all entirely true.

"I know, but what assurances do we have? None. I go through each day not knowing when I will see you again or *if* I will ever see you again."

"You will, I promise. Now, did you do that thing I asked you to?" Sean asked mysteriously.

"Yes, but I still don't understand why," the voice answered.

"You will, trust me. As long as it is done, then we are okay. Listen, I want to talk to you all night and fall asleep to your voice, but I have to return this phone before the guard comes looking for me. I promise I will call you back when I can," said Sean.

"How will I know when to expect your call? "the voice asked.

"I will send you a message, just like last time. Good night, honey. I love you," Sean said, hoping to ease his pain of having to hang up the phone.

"I love you too," said a teary voice on the other end.

Just as Sean was about to end the call, he could hear the voice say, "I'll be right down. Make sure Gio and Angela are ready. I don't want to be late to the movie."

Part II

Chapter 21
Four Months Later

"All rise!" the bailiff instructed everyone in the courtroom. "This court, with the Honorable Nicholas DeSanto presiding, is now in session."

By the time Judge DeSanto walked into the courtroom, I had gotten a good look at how the jury was reacting to what was happening. Even though it was just an introduction, I could tell which ones were going to be a potential issue and which ones I would need to play to their ego. I had excused eleven jurors during the *voir dire* using preemptory challenges; however, Bryce Weatherford had managed to get the upper hand and have nine jurors of his choosing to be sworn in by Judge DeSanto. I knew this was going to be a challenge to convince the jury that my client was innocent, even though it is not my responsibility to prove his innocence. I always found that the phrase "innocent until proven guilty" was a bunch of bullshit. Everyone knows that most members of the jury have their minds made up before the trial begins. When the jury deliberates, those members will tend to argue their beliefs or feelings rather than the facts. I win most of my cases by believing that I need to prove innocence and use my ability to read people as a main tactic. This jury looked to be more than I could handle.

"Good morning, everyone, please take a seat," Judge DeSanto said stoically. "Calling the case of the People of the State of New York versus Sean Lancaster. Are both sides ready to begin?"

"Yes, Your Honor," Bryce Weatherford said.

"Yes, Your Honor," I repeated.

"Very well, will the bailiff administer the oath to the jury?" Judge DeSanto instructed.

After the jury was sworn in, reality set it in. I have been through this process dozens of times and knew exactly what to expect; however, this time felt much different. It felt like I needed to try harder and work longer. I knew why this was happening, even after all this time. David Flores was still in my head and, although he was about to have his own trial, for some reason I could not shake the guilt I had over what he had done. I was so consumed in my thoughts and struggling with my anxiety that not only did I *not* hear Bryce's opening statement, I also didn't hear the judge when he subsequently asked me for mine.

"Mr. Amici, are you there? The prosecution has concluded its opening statement and you now have the opportunity to have your own. Do you wish to enter an opening statement?" Judge DeSanto said angrily.

"Uh, yes, Your Honor. Sorry, I have not been sleeping too well, and Bryce's statement put me in deeper trance," I said, getting a laugh from both the jury and audience. A great start.

"Ladies and Gentlemen of the jury, good morning. I would first like to thank you for your service and willingness to serve on this trial. You are in for quite a ride. But I do want to warn you about something. You will hear two versions of what happened. Mine and theirs," I said as I pointed directly at Bryce Weatherford and his team. "Which version you choose to believe is up to you; however, as you were told earlier, you can only review and consider the facts of this case when you deliberate, *not* what your hunch or your feelings are." I paused for dramatic effect before continuing. "Look, we all know who my client is. We all know how much he has given back to this city, how much he has donated to various charities. It is no secret how Mr. Lancaster made his money and how he lives his life. If that is a source of jealousy, then so be it. Does having millions of dollars many times over make someone a murderer? It might. But in this case, Sean Lancaster is as innocent as they come. The state will want you to believe that a loving husband and father of three can savagely butcher his family in cold blood and then act as though nothing happened. We all saw the emotion on Sean's face when he was being arrested and brought downtown. Does that look like the face of someone who just murdered four people? Now, you cannot acquit based on what someone's face looks like, but you can acquit on the lack of evidence and motive. The state will present you with dazzling evidence and technical testimony from law enforcement officers and forensic experts in an effort to wow and confuse you. But I will tell you that behind *all* the technical jargon, behind *all* that razzle-dazzle, they will have accomplished one thing:

failure to produce evidence and motive. Why? Because there is no evidence or motive. Sean Lancaster did not commit these crimes. You will come to realize that as well. Thank you," I concluded and went back to my seat.

"Mr. Weatherford, you may call your first witness," the judge ordered.

"Thank you, Your Honor. The state would like to call Detective Harris," Bryce said with a smirk on his face.

Anthony Harris was the lead detective on the murder scene at Sean's house. He was a pudgy man with a bald head and a badly trimmed goatee. He looked like he worked in the bathroom at Penn Station rather than as an NYPD detective. After Detective Harris was administered his oath, Bryce began his case.

"Mr. Harris, thank you for your time today. Can you please state your name and position for the court, please?" Bryce politely asked.

"Anthony Phillip Harris, New York City Police Department Detective," Detective Harris answered.

"Thank you. Can you please tell the court the nature of your investigation on the night of July 17, 2021?"

"I was called to a murder scene that took place in the Upper East Side," answered Detective Harris.

"Can you please describe the scene for the court?" Bryce asked.

"It was one of the most brutal and gruesome scenes I have seen in over twenty years as a detective. There were four victims; two of which were badly beaten on top of being stabbed."

"Were you able to identify those bodies at the crime scene?"

"Not positively, but we had a speculation that they were the family of the defendant."

"Objection!" I shouted for the first time. "Speculation."

"I didn't hear Mr. Weatherford ask for the detective's opinion. He simply asked if he was able to identify the bodies. Overruled," Judge DeSanto said calmly.

I sat down next to Sean after I was shot down and felt a small pinch on my leg. I looked over at Sean and he had a surprised look on his face. It was almost as if he expected something more out of me. If this was how he was going to react to something as trivial as an objection, what would he be like when something cataclysmic happened?

"I'm paying you one thousand dollars an hour for *that*? Aren't you supposed to argue some more to get it on record or something?" Sean asked me with anger in his eyes.

"Stop watching so much television, you twat. It doesn't work like that. It is the first objection of the case. There will be plenty more for you to be happy about," I responded dismissingly.

"Detective Harris, can you describe the process in which you and your team processed the murder scene?" Bryce asked, knowing it would take a while for the detective to answer.

This is a technique I often used to confuse the jury. When an expert witness begins to speak on his or her craft, the jury will oftentimes get confused or bored and tune out most of the explanation. They usually will only remember the first few minutes, which generally does not have any incriminating information. As a defense attorney, it is a great way to distract the jury and put doubt in their minds. I had never seen a prosecutor use this strategy before. Then again, I had never gone up against Bryce Weatherford.

"Finally, we put crime scene tape on the door and sent the evidence collected to the lab for analysis," concluded Detective Harris.

"Thank you, Detective. One more question. In your decades of experience, how many times have you led a team that collected evidence at a crime scene that led to a wrongful conviction?"

"Objection! Relevance?" I shouted as I stood up faster than before, hoping to please Sean.

"Sustained!" Judge DeSanto replied.

"Withdrawn, Your Honor. No more questions," Bryce answered as he went back to his table.

"Mr. Amici, do you wish to cross?" the judge asked me.

"Yes, Your Honor, I do. Thank you."

"Detective Harris," I began, "I have but one question for you. From the time you arrived on the scene until the time you left, did you see Mr. Lancaster?" I asked, already knowing the answer.

"No, sir," Detective Harris answered.

"Thank you. No further questions."

"Detective Harris, you may step down," Judge DeSanto commanded.

"What the hell was that? One fucking question for the lead detective? I might as well pick out a cell at Sing Sing now," Sean said to me, even more angry than he was earlier.

"Relax, Sean. It's all part of my strategy," I replied.

"Strategy to what? Get me convicted in record time?"

"We will go over the strategy after this court session is over, but just know that if I can place you somewhere else that night, you could not have committed these crimes. Got it?" I told Sean.

It didn't take long for Sean to understand what I meant and what the defense strategy was going to be. He relaxed in his chair and, with as much humility as he could muster, responded, "Okay. It's your show. Lead the way."

Chapter 22

The rest of the afternoon was uneventful. It was a typical feeling-out period of boring witnesses talking a lot of technical jargon. After the judge dismissed us for the day, I went to call Danielle. I had not spoken to her in the three days since she went to stay with her best friend, and I was beginning to worry. We had been going through a very rough time, and I knew I was not her favorite person right now.

"Yeah," Danielle answered, annoyed.

"Hey, just wanted to call and see how you are," I answered, hoping to get more emotion out of her.

"I'm good. Everything okay?"

"Yeah, just wrapped up day one in court."

"How did it go? Is he convicted yet?" Danielle said sarcastically.

"What does that mean?" I asked her, equally annoyed.

"Nothing. I don't want to do this again with you, Sal."

"Danielle, if I did something wrong, said something wrong, please tell me so I can fix it."

"You didn't do anything, Sal. You *never* do anything," Danielle answered abruptly.

"What the fuck is with the attitude? The 'oh shucks, I'm miserable' attitude. I don't get it. What happened?" I asked genuinely, not knowing what was wrong.

"Sal, if you don't know, then I don't know what to tell you. I gotta go."

"No, wait. Just give me five more minutes," I pleaded.

"What?" Danielle yelled, sighing loudly at the same time.

"Can we have dinner tonight to talk things over? Come home and I will cook for you."

"No. It's too soon. I can't."

"Danielle, this is not fair," I said as I decided to just go for it and stop walking on eggshells. "You have been acting like this for months now, and it is about time you told me why. I have been very fucking patient with you. Not pushing and not bothering you. I have given you space and time and all that shit you women say you need. And still, you treat me this way. If you aren't going to tell me why you are acting like this, that's fine, but at least have the balls to tell me to fuck off."

"Fuck off, you prick!" Danielle shouted and hung up.

Well, there it was. The moment that I knew our marriage was in serious trouble. I honestly did not know why Danielle was being so cold-hearted and detached, but I did know it had started when I took this case on. I had asked Thomas Greenwood to get me off the case the morning I snapped at my kids, and he suggested I give it two weeks to see how things went; that was four months ago. Somehow, I had forgotten all about my request once I dug into the files on this case. Maybe Thomas knew that would happen and just wanted me to agree to stay for any amount of time. He was very slick like that, which is why his firm was so successful. I knew I was taking my frustrations out on my family, but could they blame me? I needed to visit with Thomas again, but first, I would have to speak to Sean about our defense strategy so he wouldn't throw another hissy fit in court.

Chapter 23

I arrived at Rikers Island a little after six o'clock in the evening and was given special privilege to speak to Sean. I know a lot of people in the criminal justice system and have always treated them well in case I need a favor. Well, today I was able to cash in on that favor with one of the prison guards: James "Jimbo" Duncan.

"Thank you, Jimbo. I appreciate you letting me see my client at this hour. Tell Hailey I said hi," I said as I walked through the gated door.

"Will do, Sal," Jimbo said as he gave me a salute.

The halls at Rikers are straight out of a horror film. You know there is evil behind them, yet you don't know what they are capable of. The path to the meeting room was a straight, short one, although it seemed like it was a never-ending hallway. I passed by cell after cell of inmates screaming, spitting, and cursing at me, none of which bothered me. I had grown immune to such antics because of the number of criminals I have defended and subsequently visited in jail. When I finally reached our meeting room, I saw there were two chairs, one table, and an excruciatingly bright light.

I sat down at one of the chairs and waited for the guards to bring in Sean. While I was waiting, I pulled out Sean's file and began to organize my talking points. I wanted to let him know what the strategy was, but I did not want to tell him too much. In the months leading up to the trial, I had gotten to know Sean pretty well and felt comfortable asking him any question. Before we began to talk about the case, I wanted to know a little more about him. I was able to find out that although he lived most of his life in New York City, he was actually born in Toronto. His family moved to the United States when he was four years old because his father got a job as a professor at NYU.

When it was finally time to ask Sean about the murders, he was very guarded. For someone as outgoing and sarcastic as he was, to be quiet on the topic was a red flag. My job as a defense attorney is to have my clients acquitted. I accomplish this by gaining their trust and asking for complete transparency. With Sean, I never knew when or if I was getting that.

Sean walked into the room with his hands in cuffs and legs in shackles. He was being escorted by two guards, one on each side of him. After Sean sat down, they chained his shackles to the bolt in the floor and secured his handcuffs to the table. Standard procedure and something I had seen them do before. Once he was secure, the guards left Sean and I alone to talk.

"So you going to tell me what's going on, or do I need to cause another scene tomorrow?" Sean asked with as much an attitude as he could give.

"Let's get one thing straight here. Whether I win or lose this case, I still get to go home as a free ma—"

"Maybe a divorced man, too, huh?" Sean said, interrupting me.

"What are you talking about?" I asked him with concern.

"Oh, please. You think I don't have my sources digging into you also? You think because we spent the last four months bonding and talking about my childhood that I am going to trust you? Wake up, dude!" Sean yelled back at me.

I was stunned. Actually stunned. I had not seen this coming, and I am great at reading people. How was Sean able to slip this one past me? Was he lying about something else? Was this going to turn into another David Flores situation where I set him free, and he killed again because I was deceived?

"I, uh..." was all I could manage to get out.

"Alright, listen, I'm sorry. I know you are doing your best and need me to cooperate. I just wanted you to know that I still control things here, and as long as you don't get out of line, I will never need to exercise that advantage. I defer to you, good sir. Carry on," Sean said in a bad British accent.

"Okay, I get it. You don't have to be such an asshole about it."

"That's me, man. So tell me what's going on," Sean said as if nothing was wrong.

"Based on the evidence presented during discovery, they have your fingerprints on the knife that was recovered in the trash outside. That knife was tested for DNA and matched all four victims; however, your DNA was not present. We will need to use every opportunity we have. I am going to keep reiterating that your fingerprints were on the knife because you live there, and it would make sense that they are." For the first time since I met him, I can tell Sean was intrigued and was waiting to hear what was next instead of coming up with some smartass comment. "Because your DNA was not on the knife, we are going to need to drive home the fact that you were not in the home at all that night. If you weren't there, then you didn't commit these crimes."

"I see. That makes sense, but why not question the detective more and poke holes in his story?" Sean inquired.

"Because Detective Harris has over twenty years on the force, and his reputation is as good as it gets. If I start attacking him, questioning his credibility, it looks like we have something to hide. Do we?" I asked, knowing I was going to pay for asking that.

"No!" shouted Sean. "I told you everything already. Are we going to continue to play this game?"

"No, but I wouldn't be doing my job if I didn't ask," I said, hoping to calm him down.

"Okay, I get it. Just know that I understand you are my lawyer and my best chance of going free, so I will never hide anything from you. *Never*," Sean told me with a hint of anger.

"Good. As long as we understand each other, we will be fine. Now, I am going to go work on my cross-examination of tomorrow's witnesses."

"Who are they calling to the stand?" Sean asked.

"The medical examiner and Joseph Love," I said timidly.

"Joseph Love? What the hell for?" Sean exclaimed with significant anxiety.

"No idea, but we will find out tomorrow."

Chapter 24

After his meeting with Sal, Sean was escorted back to his cell by the same two guards who had brought him into the meeting room. Once they reached his cell, they unlocked his cuffs and shackles and held out their hands. Sean gave them each a fifty he pulled out of this sock and patted them on the shoulder. As he went to lay down on his metal bed, Sean saw someone he needed to talk to.

"Hey, Jimbo. How's Hailey? She pass the board exam yet? Oh, that's right, she's a little under the weather. It is the season, after all," Sean teased Jimbo.

"How long is this going to go on for? Why me? What did I do to you?" Jimbo asked.

"I'll let you figure that out. And this will last as long as I am in this shithole. I have to have fun somehow."

Jimbo ignored his last comment and moved on. Sean knew that he had gotten under his skin and that Jimbo was afraid of him. This was one of the advantages of partnering with someone like Titus Baxter. He now held a certain level of leeway with the guards and had created an understanding that he was not someone they wanted to mess with.

After Jimbo left, there was nothing but silence. Sean rather liked this time because it gave him a chance to reflect and plan. He knew an escape was not possible, especially for someone of his stature. That left him with few options, most of which required the help of others, which Sean did not like because he was very much an independent man. However, he had become reliant on Titus's help, so he knew he could rely on him to help him with his plans.

As the minutes of deep thought passed, Sean became more and more tired from the excursions of the day. He had to fight off the urge to fall asleep because he needed to get a message to Titus, who was three cells to his left. The night guards did not make regular rounds like the day guards did, so it would easier for Sean to send a message at night rather than during the day. He whistled to get the attention of his cellmate next to him but got no response. He whistled again. This time loud enough for the whole row to hear him. Still, no response. Dejected, Sean knew he had to resort to a way that would not only get Titus's attention, but also the attention of the guard.

"Hey, Ricky!" Sean screamed as loud as he could. That certainly got Ricky's attention. Surprisingly, the guard didn't take notice of him.

"What, for fuck's sake?" replied Ricky, still half asleep.

"I need you to pass along a message to Titus," Sean said at a whisper.

"Two packs this time because I was sleeping," Ricky demanded, referring to his habit of chain-smoking Marlboro Menthol Lights.

"Fine. I will get them for you in the morning. Pass along this message. You ready?"

"Yeah."

"Ship is wrecked. Got it. *Ship is wrecked.*"

"What does that mean?" Ricky asked.

"Don't worry about it. Just pass it along," Sean said, annoyed.

"Fine. I want my two packs after roll call," Ricky insisted.

The next ten minutes seemed to take an hour to pass. Sean knew that Titus would have questions, but he would worry about that later. For now, he needed to let Titus know that the time to set things in motion was now.

"Hey, Sean," Ricky whispered.

"Yeah?"

"Throw the anchor," Ricky said.

"Thank you."

Sean was happier than a pig in mud. He knew that Titus was on board and had no issues with what they were about to do. His trial had just begun, yet Sean felt the end was already in sight.

Chapter 25

Before the trial resumed later in the morning, I needed to stop by the office to pick up some documents I left there. I had been driving to work for the past few months because I cherished that time to myself, which meant my MTA card would have to get a workout some other time. On my way in, I listened to *Boomer & Gio* on WFAN, the number-one sports radio station in New York City. They were discussing pitchers and catchers reporting to camp later in the week. I love this time of year. The Super Bowl is played, baseball is right around the corner, and the hockey and basketball seasons are in full swing. Sports is a huge part of my life; sometimes it's a little too huge. The topic this morning was what the Yankees season would like with the roster overhaul they had done. Last season had ended in heartbreak as they lost in the division round to the Tampa Bay Rays after being ahead 2-1 in the series. It had been twelve years without a World Series title, something Yankee fans are not used to. The loss last year affected me in a big way, as I had hoped the drought would end. I promised myself to not let sports affect me in that way anymore, but here I was, getting pumped beyond belief for pitchers and catchers. When the discussion on the radio ended, they went to their usual update, which occurs every twenty minutes.

"Before we get to the latest sports news, we have major breaking news out of Rikers Island," the broadcaster said. "Many of you have been following the Sean Lancaster case the past few months. Well, there has been a new development. Earlier this morning, Sean and a few other inmates were involved in a massive riot that left two dead and several more injured. We will have more details as they come in. Meanwhile, the Yankees..."

My heart both dropped and raced at the same time. What the hell happened and why wasn't I notified? I was so panicked that I missed the exit for the office and had to go two miles out of my way to turn around. When I reached the office, I threw the car in park and rushed out into the parking lot without locking the car. I ran into the lobby and blew past everyone I normally stopped to greet hello. Instead of taking the elevator,

I took the stairs, climbing two at a time to get to my office quicker. Sweat began to pour down my face, and my dress shirt showed wet patches on my back and under my arms. When I reached the third floor, I flung the door open, thus creating a hole in the wall when the knob made extreme contact with the drywall. I continued to run down the hallway to my office, signaling to Jill to follow me.

As soon as I entered my office, I reached into my fridge and opened a bottle of Poland Spring and drank the entire contents in record time. I grabbed another and did the same. I was still breathing very heavy, and my heart was racing at around 150 beats per minute. I knew I would calm down eventually, but I felt like the walls were caving in at that moment.

"What's going on, Sal? Jesus," Jill said, worried.

"Sean... Sean... Sean," was all I could say in between deep, exasperating breaths.

"What did he do now?" Jill asked.

"G-get Thomas, Alan, and S-Steve right away," I stuttered, starting to finally calm down.

"They are in a meeting."

"I don't care. This is more important than that. Go!" I ordered Jill.

Jill left my office and slammed the door behind her. For the next few minutes, I was alone with my thoughts—never a good thing. I wanted to find out right away what happened. Had Sean started it? Was he attacked? How was he? As these questions went through my mind, another possibility popped up. One that I thought could be an explanation for this. One that wasn't so far-fetched to be impossible. Before I could develop this theory, Thomas, Alan, and Steven walked in.

"This better be good, Sal," Thomas said with as much anger as I'd seen in a while.

"Sean was involved in a riot last night. Two people are dead and several more are injured," I explained to all three of them.

"How do you know this?" asked Steven.

"I heard it on the radio on the way in."

"So why are you all bent out of shape? The man probably got the beating he deserved," Alan remarked.

"No, that's not it. I had just met with him last night and explained to him our strategy. He seemed to like the direction we are going and was calm—for once. He is too smart to mess it all up, unless..."

"Unless what?" asked Thomas.

I paused for a few seconds. Not for dramatic effect, although I did accomplish that, but to gather my thoughts on how I was going to present the theory that came into my head when they walked in.

"He had help," I uttered.

"Help? Help with what?" Alan questioned with apprehension.

"Creating a diversion. Making everyone think he is the victim. Getting sympathy from the jurors," I explained.

"I'm not buying it, Sal. Why would he need to do that?" Steven asked me.

"Because that is who is he is. Remember when I first met him? How he toyed with me by not answering my questions and trying to irritate me? That was his way of getting control over me. He needs to be in control, no matter what the situation is. In this case, he felt like he needed to get control over the trial, and what better way to do that than to cause a riot to gain both sympathy from the jury and judge," I explained, giving it all I had.

I could see that I was making sense to everyone because nobody said a word. All I saw were heads nodding and lips curling. I knew not to say anything else because this was like a sales pitch, and the first one to speak always loses.

"It actually makes sense," Thomas said as he continued to nod his head. "What are you going to do about it?"

"I'm going to visit Sean in the infirmary and beat the truth out of him if I have to. But first, I have a little family business to take care of."

Chapter 26

I knew that Danielle was staying at her friend's house in New Jersey, and she didn't want me to come see her. But that wasn't going to stop me. I needed at least one thing in my life to get better. I hadn't seen my kids in over a week, and I missed them like crazy. The entire drive into New Jersey was spent pondering what I was going to say to her and how I was going to get her to tell me what was bothering her. By the time I got onto the Garden State Parkway headed to Short Hills, I had nothing. Not a single idea had come to fruition in my head. I thought about turning around and forgetting the whole idea, but something inside of me kept pushing me to continue. I finally arrived at her friend's house and got out of the car not knowing what I was going to say or how she would react.

I slowly walked up to the door, my heart pounding so hard I felt everyone in the neighborhood could hear it. I rang the doorbell before I gave myself the chance to chicken out. A little girl answered the door, looking confused as to who I was.

"Who are you?" the little girl asked.

"My name is Sal, and I am married to Danielle. Is she here?" I asked, hoping the answer was yes.

"I don't know if I am allowed to tell a stranger who is with me," the girl said shyly.

"That's smart. You shouldn't give strangers information," I said to her as I looked up and saw Danielle in the background.

"Julia, it's okay. I know him. Why don't you go play with Angela?" Danielle said to the girl.

"What are you doing here?" Danielle asked after the girl had left.

"We need to talk. I know you said not to come here, but you left me no choice."

"That's right. I said don't come here. You can't even follow one simple goddamn direction."

"It's really cold out here. Can I come in, please? At least to see my kids?" I pleaded.

"Fine. Just not for too long. We are going out soon."

As soon as I entered the house, Angela came running up to me and gave me the monster hug I needed.

"Daddy! I missed you. Where have you been? Mommy said you went away on a business trip," Angela said joyfully.

"That's right, sweetheart, I was on a business trip, but now I am back, and you will be seeing a lot more of me," I said, knowing that would piss Danielle off.

"Yay!" exclaimed Angela as she began to run around the house.

"Let's go in the study to talk," Danielle said, clearly unhappy.

As we were walking to the study, Danielle got a text message and stopped dead in her tracks. Something was clearly bothering her because she just stood there with a look of disappointment on her face.

"What is it?" I asked her.

"Nothing. It's just something I have been waiting for and now have to delay because you want to talk."

"Glad I can be of service," I said as we entered the study and Danielle closed the door.

"Now, what do you want?"

"Why do you have to be like this? You're not acting like yourself. I could understand if I did something, but I haven't. Like I said before, if I did, then why aren't you telling me?" I asked her in a voice that raised an octave with each sentence.

"Fine, you want to know what is going on? I'll tell you." I knew what was coming was not going to be pretty. "You became so consumed with your job, you let it do the one thing you promised me it would never do: change who you are. You used to be such a sweet, caring, and romantic guy. One who made all the women in the neighborhood jealous. I remember lying down with you while we watched TV or rubbing your back as we both drifted off to sleep. I loved that about us back in the day. That all changed when you took on this case. You became stressed and annoyed so much faster than you had in the past that you began to take it out on me and the kids. I understand the pressure of this case. And what happened with David Flores is a lot to handle; it would be for anyone. But you never did the one thing that I expected you to do. You never asked me for help," Danielle said as she began to cry.

I had no idea this was how she felt about my current case. Suddenly, it was all starting to make sense. All she wanted me to do was be my old self again, which was something I knew would be difficult. I wanted to run up to her, hug her, and tell her everything was going to be okay, but that would have been a lie. Truth is, everything would not be okay, especially with the latest development. I had been spending twelve to fourteen hours a day working on this case over the last four months. It consumed every ounce of energy I had, not to mention all my time. I couldn't just switch it off now and scale back.

"Danielle, I'm so sorry. I had no idea," I said with remorse in my voice.

"I know you didn't, and that's the problem. You couldn't see what it was doing to us."

"Us?" I asked, confused.

"Yes, us. Do you have any idea how many nights I had to explain to Gio and Angela why you were behaving the way you were? Why were you basically ignoring them? It was torture for all of us."

I knew that Danielle was upset about this, but I had absolutely no idea that the kids noticed. That got to me more than anything else. I tried to keep my composure but couldn't at the thought of not only hurting my wife, but my kids as well. What had happened to me? Why was I so blind to this?

"Danielle," I said through my tears. "I want you to know that I asked to be off of this case early on. Remember that morning when I blew up at Gio for not getting ready for school and stormed out the door? The first time you got visibly mad at me. Well, I went to Thomas's office that day and asked to be taken off the Lancaster case because I did not like how I behaved. I had a meltdown in my car before I went into the office. He convinced me to give it two more weeks and before I knew it, it had been two months. By that point, I was in too deep to turn my back on the firm and my client. I hope you understand that."

"I do understand that," Danielle said as her tears started up again. "What I don't understand is that after fourteen years, you feel like you couldn't tell me. Or worse yet, didn't realize that you should tell me."

"I don't know what to say. I'm sorry. I am truly sorry. What would you like me to do? I will do anything to make this right. I just want you and the kids to come home. I miss you," I said fighting back tears.

"I want you to leave, Sal. I think we need to take a break from each other. I don't know if I can move past this," Danielle said as she began to cry a little harder.

"No, that can't be what you want. You love me. I know you do. We can work this out. We have never let anything get in the way of us before, and we certainly aren't going to start now."

"Not this time, Sal. I'm sorry, but I don't want this right now. Maybe things will change in the future, but right now I need time to think. I think it is best if you just go," Danielle uttered quietly.

"For how long, Danielle?"

"As long as it takes. I'm sorry if I hurt you, but if you love me, you will honor my request."

I am a defense attorney for the second largest law firm in the city. I have gotten juries to doubt my clients' guilt when there was no way I supposed to be able to do that. I had a rebuttal for everything. Every argument and contradiction. But not this time. This time I was so heartbroken I had no comeback. No clever question or statement. All I could do was stare at the floor in disbelief. My marriage of ten years seemed to be ending right before my eyes, and there was not a damn thing I could do about it. I started crying again. Within seconds, I could not hold back the waterworks.

"The kids?" I asked Danielle, although I don't think she understood me because of how hard I was crying.

"You can say goodbye now, then we will talk about when you can see them again," Danielle said cold-heartedly.

"I don't want them to see me like this. Just tell them I had an emergency and had to leave."

"Okay," Danielle replied softly, now crying even harder.

"So, this is it?" I asked, hoping she would say no.

"Yeah, it looks that way," Danielle agreed, turning away so she didn't have to see me leave.

I peeked my head out of the study to make sure nobody was there. I did not want anyone to see me like this, especially my kids. The coast was clear so I headed to the front door as fast as I could. I opened the door slowly and looked back to see if Danielle was behind me to tell me she had changed her mind. That she realized she was mistaken and wanted to reconcile our differences. That our kids were too important to her to let this come between us. However, she was not there. All I could see was the study door closing. Nobody else was in the hallway. I was all alone. I walked out of the house and closed the door ever so softly behind me, not knowing when I would see my wife or kids again.

Chapter 27

On the drive over to see Sean at Rikers after the riot, I felt like I was living someone else's life. Danielle and I had never had an argument last more than a few hours, so for this to happen was completely new territory. I was trying to wrap my head around the idea that there must be some other reason why she wanted to separate. After all the time we had spent together, to possibly end our marriage over my recent behavior change because of a heavy workload seemed ludicrous. What was I missing?

When I pulled up to Rikers, I sat in my car and didn't move. I didn't have any clue what to do or what to say to Sean when I saw him. He was in the infirmary for internal bruising and a few lacerations across his forehead stemming from the riot. Before meeting with Danielle, my intention was to be rough with him to see if my theory was correct. But now, I wasn't sure if I could even get out of my car. I began to replay all the happy moments with Danielle, starting with that baseball game where I first met her. She was so beautiful and shy that I knew I had to seize the opportunity to ask her out. Our first date was spectacular. I went all out for her. We had dinner at Carmine's and then went to see *Mamma Mia!* with front row seats. We instantly fell in love and had a lavish wedding that included over two hundred guests. All of these memories came rushing back to me like a tidal wave headed for shore. I was so overcome with emotion that I again broke down and started crying tears I didn't know I had left.

I knew I could not let Sean see me like this, so I tried to calm myself down by focusing on the task at hand. It seemed to work a little bit, as I forced myself out of the car. I dried my eyes as best I could and walked with my head down so people would not see me. I must not have done a good enough job because everyone was looking at me with a look that implied, *I hope he is okay*.

I went through the annoying process I always do when I visit Sean, only this time I did it in complete silence. No talking with the guards. No flirting with the prison doctor. Nothing. I needed to concentrate not only on what I would ask Sean, but on how I would prevent myself from letting him see me like this.

When I walked into the infirmary, Sean was hooked up to a few IV lines that I assumed had some type of painkiller in them. I would use this to my advantage because he would not be at his sharpest with all those meds coursing through his body. Once again, I underestimated Sean Lancaster.

"Rough morning, huh?" Sean said.

"What do you mean?" I asked, hoping he had not noticed.

"Well, besides the puffy eyes and red nose, word is that your wife is leaving you," Sean said with a hint of joy.

How the hell did he know that? He said he has sources on the outside, but this had *just* happened. I hadn't calmed down yet, and he already knew? Was I being bugged or followed? I took a few moments to compose myself, not allowing the tears to come back in front of this asshole. Once I was able to speak, I let him have it.

"Okay, enough games, fuckface. How did you know that? Who do you have tailing me? If you want me to continue to represent you, you'd better start talking. And I meant *right now*."

"Wow. Quite the temper there. No wonder Danielle is leaving you," Sean teased.

"I will ask you again, how do you know that?" I demanded, ignoring his comment. "You better tell me, or your face will look a lot worse than it does right now."

"Is that a threat, Counselor? I didn't think lawyers were allowed to make threats, especially to their clients."

"You will tell me eventually, even if I have to beat it out of you when this is all over," I said with as much anger as I have ever had.

"Promise?" Sean said with a smile.

"Tell me what happened to you, and no lying."

"Aw, no more games? No more Mr. Hothead? Okay, fine. What does it look like? I got the wrong side of a riot gone bad," Sean declared.

"How did it start?

"I don't remember. One moment I was in my cell, then doors opened for chow time, and the next moment I was being pounded on by three or four guys."

"Come on. You expect me to believe that bullshit?" I said, annoyed.

"Believe what you want, but that's what happened."

I could see Sean wasn't going to budge on his story, and I did not feel this was the right time to ask him if he started it, so I just went along with what he said and explained what would happen next.

"Fine. I was able to ask the judge to allow you a few days to recover. He is giving you two days. We will resume the trial on Friday morning at nine o'clock," I told Sean, not caring what he thought about his court schedule.

"Two days? That's it? Why the short amount of time?" Sean asked, seemingly nervous.

"Why do you ask? Do you need more time? Your injuries aren't that severe. Besides, you will be on painkillers, so you will be flying high through the whole thing."

"That isn't enough time for me. You need to go back to DeSanto and ask for more time. I need at least a week. Dr. Rivera will confirm that," Sean demanded, even more nervous now.

"She will, huh? Will she also confirm the fact that you started the riot?"

I saw a dramatic change in Sean's demeanor when I told him that the judge was only allowing him two days. Truth is, I never spoke to Judge DeSanto. I wanted to gauge how much Sean was really hurt and when the appropriate time was to strike. My ability to read people was finally coming back. I had to strike while the iron was hot.

"What do you mean?" Sean asked, acting confused.

"Sean, please. Give it up. I am your lawyer, for Christ's sake. Anything you tell me is strictly protected by the attorney-client privilege unless you confess to a crime. So please, just come out with it because I already know. Why did you start the riot this morning?"

I knew I had him cornered. It felt good to have the upper hand with Sean for the first time. I couldn't wait to hear what he had to say. How he would try to squirm his way out of this one. His wit and charm could not save him now. Not even his money would do him any good with me. I just waited patiently for him to spill what happened so we could move on to the trial.

"I'm not feeling so good. Doctor, can you please ask my attorney to leave. I would like to get some sleep," Sean said without emotion.

I was surprised but not shocked I had not gotten Sean to admit what he had done. He is very meticulous in everything he does, which is to say he does not make many mistakes. As I was leaving the infirmary, Sean whistled at me to get my attention.

"See you on Friday, Counselor," Sean said, giving me a wink and a smile.

"Actually, I will see you tomorrow. I never spoke to the judge. Wear your black suit. It matches your soul."

Chapter 28

The courtroom was at capacity when I entered a little before nine o'clock. There were TV and newspaper reporters lined up in the back row. Sean and Denise's families occupied the first two rows, and curious spectators filled the rows in between. I had never been involved in a case with this much press before, and it was little unnerving, which surprised me. Sean was brought in a few minutes after me and right away went into attack mode.

"You son of a bitch. You lied to me, you prick."

"And?" I gloated.

"I should file a complaint against you and have you removed," Sean uttered.

"All rise."

"Too late," I said with a big smile on my face.

"Ladies and Gentlemen, I want to apologize for the delay we had yesterday. It is a good thing Mr. Lancaster is okay and is able to continue so quickly. I was expecting to give him some time to recover, but Mr. Amici assured me he did not need it," Judge DeSanto remarked.

The look Sean gave me after that should have been one of fear. He was trying to intimidate me by squinting his eyes and curling his upper lip. He thought I would be scared off by him making a fist and letting me see that he had no intention of taking it easy on me. None of that worked. I had gotten a call from the court clerk to ask if Sean needed extra time, and I said he did not before I even met with him. I played a hunch that he would not admit to me what he had done once I accused him of it, and I was right. It felt good. Really good.

"Something you want to say *Sean baby*?" I whispered to him.

"Not now. Later," Sean said beneath his breath.

"Mr. Weatherford, are you ready to call your next witness?" Judge DeSanto asked.

"Yes, Your Honor. The state would like to call Dr. Davis," Bryce stated.

After being administered the oath, Bryce began his questioning of Dr. Davis.

"Would you please state your name and position for the court, please, sir?"

"Dr. Randolph Davis, chief medical examiner for New York County."

"Thank you. Dr. Davis, how many years of experience have you had in the medical field?" Bryce asked.

"Thirty-one," Dr. Davis answered proudly.

"That's quite impressive. And how many of them have been spent as chief medical examiner?"

"Twenty-seven," Dr. Davis answered proudly again.

"In your twenty-seven years of experience as a chief medical examiner, have you ever been doubted in regard to your findings during an autopsy?" Bryce questioned.

"All the time, sir. It is natural to second guess the person determining the cause of death."

"How does that make you feel?"

"Objection!" I shouted. "What do the doctor's feelings have to do with what he found?"

"Overruled!" Judge DeSanto barked.

"Doctor?" Bryce asked, redirecting Dr. Harris.

"It doesn't bother me. It is part of the job."

"Can you describe for the court what your findings were on the four victims in the Lancaster murders?" Bryce asked.

"Each victim had multiple stab wounds. The female victims had more stab wounds than the male victims. The female victims also had several bruises all over their bodies, indicating they were also beaten," Dr. Davis explained.

I felt Sean pinch my leg, which was our signal that he wanted me to object, but I could not in this instance. What Dr. Davis had described was fact, and objecting to that would show fear of the truth. I slapped his hand away and turned my face from him.

"Can you tell the court what type of knife was used for the stabbings?"

"Objection, Your Honor! The witness is a medical doctor, not a knife expert," I stated.

"Sustained. Rephrase your question, Mr. Weatherford," Judge DeSanto ordered.

"Yes, Your Honor. Is it possible to determine what type of knife was used in this crime?" Bryce said, looking over at me with a look of disdain.

"It is possible if I am looking for it; however, in this case, I was concerned with cause and time of death, not the type of weapon used," the doctor replied.

"So you don't know what type of knife was used?"

"No."

"Were you able to determine time of death?" Bryce asked, hope filling his tone.

"Yes. I was able to determine that time of death occurred somewhere between ten p.m. and one a.m.," Dr. Davis answered.

"Thank you, Dr. Davis. No further questions," Bryce concluded.

"Mr. Amici!" Judge DeSanto spoke.

"Thank you, Judge. Dr. Davis, where did you go to medical school?"

"Harvard," Dr. Davis said as he rose his chest to brag.

"Wow, that's impressive. What type of grades did you get?" I asked.

"Objection!" yelled Bryce. "Relevance?"

"Relevance is coming up, Your Honor. I am asking for a few more minutes, please," I pleaded.

"Very well. Objection overruled."

I looked at Dr. Davis to signal him to continue, which he did because he knew what was coming.

"I was an A and B student," Dr. Davis said.

"I see. And what was your method of study? Was it group, individual, office hours with the professors?"

"All of the above. What does this have to do with my examinations?" Dr. Davis asked, clearly getting annoyed.

"Oh, I'm sorry, Doctor. I am the lawyer, so I ask the questions here. And it has to do with your examinations because you were not quite the top student you make yourself out to be, were you?" I accused.

"Objection! Speculation, Your Honor!" Bryce yelled.

"Overruled!" Judge DeSanto yelled back.

I was shocked that the judge had overruled this objection. I had a backup question because I was fully expecting him to do so.

"I am not sure what you mean, Mr. Amici," Dr. Davis stated nervously.

"Do you know a man by the name of James Whitfield?" I asked the doctor, knowing that he did.

The face of Dr. Davis turned whiter than Casper the Ghost. He was clearly rattled and did not know how to respond. I had decided in my prep the night before that I was going to go for it right away and not beat around the bush. The state had too much evidence against Sean, so I needed to establish doubt in credibility right away. There was no better way to do that than with the second witness.

"Yes, I do. He was my roommate at med school."

"He also just happened to be the teacher's assistant in over seventy-five percent of your classes, wasn't he?" I questioned as I continued to squeeze the air out of Dr. Davis.

"Yes."

"Was he something else to you as well?" I asked, looking back at Dr. Davis's wife.

"What do you mean?" asked Dr. Davis, shifting uncomfortably in his chair.

"Oh, you know what I mean. Come on... you *know*."

"Objection! He is intimidating the witness, Your Honor!" Bryce interjected.

"Sustained. Mr. Amici, watch yourself."

"Yes, sir. Dr. Davis. Mr. Whitfield was, in fact, your boyfriend, wasn't he?" I finally revealed.

"No, not at all. I have no idea what you are talking about. I am not gay. Honey, I'm not gay!" Dr. Davis shouted to his wife as he stood up in his chair.

Judge DeSanto banged his gavel with all his might and almost broke the judge's bench. "Order! I want order right now!" Judge DeSanto screamed.

The courtroom became deathly silent out of fear more than instruction. My job was done with Dr. Davis. I did not feel the need to humiliate him any more than I already had.

"No more questions, Your Honor," I concluded.

As Dr. Davis stepped down from the witness stand, he hung his head in shame. I had only found this out a week ago and was not planning on using it, but something inside me drove me to bring it out now. Was it my anger at what was going on with Danielle or my desire to make Sean happy so he would back off? Whatever it was, it worked. It was a complete shift in how I normally question witnesses. And I have to admit, I liked it.

"Atta boy! My hero," Sean said as he patted me on the shoulder.

"Oh, I am just getting started. Buckle up," I replied, winking at him.

Chapter 29

The next few witnesses were more technical than anything else. They provided testimony of how they suspect the murders took place and where in the home they did. I had warned Sean about these testimonies not painting a good picture for him before the trial because they would show he had the means beyond a reasonable doubt. I coached him to remain stoic and not react to anything that was said. I further explained that this was vital because it would show the jury that he had nothing to hide and, in fact, expected what was said. To my surprise, Sean actually listened to me and didn't move a muscle during the three hours of testimony. With each passing question, I was waiting for him to show his true emotion. It never happened, which made my job a lot easier. After the last witness, the judge ordered a recess for lunch. Instead of grabbing a bite to eat, I decided to head back to the office to check in with the partners.

When I arrived at the office, there was an eerie silence not often seen these days. There was nobody running to the copier or bathroom. The phones were not ringing off the hook, and most of the offices were dark. It felt like I had stepped into a scene from a horror movie, waiting for Freddy or Jason to come out and kill me.

I went to my office and sat down in my chair. Jill was not at her desk, so I called her to try and find out what was going on. Her phone went right to voicemail, which meant it was completely off. I then sent her a text, not expecting an answer right away because her phone was off. Five minutes later I got a text message back that rocked me to my core.

I can't believe you haven't heard. We are all at New York Presbyterian. Thomas had a stroke.

I didn't know what to do. I had been dealing with so much lately that I seemed to be immune to this news affecting me. Thomas Greenwood was like a second father to me. He gave me the opportunity at Lowery, Hill, and Greenwood and had been by my side ever since. He showed amazing confidence in me by assigning me the Lancaster case, even when I wanted to be taken off of it. I couldn't go to the hospital now because I was due back in court in fifty minutes, and Judge DeSanto would never grant me a continuance until tomorrow. I sat at my desk, pondering what to do next. Instinctively, I went to call Danielle, but I knew that was the wrong move. I called anyway and got her voicemail, which, surprisingly, filled me with relief. In the message, I detailed what had happened and asked her to call me if she wanted. I said nothing else, although the urge to let her know I was thinking of her was strong.

I quickly refocused my attention back to Thomas and what was going on. I thought of the meeting we had when I told him I wanted off the case and how he refused to let it happen. He had a way of making me feel I was a better person than I believed myself to be. After our conversation that day, I believed I could conquer the world. Amazingly, two months had passed before I realized I had promised him two weeks, not two months. It didn't matter because by then, I was well into the case and making good strides. A half smile formed on my face, and I realized that Thomas was right... again.

I recalled the advice he gave me a week before the trial began. He told me I was no longer just a cog in the wheel at the firm. I was now one of the microchips that powered the motor. He trusted so much in my ability and dedication; it didn't matter to him what the other partners thought. He pushed me to reach outside my comfort zone, and now he was lying in a hospital bed.

How was I supposed to go into court with this on my mind and no details? That would not be fair to Sean or the court, but I would have to push through somehow.

I texted Jill back.

> Let me know if there are any developments. I have a big afternoon ahead of me, so I won't be able to visit right now.

She never responded.

I entered the courtroom after lunch, trying not to let my emotions show. Right away, Sean noticed something different. I explained to him what happened and that I would try my hardest in that afternoon to put it aside so I could cross-examine the next witness. When I told him the next witness was Joseph Love, he immediately turned around in his chair to see his old friend and partner sitting in the back of the courtroom, wondering if he was there to seal his fate or help set him free.

Chapter 30

The afternoon session of the trial began with the judge providing the jury some further instructions about following the case on TV or on the Internet. He made sure they understood they were not to have any outside influences under any circumstances. Once his instructions were complete, Bryce Weatherford called Joseph Love to the stand.

"Good afternoon, Mr. Love," Bryce said.

"Joseph, please. Just Joseph. You say Mr. Love, and I turn around to look for my father," Joseph joked. The audience members in the courtroom chuckled a bit at his humor.

"Okay then, Joseph," Bryce said through a smile. "Can you tell the court how you know the defendant?"

"Sean and I were business partners and close friends."

"When was this?"

"We met in 1999 at college and became business partners shortly thereafter," Joseph answered.

"And where was that?"

"Boston University," Joseph said proudly.

"How did you become business partners?"

"We were both hungry for money and girls. We knew the girls would come if the money did. Plus, the corporate life was not for us. We wanted to go into business for ourselves, so we spent the next few years trying to develop innovative ideas."

"And what was the last innovative idea you both decided on?" Bryce asked.

"Have you ever been in a NYC taxi, Mr. Weatherford?" Joseph said with a big grin. Once again, the audience in the courtroom laughed. Making people laugh seemed to be Joseph's comfort zone. I made sure to make a mental note of that.

"Yes, of course I have. So you and Sean developed the touchless payment pads now used in taxis?"

"We developed the idea and practical uses. We hired one team to develop the technology and another team to build the devices."

"So is it fair to say that you and Sean were equal partners?" Bryce continued.

"Yes, that is fair to say, but he didn't see it that way."

"Objection, Your Honor. Hearsay!" I said as I stood up and banged my knee on the table.

"Please explain, Mr. Amici," Judge DeSanto stated.

"There is no possible way that Mr. Love could have known what my client was feeling when they were business partners," I answered.

"Sustained!" Judge DeSanto ruled.

"Joseph, how would you describe your business relationship with the defendant?" Bryce redirected.

"It was great in the beginning. We saw eye to eye on everything and were thrilled we had so many investors interested in our idea. We had to hire several attorneys to help us dig through the legal stuff, but when we finally got the product off the ground, it really took off. Money started flying in, and we didn't know what to do with any of it."

"When did it begin to go south?"

"When Sean decided that he didn't want to share the profits with me anymore, which was about five years ago," Joseph said in a much more serious tone.

"Can you talk about what happened between the two of you?"

"Well, basically, Sean told me one day that he was spinning the company off to manufacture devices for other industries. I asked him when he started thinking about this, and he told me he'd begun planning it the moment we made our first million."

"How did that make you feel?"

"Angry and betrayed. Sean and I weren't just business partners; we were best friends. I never thought he could do something like this," Joseph said, trying to hold back tears.

"What did you say to him at that time?"

"I asked him why I wasn't included and what that meant for our partnership."

"What was his response?" Bryce asked softly, walking toward the jury box.

After taking several moments to pause and collect himself, Joseph finally uttered, "He told me I wasn't in his future plans anymore and that he would kill anyone who stood in his way."

I looked at the jury immediately after that statement and saw shock and horror on the majority of their faces. It was obviously a very damning statement; one which I could not object to because there was no legal reason to do so. I looked at Sean, and his face remained unfazed and stone cold. If he did indeed say that, then he was doing a masterful job of hiding his true feelings.

"Thank you, Mr. Love. No further questions," Bryce said as he motioned to me to take over.

"Mr. Love, thank you for joining us today. I hope it is not too much of an inconvenience for you," I said, intending to cause confusion.

"I am sorry. I don't follow," Joseph said with the confusion I was looking for.

"There is nothing to follow. I was just saying I hope we are not causing too much of an inconvenience pulling you away from your job as CEO of Love-Bannister Technologies."

"Oh, I see. No, it's fine, just doing my part," Joseph said nervously.

"What part is that, sir?" I asked.

"You know, helping serve justice."

"I see. You sure you don't mean fulfilling your desire to get revenge?" I stated, now in full-on attack mode.

"Objection, Your Honor! Move to strike!" Bryce screamed.

"Sustained! The jury will disregard counsel's last question. Mr. Amici, I am not going to tell you again. Watch yourself," Judge DeSanto said while pointing his finger at me.

"I apologize, Your Honor. Mr. Love, please tell the court what it is that you do."

"Well, as you mentioned, I am CEO of Love-Bannister Technologies. We manufacture many of the components that go into high-end electronics," Joseph Love answered.

"Love-Bannister? Are you partners with someone else?"

"Yes, Peter Bannister."

"I see. And how did the two of you meet?"

"Actually, we met through Sean."

"Interesting. When did you first meet Peter?" I asked, causing at least two jurors to sit forward in their seats.

"In February of 2000," Joseph said, seeming to know where this was going.

"I'm sorry, did you say February of 2000?" I asked.

"Yes."

"Wasn't that around the time you began getting investors for your project with Sean?"

"Yes. We actually signed our first contract in late 1999," Joseph answered, realizing he had taken the bait.

"Well, if you signed your first contract in late 1999, and you met Peter in 2000, when was it that Sean allegedly betrayed you and said he wanted to go off on his own?" I asked with an edge to my voice.

"I don't recall," Joseph answered angrily.

"You don't recall? Mr. Love, you testified earlier that you felt angry and betrayed that Sean would venture off without consulting you, and when you confronted him about it, he told you he would kill anyone who stood in his way. How can you not remember when that occurred?" I asked, beginning to raise my voice.

"Objection! Defense is badgering the witness," Bryce said.

"Overruled!"

"Please explain that to me, Mr. Love," I said, waiting for an answer.

"Peter and I did not venture into business together until after Sean had disclosed, he was going off on his own. I had no choice but seek out another partner if I wanted to make money. I sure couldn't use the idea that Sean and I came up with, so Peter and I had to come up with something different."

"Why were you not able to use the idea you and Sean came up with together? It was just as much yours as it was his. Didn't you want to argue that in court?" I asked, moving toward the jury box.

"I just wanted it to be over, so I let Sean have it," Joseph answered, annoyed.

"You let him have it? Mr. Love, you just stated that the idea for the touchless payment pads was yours and Sean's. That implies an equal partnership. Yet now, you are testifying that you let him have it. Was that because it was his idea and not yours?"

"Objection!" Bryce immediately interrupted, hoping to disrupt my flow.

"Overruled!" Judge DeSanto said, with a hint of joy lacing his tone.

The jury was now fully engaged with my cross-examination. I carefully watched their reaction to my questioning because they were offering up valuable non-verbal clues that aided me in how I should continue and what missions I would abort. They were clearly interested in what I was saying, so I decided to press the gas pedal a little farther.

"Well, Mr. Love. Was it Sean's idea and not yours to create the touchless pads?"

"Yes, it was," Joseph answered, lowering his head in shame.

"And it was, in fact, you who broke things off with Sean, wasn't it?"

"Yes," Joseph shamefully echoed his previous answer.

"When did Peter Bannister approach you to go into business with him?" I asked, not knowing the answer.

"Around three months after we met. Sean had just secured another investor and needed me to sign some contracts. It was at that time I told him I wanted out and was going into business with Peter."

"Aha, I see. Well, thank you for your candor, Mr. Love. It is nice to finally have the truth be told. No more questions, Your Honor."

When I returned to the defense table, Sean had a smile from ear to ear and patted me on the knee.

"This is easier than I thought it would be. You really are as good as advertised," Sean said, bright-white teeth showing from his arrogant mouth.

"Relax, tiger. This is the easy part. We still need to explain the forensic evidence."

Chapter 31

On my way to New York Presbyterian, I called Danielle to tell her what had happened with Thomas. I knew she wasn't going to answer, so I had a voice message preplanned in my mind.

"Hey, it's me. I know you are mad at me, but I am not calling about us. Thomas had a stroke this morning, and it's not looking too good. He is at New York Presbyterian. I am headed over there now. It would be nice if you could stop by. Okay, talk to you soon. Bye."

When I got to Thomas's room, there was barely any room to stand. The allowable visitors per room was four, which was clearly being violated. After I shook hands, hugged, and kissed everyone in the room, I got my first look at Thomas. It was a sight I was not prepared for. He was lying in the bed, motionless, with numerous tubes attached to his upper body. He was on a ventilator and had an IV in his right arm, which was dripping three different medications into his body. A machine stood next to his bed, flashing his vital signs, prepared to beep when something abnormal occurred. It took all of five seconds for me to lose control. I covered my mouth and tried to prevent a meltdown, but it could not be avoided. Alan Lowery put his arm around me, which made it worse. I wanted to find out Thomas's prognosis but was simultaneously afraid to hear it.

I finally was able to track down Thomas's doctor and ask what was going on. I told him I wanted to know the truth and to offer up no bullshit. After some pushback because of HIPAA, he finally relented and told me that Thomas had suffered a major stroke. As a result, he had massive swelling of the brain, and his reticular activating system (RAS) had suffered severe damage. He further explained that the RAS is the part of the brain that is responsible for waking and sleeping. When there is damage done to that system, the person will fall into a coma, and there is no telling if or when he will come out. The doctor then went on to tell me that they were also treating him with heparin prophylaxis, which was to prevent potential blood clots that can occur from immobility.

I thanked the doctor for his honesty and went to call Danielle again. She didn't answer, so I left another message letting her know how severe the situation was. After I hung up, I tried to process everything the doctor had told me, but couldn't. All I could think of was that Thomas would get better soon and be back at the office before I finished cross-examining my next witness. While I was in the hallway deep in thought, loud synchronized beeps began coming from Thomas's room, followed by a flock of running nurses. Everyone was rushed out of the room as the nurses lowered Thomas's bed, laying him down flat. The hallway outside of Thomas's room was crowded as all of us tried to peek inside to see what was going on, but nobody could get a clear view. The doctor with whom I was just speaking rushed into the room, nearly barreling me over.

After a few agonizing minutes, the loud beeping sounds subsided and were replaced with low-pitched, rhythmic beeps. The doctor came out and told us that the swelling in Thomas's brain was getting worse and was pressing on his spine, which is what caused the machines to sound off. He said they needed to perform a decompressive hemicraniectomy, which is a procedure that removes part of the skull so the pressure can be relieved. This surgery, he informed, had to be executed right away or he would die. That hit me like a ton of bricks. I have seen this situation on TV and in the movies but have never had to deal with it in real life. Not wanting everyone see how fragile I was, I stepped up and offered to speak to Thomas's wife, Evelyn, and explain to her what was going on. I also needed to inform her that her consent was needed to perform the procedure because she was Thomas's medical proxy.

Evelyn was in the cafeteria getting a cup of coffee and missed the entire fiasco upstairs. When I saw her sitting alone and looking up at the heavens for answers, I knew my task was going to be a difficult one; possibly one of the hardest I had ever endured.

Chapter 32

"How is the trial going?" Titus asked Sean as he revealed a pair of Aces.

"As planned, my friend, as planned," Sean said and folded his hand.

In fact, the trial was going better than Sean had anticipated. He knew that once he heard Joseph Love would be called as a witness, there was a chance his defense would be blown up before it even began. To his surprise, Sal was able to avoid such disaster and somehow shame Joseph at the same time.

"My lawyer is a genius. I knew he was good, which is why I asked for him, but I had no idea he was *this* good," Sean said with a smile that could have reached coast to coast across the United States. "I mean he keeps mowing down these witnesses and making them look like fools. He shamed the medical examiner and Joseph Love with such precision, it ought to be illegal."

"You think he can defend me? I got this dude who doesn't know his head from his asshole," Titus replied.

"Oh no, my friend, you can't afford him. It's on you," Sean said as he raised the bet.

"Fuck you, you prick," Titus said with a chuckle.

Sean and Titus had been hosting a "no limit, Texas hold 'em" game for the past few weeks. The buy-in was five packs of cigarettes, but they played with real money. Some of the inmates got their money from their commissary accounts. Some from the shitty jobs they did around the jail. But most got their money from stealing. Sean quickly began to realize just how much these inmates like to steal, so he paid a few of them handsomely to steal items for him that he could exchange for favors later on. The average stack an inmate would need for one of these games was one hundred dollars.

Titus looked Sean up and down, trying to decide whether or not he was bluffing like he had the previous four hands. After careful thought, Titus called Sean's bet with a pair of threes. When Sean flipped over a full house, Titus took the chair he was sitting in and threw it across the room. It struck the inmate sitting in the corner, who was reading a book, and startled him. When the inmate confronted Titus, Titus proceeded to beat the ever-loving shit out of him. He pounded and pounded on him like he was flattening chicken to make chicken parmigiana. It took three guards to pull Titus off the inmate and restrain him. When they finally did, they ordered him to be sent to solitary confinement. As Titus was being brought away, he looked at Sean and winked. Sean did not know what that meant, but it did not sit too well with him.

Once the beaten inmate was taken to the infirmary for what undoubtedly would be a long time, Sean continued the card game with the two inmates who were left.

"I don't believe I know your names," Sean said, implying that they'd better tell him their names.

"I am Nick, and this is Bob," one of the inmates said.

"Nick and Bob. Okay, I can deal with that. If that's what you want to be called, so be it," Sean said, not believing them.

"It's your move, Bob," Sean said.

"Before I move, I have a question for you, rich boy," Bob whispered.

"Yeah, what's that?" Sean asked.

"What are going to do now that your protection isn't here anymore?"

"Who, Titus? Oh, he's my protection alright, but he ain't the only one," Sean said as he whistled.

As soon as Sean whistled, six guards came out from behind the wall in back of both Nick and Bob. They each were holding a baton and slapping it on one hand.

"See, boys, in a place like this, money is king. I have all of it, and you have none. Got it?" Sean said proudly.

Both Nick and Bob gulped and began to back off when both of them were struck in the legs with batons. They instantly collapsed and curled up into balls as the guards continued to pummel them from all directions. It seemed as though the guards were synchronized because both Nick and Bob were being hit in the same place at the same time by two different guards. When those guards got tired, they tagged the others to replace them. This went on for five minutes before Sean put his hand up.

"Enough. I think they have learned their lesson for today. What do you think, boys?"

Each of the six guards were covered in blood, huffing and puffing, trying to catch their breath. Sean put a hundred-dollar bill in each guard's breast pocket and signaled for them to leave. Once all of the guards left, Sean had one final message for the badly beaten inmates.

"I think you got it wrong, Bob. Titus is not my protection. *I am his*," Sean said as he walked away, laughing and whistling the theme to *The Andy Griffith Show*.

Chapter 33

When Evelyn Greenwood looked my direction, she immediately burst into tears. I had known Evelyn for over a decade and regarded her as one of the most eloquent speakers I know. She was always able to express herself in a way that made me see things from her perspective, even if I disagreed with her opinion. It was painful to see her like this, a broken-down wife who seemed to have lost all hope.

As I approached Evelyn to give her what might be the most important hug of her life, my phone buzzed. I ignored it because I needed to be there for Evelyn and not get distracted. Before I could extend my arms, she fell into my arms and buried her head in my chest.

"My god, Sal. How can this happen? I can't do this without him," Evelyn said, sobbing.

"I know, I know. But Ev... I need you to listen to me right now," I said, then ducked down in front of her so I could look into her eyes. "The doctors need to perform a procedure that will relieve pressure in Thomas's brain. Right now, the pressure is causing other problems that could be fatal. They need your consent to do so. I need you to follow me right now. We can talk about this after."

Evelyn seemed to understand what I was saying because right away she stopped crying and focused on me.

"Okay, let's go. Did they tell you anything else?" she asked as we began to trot to the elevator.

"No. They only told me the necessities. I don't think there is anything more they *can* tell us right now without doing the surgery."

"Sal, I don't know what to do. Who do I call? What preparations do I make?" Evelyn asked, tears spilling down her cheeks.

"Ev, we have time to worry about that later. Let's just get upstairs so they can perform the surgery on Thomas."

After what seemed like an eternity, we finally reached Thomas's room. I walked Evelyn inside and introduced her to the neurosurgeon who would be performing the surgery and then left the room. I could hear Evelyn screaming as I walked out but did not turn around. She needed to handle this on her own and listen to what the doctor had to say on her own.

Once she gave her consent, the doctor ran out of the room and ordered transport to come and take Thomas to the operating room immediately. Most of the crowd that was there earlier had left, but I wanted to stay with Evelyn to make sure she was okay.

"Do you need anything? Is there anything I can do for you?" I asked Evelyn as I wrapped my arm around her.

"No, I don't think so. I am just so lost right now. I don't know what I want."

"Well, I will stay with you as long as you need," I reassured Evelyn.

"That is very sweet, Sal. But you need to go home and get some rest. I heard the trial is going to start getting intense very soon."

"Rest is overrated. I can sleep a few hours here."

"Sal, don't make me more upset than I already am. Go home!" Evelyn barked at me.

"Yes, ma'am. Promise me you will call if you need anything or if there is anything new developing."

"I will. I promise. Good night, Sal," Evelyn said as she kissed me on the cheek.

"Good night. Ev," I said, then walked away.

When I got to my car, I had to collect myself before I would make one last attempt to contact Danielle. The fact that she had not returned my calls really was aggravating me because Thomas's situation had nothing to do with us. I decided to send a text message instead of calling because I knew she would see it.

> Danielle, I know you have seen me try to call you. I don't know why you won't call back. This has NOTHING to do with us. Thomas is in the hospital. He had a stroke and is in bad shape. Can you please put your feelings aside and call me? Thank you.

I sent the text and began to drive home, hoping that I would hear from her soon. I was not prepared for what I would encounter when I got home.

Chapter 34

When I pulled up to my house, I saw the living room light was on. I never leave the lights on in the house, so right away I was alarmed. It was not until I saw the car parked on the street that I got out of my car to prepare for whatever battle lay ahead of me.

I opened the front door and was greeted with a bear hug that I desperately needed. My six-year-old Angela was a sight for sore eyes, and I just melted into her embrace.

"Hey, angel, how are you?" I asked, picking her up as high as I could.

"I'm good, Daddy. I have missed you so much. When can we see each other every day from now on?" Angela asked me innocently.

"Soon, honey. Soon. Is Mommy here?"

"She is in the bathroom. Where else?" Angela said jokingly.

"Hey, Dad," Gio said as he came in from the kitchen.

"What's up, dude?" I said, smiling.

"Nothing. I'm gonna watch some TV," Gio offered, hanging his head.

"Wait a second, young man. What's wrong?"

"Nothing. I just want to watch TV," Gio replied.

"Uh-uh. Not until you tell me what's wrong."

"What do you think is wrong? You and Mom fight all the time. She calls you names when you are not around to defend yourself. I never get to see or talk to you. And the worst part about all of this is nobody has once asked me how I feel or how I'm handling all of this stuff!" Gio yelled back.

I had never seen my son so upset before, but he was right. What he didn't understand was that this was Danielle's fault, something I am sure she has not acknowledged or admitted to Gio.

"I know, Gio. I am sorry things have gone the way they have. I truly am. Has your mother told you why?" I asked, afraid of his answer.

"She said she was tired of you working all the time and not spending time with us anymore. She also said that you said some mean things to her."

"Like what?" I asked with my teeth closed together.

"I'm not going to repeat. You need to ask her," Gio said.

"Okay, just know that not all of that is true."

"Whatever. Now can I go watch some TV?" Gio asked with that puppy dog look on his face.

"Yeah, go ahead."

When Gio went into the other room, I went into the kitchen to make myself something to eat. I was not really hungry, but it had been a long day, and I knew I needed something in my stomach. All I could think about was how the surgery was going with Thomas and what his prognosis would look like after. I tried to redirect my focus on the case but was not able to. I was completely lost in thought when Danielle came into the kitchen and surprised me.

"You alright?" Danielle asked as she began to rub my shoulders.

"Not really. I take it you got my messages?" I asked with an attitude of bitterness. The shoulder rubbing stopped.

"Yeah, I got them," Danielle said with a tone that made my anger seem like kindness. "What am I supposed to do? Just drop what I am doing because you have an emergency?"

"Huh? *I* have an emergency? My boss, our friend, had a massive stroke and is in surgery to save his life, and you can't send a simple text to see what's going on?" I yelled, feeling my blood begin to boil.

"Ugh. Let's not do this in front of the kids, huh?" Danielle whispered.

"Why? You afraid it will ruin your little lie about me being the villain? What the hell happened to you, Danielle? It's like you are a totally different person."

"Whatever. How is Thomas?" she asked, quickly changing the topic.

"It's too early to tell. He is having surgery to relieve the pressure in his brain. The doctors have given him less than a 50 percent chance of survival," I said, holding back tears.

"How's Evelyn?"

"She is a mess, as expected. I was with her right before I left the hospital. She will update me if anything changes."

"Poor woman. Maybe I should head over there to be with her," Danielle said, to my surprise.

"I think that is a good idea. She needs someone right now, and the two of you are close."

"Okay. Can the kids stay here?"

"Of course. I'm sure they will love it!" I said with as much enthusiasm as I could muster in that moment.

Danielle said goodbye to the kids and let me know she would text me with an update when she got to the hospital. I finished my meal and went into the living room to be with my kids. It had been a long time since we had spent meaningful time together, and I was going to enjoy every minute of it, even if that meant I would get little sleep.

"Have you thought anymore about the playroom for me, Daddy?" Angela asked with a huge smile on her face.

"Not yet, honey. I told you maybe someday, but not now."

"I get it," Angela replied, disappointed.

The rest of the evening was uneventful yet satisfying. Being with my kids for a few hours was a welcomed activity. For most of the night I sat on the couch and observed them play and bicker with each other. When it was bedtime, they each went to bed without an issue, which left me alone again. I had not heard from Danielle yet, so I decided to call Evelyn to see if I could get an update. When Evelyn answered the phone, crying, I knew something was terribly wrong.

Chapter 35

In preparing for his trial the following day, Sean Lancaster began to think of how he would react to the testimony he was sure would paint him in a very unfavorable light. Sal had advised him to act as though everything that was said during the trial was what he expected. That was easy to say because it was not Sal's freedom on trial. Sean thought about the dozens of people he had screwed over the past two decades and who might come back to get their revenge. That was a long list, so he decided it was best to just focus on what he could control: the guards.

Sean was going down his list of guards who were on his payroll and those who had refused his money. There were far more guards who took his generosity than those who didn't, but the ones who had refused were more powerful. That would pose a potential problem if Sean wanted to have contraband snuck in or special privileges invoked. Some of those privileges included extended yard time, phone use any time of day, visitors at any hour, and any job he wanted. As he was going through his list, one of *his* guards approached his cell.

"I don't know how much longer I can keep this up?" the guard said.

"Keep what up?"

"This sneaking around shit. The phone calls and visitors," the guard said quietly.

"What the fuck are you talking about?" Sean said angrily.

"You have a visitor, you prick."

The guard escorted Sean to his usual meeting place, trying to remain as quiet as possible. Sean followed the guard all the way the end of the hallway, trying to think of who needed to see him this late at night. It didn't matter to him, though, because it was a chance to get out of his cell and roam around the small meeting room as if he were back in his office.

"Don't take too long, Casanova," the guard said as Sean slipped a hundred-dollar bill in his pocket.

With the guard paid, Sean headed into the meeting room with a huge smile on his face. When he saw who was waiting for him, that smile quickly went away.

"What the hell are you doing here?" Sean said with a bit of rage lacing his tone.

"I had to see you. It's been a rough night," Danielle said.

"Are you crazy coming here? We had a deal. No visits."

"I know, but let me explain."

"Explain what? You shouldn't be here. You are jeopardizing everything," Sean said as he grabbed Danielle's arm to escort her out.

Danielle wiggled free from his grip and sat down on the one chair that was in the room.

"Listen to me for once, Sean. Nobody knows I am here. Thomas Greenwood had a stroke this morning and is in the hospital. Sal thinks I went to visit his wife at the hospital. I made sure to say it loud enough so my kids heard it as well," Danielle explained.

"And what happens when Sal calls Thomas's wife and she tells him you never came to see her?"

"Got that covered. I called Evelyn on my way here and told her that I was on my way and was stuck in traffic. Manhattan always has construction going on overnight, which makes that believable," Danielle said and winked at Sean.

"Clever. I taught you well, huh?" Sean said as he leaned in to give Danielle a kiss.

"Very well. But there are a few things I need to teach you," Danielle replied as she began to tear off Sean's jumpsuit.

Sean had not expected this, but he was going to enjoy it. He and Danielle had not been intimate in months, and he missed her scent and touch. There was no bed or soft area in the room, so Sean had to bear the cold metal floor while Danielle sat on top of him. They climaxed together, which caught the attention of the guard patrolling the area. Neither Sean nor Danielle cared that the guard walked in on them and ordered them to get dressed. Sean stood up and looked at guard as he stepped one leg into his prison jumpsuit, which made the man look away. Danielle put on a reverse strip show for the guard, even getting close enough to tease him.

"Let's go, Lancaster," the guard ordered, trying to hide his discomfort.

"In a minute, boss. Can't you see I am on a date here?" Sean said sarcastically.

"I'll show you a date," the guard said as he took out his baton and went to hit Sean behind the knee with it. What the guard did not know was that Sean was a black belt in Taekwondo and had quick reflexes, which always took people by surprise. Sean grabbed the baton from the guard and, in the same motion, swung it across the guard's face. The guard's nose shattered, and blood went all over the room. Sean continued to beat the guard until he was knocked out. Danielle was surprisingly aroused by Sean's behavior. Although covered in blood, she was ready for round two.

"Not now. Not with all that blood on you. How am I going to explain the blood on me when I go back to my cell?" Sean said to Danielle.

"You're right. I'm sorry. It's just I miss you and want you so bad."

"Me, too, but we need to get you cleaned up first."

Sean peaked out of the room he was in and saw a guard walking toward him. He was happy to see him because he knew this was his way out.

"Jimbo! Hey, Jimbo, come here. I need your help," Sean whispered.

Jimbo Duncan rolled his eyes and let out a loud, deep breath. He had no idea Sean was in that room and was completely taken back when he saw what had happened.

"What the hell, man!" Jimbo yelled as he jumped backward into the hallway.

"No time for that now. I need your help. We have to get this body out of here and clean up the room," Sean instructed as he grabbed the beaten guard's feet.

"You want me to help you cover up a crime? That is too far, man. No way," Jimbo objected.

"Oh, really? Do I need to remind you of the weekly deposit you get and the meaning of the gray van that is always parked outside of your house?"

"No, you don't, but Sean, there has to be a limit to what is expected of me. I am studying to be a cop. I can't get involved in something like this. Please," Jimbo begged.

For the first time since he was in Rikers, Sean felt guilty about the way he was treating someone. He understood what Jimbo was saying, and the poor guy did not deserve to have his job put in jeopardy.

"Okay, okay. I get it. Can you at least help get Ms. Smith cleaned up?" Sean asked politely.

"Ms. Smith?" Jimbo repeated with sarcasm.

"Yeah, Ms. Smith. That okay with you?"

"Sure thing. Right this way, Ms. Smith," Jimbo said, glancing back at Sean with squinted eyes.

Sean winked at Danielle and mouthed *I love you* to her. She mouthed she loved him back and went off with Jimbo to get cleaned up. After Danielle left, Sean finished getting dressed, moved the body of the beaten guard into a nearby locker, and headed back to his cell to get some much-needed rest. He was going to need it for the long day in court tomorrow.

Chapter 36

"Evelyn, what's wrong?" I asked nervously.

"Thomas stopped breathing for a minute or two. The doctors said that can happen when the brain cells are destroyed because of a stroke... or something like that. I don't know," Evelyn said, barely able to get the words out.

"Oh my god. Ev, I'm so sorry. I was going to stay home with my kids, but if you need me there—"

"Yes! Yes, I do, Sal. Please come as quick as you can. I need someone with me," Evelyn pleaded.

"Wait, where is Danielle? Isn't she with you?"

"No, not yet. She called a little while ago and said she was in traffic."

"That's strange. Traffic at this hour? Anyway, I am on my way," I assured Evelyn.

I called our neighbor and asked if she could watch the kids after explaining what had happened. She agreed and came over after she changed into a sweat outfit. I checked on the kids one more time before I left. However, I could not get one thing out of my head. Why was Danielle not at the hospital? Even if she was stuck in traffic, she should have been there by now. I tried calling Danielle from the car but got her voicemail again. I didn't want to leave a voicemail, so I sent her an angry text message.

Where the fuck are you? Evelyn said you haven't gotten there yet. Where did you go instead? And don't lie.

I was unsure when she would receive the text, and frankly, I didn't care. The only thing on my mind right now was getting to the hospital and being there for Evelyn. When I arrived at the hospital, I was fortunate to find a parking spot in the first row. Even at one in the morning, the parking lot was three-quarters full. The walk to Thomas's room on the fourth floor seemed like an eternity. I was speed walking as fast as I could, but it was still not fast enough. With each step I took, I was getting more and more nervous and scared. I felt something in the pit of my stomach that I don't normally feel, which is why I didn't know what it meant. I finally arrived at Thomas's room to find Evelyn sitting in a chair next to Thomas's bed. She was holding his hand and stroking his hair while singing their wedding song to him: "Can't Help Falling in Love" by Elvis Presley.

"Ahem." I cleared my throat to announce my arrival. "Evelyn," I said, trying to be as quiet as I could be.

"Oh, hey, Sal. I know he can hear me. He loves this song so much," Evelyn said as she broke down yet again in my arms.

I have been around grieving people many times. Some have been family and friends; others have been the victims of the clients I've defended. Most of them are consolable when they are around other people, but I had never seen someone so grief stricken as Evelyn was in that moment. Thomas was still alive, but only barely. I knew Evelyn was a strong woman, so to see her like this really broke my heart.

"I'm so sorry, Ev. Is there anything I can do? Do you need anything?"

"Yeah, can you get me some coffee, please? I have been up for God knows how long and am running on fumes."

"Sure thing. Black, right?" I asked her.

"Normally, yes. Tonight, I need some sugar as well."

"You got it. I will be right back," I said, turning around to leave the room.

Just as exited, I heard loud beeping and screaming coming from Thomas's room.

"Nurse! Nurse! Come quick!" Evelyn screamed frantically.

Three nurses came running into Thomas's room to assess the situation. The charge nurse immediately paged Dr. James, Thomas's doctor, and called for a stroke code, which let the doctors and staff on the floor know there was an emergency. I grabbed Evelyn to move her out of the way, and she started kicking and screaming that she wanted to stay, but the doctors and nurses had ordered both of us out of the room.

In the hallway, Evelyn continued to cry and scream, so I did my best to calm her down. I felt the best way to do that was to remove her from the situation and let her cool off. I also felt that being so close to Thomas's room and hearing what was going on was not helping her. She finally agreed to take a walk with me to try and gather herself. As we walked to the waiting area, I called Alan and Steven to let them know they'd better come down to the hospital and double-time it.

Alan and Steve arrived in record time and immediately went to Evelyn to console her. They both asked me what was going on, and I tried to explain the best I could what had happened, but my mind was all over the place. Just as I finished explaining my gibberish to Alan and Steven, Dr. James finally found us to provide an update.

"Mrs. Greenwood, your husband stopped breathing again, even though he is on a ventilator. However, this time it was for several minutes. This is called respiratory distress. It typically takes about five minutes for brain cells to begin dying without oxygen, which is why we had to rush as fast as we did." Dr. James took a deep breath and was about to tell us the news we knew was coming yet did not want to hear. "Mrs. Greenwood, your husband went over seven minutes without oxygen flowing to his brain. That is far too long. We were able to help him breathe again with the life support machine, but I do not expect a full recovery. I am so very sorry. There is nothing more we can do. I will give you some time," Dr. James said as he walked away slowly and kept his head bowed respectfully.

I glanced over at Evelyn after hearing the devastating news to see her reaction. Her hand was over her wide-open mouth, and she was staring at the floor. She was motionless, almost as if she were a mannequin. She wasn't crying or screaming or saying anything for that matter. I motioned to Alan and Steven to console her and said I was going to ask the doctor a few questions.

I ran down the hallway after the doctor, waking up some patients in the process.

"Doctor James! Doctor James!" I yelled to get his attention.

"Sal, what is it?" Dr. James asked, shocked that I was running after him.

"Doc, I appreciate your frankness with us, but what do we do next?" I asked, out of breath.

"Well, that is up to Mrs. Greenwood. Like I said, I do not expect a full recovery from Mr. Greenwood, so it is up to her how to proceed."

"Not a full recovery? So there will be a partial recovery? What does that mean?" I asked, using my experience as an attorney to solicit an answer from Dr. James.

"No, Sal. No recovery at all. Full recovery is medical jargon for the patient not getting better," Dr. James said bluntly. "I am sorry, but sooner or later, Mrs. Greenwood is going to have to decide when to turn life support off."

"How much time before he goes after the machine is turned off?" I asked, fighting back tears.

"It depends. Sometimes it can be hours, days, even weeks. In Mr. Greenwood's case, I suspect it will be quick."

"Thank you, Dr. James. You have been terrific," I said and shook his hand.

I knew I had to tell Evelyn what Dr. James and I had spoken about, but how was I to tell a grieving wife to turn off the life support machine on her husband of almost forty years? I walked back slowly to the waiting room where I caught eyes with Alan and Steven. I titled my head to the right, signaling them to meet me the hallway.

"What is it, Sal?" Alan asked.

"I just spoke with Dr. James. He basically said that Evelyn needs to decide when to pull the plug because Thomas will not recover."

"Geez," Steven said, taking a deep breath and rubbing his forehead with his left thumb and forefinger.

"What do we do?" Alan asked.

"Well, we need to tell her what she needs to do, although I think she already knows," I answered.

"Guys. Let's get this over with," Evelyn said as she walked right past us toward Thomas's room.

"Do what, Ev?" I asked her.

"You know. Don't make me say it, Sal. Please?" Evelyn said as she entered Thomas's room.

The four of us stood in the hospital room, not saying a word. We all knew what had to be done, yet none of us wanted to do it. Thomas was the patriarch of our family and the backbone of the firm. I was still in denial that this had happened to him. A part of me still clung to the hope that there was something we could do. I thought of mentioning the idea of getting a second opinion but thought better of it when Evelyn started sobbing again.

The silence in the room was broken when my phone rang. I looked at the caller ID and saw it was Danielle, so I rejected the call. I was in no mood to deal with her shit at that moment. Quite honestly, I wasn't up for her fake sympathy. My phone rang again. This time, instead of rejecting the call, I threw it against wall. The phone shattered into pieces, but I didn't care. All I wanted was for Thomas to wake up and yell at me for breaking my phone.

The four of us decided it was best if I stayed with Evelyn while Alan and Steven worked on getting a continuance. I told them I did not want one because that is not what Thomas would have wanted, but I was overruled. As soon as Alan and Steven left the room, Thomas's machines began to beep again. I looked at his vital signs on the patient monitor and saw that his oxygen level was plummeting and rapidly falling into the eighties. His heart rate slowed to a crawl, and his blood pressure took a nosedive as well. His temperature rose to over 102 degrees, and his breathing became labored, even while on a ventilator. Alan and Steven came rushing into the room and immediately went to call the doctor. I grabbed Alan's arm and shook my head no, but he managed to break free and run to the nurse's station. Three nurses came charging in and paged Dr. James STAT. After a few minutes, the nurses and Dr. James managed to stabilize Thomas, but we all knew what had to be done.

Evelyn was looking at me with great fear. It was the most fear I had ever seen in someone. Her eyes got wide, and she was shaking uncontrollably. She gave me the slightest nod and then looked away. I told Dr. James that Evelyn did not want Thomas to suffer anymore and asked him to remove the tubes and shut down the life-support machine. Once Dr. James explained how Thomas would be taken off life support and the proper paperwork was signed, he and the nurses began the devastating process of shutting everything down. Evelyn was kneeling beside his bed, squeezing his hand and telling him how much she loved him. Alan and Steven were leaning against the wall with their hands over their mouths. I stood at the foot of Thomas's bed and said a prayer for him. Over the next few minutes, nobody made a sound or moved a muscle. At 2:13 a.m., we all watched Thomas Greenwood take his last breath.

Chapter 37

The drive home was very quiet. I needed it to be. No music. No phone calls, though I'd broken my phone at the hospital. Nothing fought for my attention. I felt as though a part of me had been ripped out and thrown into the garbage. The pain was so intense, it clogged up my throat. Thomas Greenwood, my mentor and father figure, was gone. How would I be able to move on in the trial or any other trial? I began to doubt myself when I remembered something Thomas had told me when I first came to Lowery, Hill, and Greenwood: "Son, you are about enter a world of deceit and lies. As long as you are always cognizant of where you are going and how to get there, you will be okay."

Those words were never truer than they were in that moment because I did not know where I was going. I was grieving the loss of Thomas, yet knew I had to regain focus because there was another long day in court set to begin in six hours. I had not felt this much pain since my brother Peter was killed in college back in the late nineties. He was killed in a hit-and-run in one of the parking lots on campus. The driver fled and was never found. That is what led me to become a lawyer. I wanted to put people away who committed violent crimes but ended up being a defense attorney because of the money. Plus, I do believe in defending those who have been done wrong by the justice system. After driving around aimlessly for a while, I figured there was no use sleeping, so I went straight to the office to begin preparing for the next round of witnesses.

When I got to office a little after three in the morning, only the front desk security guard was there. It is an inexplicable feeling being the only one in the building with all of the lights off. I could hear every noise there was, from the heat kicking on to the creaking of the walls. It seemed as though I was paying too much attention to my surroundings, almost as if I was subconsciously telling myself to slow down and enjoy life. It was in that moment I began to feel a peace come over me for the first time that night. Not that I had accepted Thomas's death; far from it. But that I was ready to continue on because I knew I had Thomas watching over me.

I finally got to my office a few moments later and was surprised when I saw a fruit basket on my desk. I immediately had an idea who it was from and became really angry. I grabbed the card attached to the basket and read it out loud.

Sorry for your loss. I know it must be difficult, but I am here if you need me.

—Sean

My first thought was, *How the hell did Sean find out what happened from a jail cell?* That thought was followed by, *Who is feeding him information?* I began thinking about all of the contacts Sean told me about when we first met, and none of them made sense. The people on his list were business associates, family, and prominent figures in New York City. None of them would qualify as a spy and certainly would not want to get mixed up with Sean Lancaster and his mess. I continued to rack my brain but could not come up with anything. I was missing something and felt frustrated I was not able to figure out the critical piece of information. I would have to confront Sean when I saw him later that morning.

As the hours passed by and the sun began to rise, I realized that I was due in court in one hour and had not showered or changed my clothes. I always keep a spare suit in my office for situations like this, so I quickly redressed and hoped nobody would notice that I hadn't showered. I gathered the paperwork I had been working on all night and headed to the courthouse without any sleep over the past twenty-six hours. It was going to be a longer day than usual.

Chapter 38

Being in a courtroom is oftentimes my sanctuary. I feel alive and free when I am at the defendant table. I am in control of what happens because I ask the questions no one else thinks of. I am the one who gets to pick apart a witness for the prosecution and put doubt into the minds of the jury. That is a lot of power to hold, and with it comes great responsibility. It takes skill to not let that power get to my head so I can remain laser focused. That morning, however, I was having such a hard time concentrating on what I was doing that I walked into the wrong courtroom.

When I located the correct courtroom, everyone was waiting for me. I felt like I was on the stage of a Broadway play because all eyes were on me. I could feel the sympathy from those who knew what had happened, which is something I did not want. If I had my way, I wanted this day to be as normal as possible, but I knew that was a pipe dream.

As soon as I sat down, Judge DeSanto asked both myself and Bryce to join him at the sidebar.

"Mr. Amici, first let me say that I am terribly sorry for your loss. Thomas was a great friend to everyone in this courtroom," Judge DeSanto said with as much sympathy as I had ever felt from him.

"Thank you, Your Honor."

"Second, as I'm sure you are aware, Alan and Steven asked me if I would consider a continuance, given the circumstances. I have absolutely no problem granting one, and I spoke with Mr. Weatherford as well. He also is okay with a continuance."

"I appreciate that, Judge and Bryce. However, I would like to continue as scheduled, if that is okay with you. Thomas would not have wanted us to stop the trial, and frankly, I could use the distraction."

"Are you sure, Mr. Amici? This is a one-time offer," Judge DeSanto warned me.

"I am sure, Your Honor. Thank you for your consideration."

"Very well. We shall proceed as scheduled. That's all."

I went back the defendant table where Sean relayed his condolences. Strangely enough, I felt he was sincere. Sean was a very difficult person to read, but now he was wearing his emotions on his sleeve and really seemed genuinely sorry for me.

"Call your next witness, Mr. Weatherford," Judge DeSanto said, kicking off the morning session.

"Yes, Your Honor. The state would like to call Julie Grimaldi," Bryce responded.

"Oh *fuck*!" Sean said to himself.

"What? What's wrong? She worked with your wife, right? She will be an asset to us," I said trying to reassure Sean.

"She didn't just work with her. She was her fucking *boss*. Oh, and she just happened to witness a number of our ugly spats at both the office and our home," Sean said, seemingly scared for the first time.

"Oh fuck is right," I replied.

Either I had missed that little detail during discovery, or it was omitted because I was not prepared to cross-examine Julie if she painted Sean in any kind of violent way. I began to scramble through my notes, turning page after page with determination. Soon, the entire courtroom was looking at me like I was a madman. I realized what was happening and quickly stopped shuffling papers. I apologized to the court and reclined in my seat. The questioning had not yet begun, but already I was feeling the walls caving in.

"Ms. Grimaldi, can you please explain how you know the defendant?" Bryce calmly asked.

"He is the husband of my now-deceased employee, Denise Lancaster," Julie said as she squinted her eyes at Sean.

"And how long have you known him for?"

"I don't really know. Maybe ten years," Julie responded while shrugging her shoulders.

"And in all that time, have you ever witnessed the defendant getting violent?"

"Yes, there were plenty of times. I saw it at the office and at their home when I would come over for dinner parties. Sean has a bad temper, and he was not one to try and hide it. He seemed to thrive on making people think he was a bad ass."

"I see. Can you describe some of those violent episodes you witnessed?" Bryce asked, looking over at me.

I suddenly felt a sharp pinch on my leg and looked over at Sean. He had an angry look on his face and, as usual, began offering advice on how to do my job.

"Hey, Sal, wake up! Aren't you going to object to anything? You are just allowing them to ask questions that will damage my case," Sean whispered to me.

"Objection!" I yelled, then went silent.

"To what, Mr. Amici?" Judge DeSanto asked.

"Uh, the questioning, Your Honor," I answered, unsure of myself.

"Overruled! Please answer the question, Ms. Grimaldi," Judge DeSanto instructed.

"There was a time about a year ago when Sean came to the office to take Denise out to lunch, but she was in a meeting. Apparently, she had not told him she had a meeting in the morning, and he got really pissed and started yelling in her office at nobody that he was wasting his time and that she was an irresponsible bitch. When Denise was told about this, she went to her office to try and calm him down, but all Sean did was yell and berate her. He stormed out of the office and threw a chair in the lobby. Denise was so embarrassed she didn't come out of her office the rest of the day."

"Did she ever talk about it after that?"

"No."

"Are there any other incidents you can recall?"

"Yes. At their house four years ago. We were celebrating a promotion for Denise, and she accidentally spilled red wine on their brand-new white carpet. Sean went crazy. He threw her down on the floor and stormed into the kitchen. Once he cleaned up the mess, he took her wine glass and threw it into the fireplace and told her she couldn't have any more because she was drunk and a klutz. She yelled back at him, and then he slapped her across the face."

"Objection, Your Honor! There is no record of this ever happening!" I shouted, feeling myself coming alive again.

"Ms. Grimaldi, did Mrs. Lancaster press charges?" Judge DeSanto asked.

"No. She was afraid to."

"Well, that is why there is no record of this, Mr. Amici. Overruled!" Judge DeSanto said, seemingly pleased.

I slumped into my chair and felt like a dog with a tail between its legs. This was not going well for Sean or me at all. As much as I tried to concentrate, I was not able to focus the way I normally do in court. I began to think maybe I should have taken that chance for a continuance.

I had not felt this lost since Peter was killed. I was in middle school at the time and remember getting pulled out of class by the school nurse. I broke down in the hallway and had to be sedated at the hospital to calm down. Peter and I were extremely close and did everything together. We both were fanatics about sports, especially baseball. We went to Yankee games on a regular basis and shared an admiration for Mariano Rivera. We also went fishing almost every weekend in New Jersey, where one of his closest friends lived. I loved spending time with Peter, which is what made his death such a devastating event. In fact, it took me almost six months to be able to enjoy life again; time I did not have to mourn Thomas.

"Please continue, Ms. Grimaldi," Bryce said.

"After that incident, I was never invited back to their house, but Denise would tell me that the abuse continued on a regular basis. She was looking for a way out but was too afraid to make a move," Julie testified as she began to cry.

"Thank you, Ms. Grimaldi. No further questions, Your Honor."

"Mr. Amici, do you wish to cross?" Judge DeSanto asked.

I wanted to jump out of my seat and interrogate Julie Grimaldi and expose her for the liar she was, but I did not have the energy to do so. I was going on almost thirty hours of no sleep and was still in shock over Thomas's death. I was unsure of how to question Julie; therefore, I declined to cross-examine her. Instead, I gained permission by the judge to approach the bench.

"Your Honor, I know I said I did not need it, but it is obvious I cannot defend my client to the best of my ability at this moment. Is it possible to reconsider the continuance that was offered earlier?" I asked Judge DeSanto quietly.

"No, it is not. I told you, Mr. Amici, that it was a one-time offer. You chose to be arrogant about the situation, and now you must deal with those consequences. If you feel you need to time away from this case, then you should have thought more about it when it was offered. However, I can see that you have not slept in forever and you are clearly not in the right frame of mind, so I am willing to adjourn proceedings for the rest of the day if Mr. Weatherford can agree to it."

"Of course," Bryce answered quickly. "I want to win this case, but not at the expense of Sal's health."

"Very well. We will adjourn until tomorrow morning. Go get some rest, Mr. Amici," Judge DeSanto said and excused us.

Once the judge announced the adjournment, I told Sean I would see him in the morning and headed straight to my car. No press. No restroom stops. Nothing. I drove home in record time and quickly took off my suit as soon as I walked in the door. As I was about to plop down on my couch to get some much-needed sleep, I got a phone call from a blocked number on my new iPhone that replaced the one I broke the night before. I do not normally answer those calls, but I felt I needed to, given how strangely the day had gone.

"Who is this is?" I asked, having no patience for games.

"No need for hostility, Mr. Amici," the voice on the other end said. "I want to ask you a question. Do you know everything you need to know about Sean Lancaster?"

The phone went dead before I could respond. Who was that, and what did they mean by, "Do you know everything you need to know about Sean Lancaster?" I would not be able to give it much thought because as soon as I lay down, I was out.

Chapter 39

Titus Baxter had been waiting for Sean at the commissary counter for almost four hours when Sean finally emerged from his cell after a nice nap.

"Where the hell have you been?" Titus asked, pacing around.

"Getting my beauty sleep. Why? What's up?"

"We got a problem, man. My guy who supplies us with the cigarettes and other contraband got pinched last night. He is in county lock up," Titus said nervously.

"You act like this is the first time this has happened. Relax, homie, we got this," Sean said, trying to reassure Titus.

"Why are you so calm? From what I hear, your lawyer is about to crack up."

"He will be okay. The man just lost his mentor and family friend. Who wouldn't be ready to crack up?" Sean said.

"Doesn't that worry you? I mean he *is* the only way of helping you live a free life."

"He will be fine. Now about this little business of ours?" Sean said, changing the topic. "Do you know anyone else, or does your guy know anyone else?"

"No, that's the problem. There is nobody else. We are fucked, man."

"Titus, relax. We will figure it out. In the meantime, go collect from those who owe us, and let them know that things are going to get a bit tighter around here."

"With pleasure, boss. By the way, Johnny is looking for you. He told me to keep it quiet, but I don't understand why."

"You don't need to understand why. Did he say where he is?" Sean asked.

"He said the usual spot. You guys aren't like..." Titus asked, afraid of the answer.

"Why, you jealous?"

"Nah, I just have the right to know."

"Calm down, it isn't like that. Not yet, at least," Sean teased.

Sean left his meeting with Titus and went to seek out Johnny at their usual spot, which was a small hallway in the corner of the cafeteria.

"You gotta be careful with Titus. He can be a little bit of a loose cannon," Sean said to Johnny.

"I know. But how else am I supposed to get a message to you?" Johnny asked, shaking.

"You use Jimbo, like we discussed. What is wrong with you?"

"I need a fix, man. I'm dying over here."

"You still on that shit? I told you, you need to get off that stuff to make me feel safe. I am not a drug dealer, so you need to speak to Titus about that," Sean said, annoyed. "Anyway, did you do what I asked?"

"Yes, I did. It went as perfect as you said it would. He was caught totally off guard. And I did it like you told me and hung up right away," Johnny said proudly.

"Good job. You sure you did not give him a chance to speak?"

"Yes, I am sure. I am just curious though. Why did I have to do that?"

"So he didn't have a chance to hear too much of your voice and discover your identity," Sean explained.

"How would he be able to identify me by my voice? He doesn't even know who I am," Johnny asked, confused.

"He doesn't know now, but he will. People never forget a face or voice when they suffer a traumatic event," Sean whispered to Johnny. "Anyway, we need to keep Sal in the dark as long as we can so he can concentrate on my defense. Because when he finds out, he will be even more batshit crazy than he is now."

"Finds out what?" Johnny asked.

"That I was driving the car that killed his brother."

Chapter 40

Over the next few days, everything went as planned. The witnesses who were called by the prosecution did not do anything to hurt my case, and I was getting more sleep because of that fact. The prosecution's case was winding down, and soon I would be able to start my case. I did not have a lot of witnesses who would blow the case open, but the ones I did have were certainly going to create some fireworks.

In what was expected to be another boring day in court, I went through the metal detector like usual and proceeded to the courtroom, when I was stopped by a tap on my shoulder. I turned around and had to blink twice to make sure I was not hallucinating.

"Mrs. Castillo, it is nice to see you," I said, still in astonishment.

"Fuck you, asshole. I came to watch you crash and burn. Don't think for one second I will ever forget what you did to my family," Paola Castillo, mother of David Flores's now deceased wife, said to me.

I had not expected Mrs. Castillo to show up. In fact, I had not even thought about her since the David Flores trial ended. Most mothers would grieve if their child was butchered, but she took the news especially hard. When David Flores was acquitted of his charges, she let out the worst yelp I have ever heard come from a human being. She was devastated that Flores was walking out of the courtroom a free man. She kept saying to me over and over that I would pay for this. She feared for her daughter's life and, in the end, she had a right to.

I did not respond to Mrs. Castillo, just kept on walking, but I was shaken. My legs were wobbly, and my heart was pounding as I entered the courtroom. When I sat down at the defendant table, waiting for Sean to be brought in, I felt a pressure in my head that I had never experienced before. My thoughts spun wildly, leaving me wondering the real reason Mrs. Castillo was here.

When Sean was brought into the courtroom, he had a smile on his face, as if he knew a piece of information that nobody else knew. I could tell he had something to say to me, but I was in no mood to deal with his arrogant crap.

"Why the glum face, Counselor?" Sean asked.

"Why the smug face, Defendant?" I replied.

"Ooh, someone is testy today. Not getting any on the home front lately?"

It took every fiber in my body to refrain from hitting him right there in his seat, but obviously that would not have been good for me. "We will talk later. For now, shut up and let me work," I said as I released my fist under the table.

"Mr. Weatherford, are you ready to continue?" Judge DeSanto asked.

"Yes, Your Honor. The state would like to call Claudia Stetson," Bryce said coolly.

"Did you know about this?" Sean asked in a nervous whisper.

"I saw the name but didn't find out too much on her. Who is she?" I whispered back.

"She is my ex-secretary. The official reason I fired her was negligence, but the real reason was because she wouldn't sleep with me."

"Jesus Christ, Sean. Do you want to win this case or just make me look bad? Didn't you think this was worth mentioning?"

Before Sean could answer, Bryce had begun his questioning.

"Ms. Stetson, thank you for joining us today. Can you tell the court how you know the defendant?" Bryce asked in a calming voice.

"He was my boss. I worked for him for three years," Claudia answered, clearly scared of something.

"Were you still working for him when he was arrested?"

"No, I was fired a few months before that."

"Why?"

There was a long pause before Claudia answered. "He said it was negligence. Want to hear my reason?"

"Objection, Your Honor. The witness's perception of why she was fired is irrelevant!" I shouted.

"Sustained! Just answer the question, Ms. Stetson," Judge DeSanto ordered.

"Sorry, Your Honor."

"Ms. Stetson, why do you think you were fired?" Bryce asked.

"Objection, Your Honor. Again, the witness's perception of why she was fired is irrelevant!" I shouted again.

"Overruled!" Judge DeSanto said and pointed at me to sit down.

"Your Honor?" I protested.

"Mr. Amici, sit down. Objection is heard and overruled. Don't make me say it again."

"Now, Ms. Stetson, why do you think you were fired?" Bryce once again asked her.

"It was because I would not sleep with him," Claudia said, seemingly ashamed.

There was a lot of noise from the crowd in the courtroom, and it took the judge several minutes to calm them down. Scandals always bring out the best reactions from people, even if they are untrue. Just the mention of sexual misconduct in a murder trial is enough to wet someone's appetite for scandal. Once the crowd was settled down and Judge DeSanto had order back in his courtroom, he instructed Bryce to continue.

"Why do you think that, Ms. Stetson?"

"Well, he was always making advances toward me and rubbing my shoulders. At first, I'll admit, I enjoyed it. It was nice having someone pay attention to me. But then it escalated to him making comments on my outfits and that he wondered what I had on underneath my clothes. That's when I began to feel uncomfortable," Claudia said, then paused to try and gather herself.

"Would you like some water?" Bryce asked as if he was caring for his daughter.

"That would be good. Yes please."

Bryce got her a glass of water and some tissues in the event she would begin to cry. It was a wonderful show the two of them were putting on, and I was eager to see where it would go. Usually, when an attorney and a witness conspire to create a performance like this, they make a mistake, and I am good at catching and exploiting these blunders.

"Why did you feel uncomfortable?"

"Because he was my boss. It was supposed to be a professional work environment. I mean, he was Sean Lancaster. I was nobody. I couldn't exactly go to human resources and report him, so I had to take it," Claudia said as she began to sniffle.

"How long did this go on for?"

"I don't know. I lost count."

"Six months, one year?" Bryce pushed on.

"Objection! Asked and answered!" I yelled.

"Sustained. Move on, Mr. Weatherford," Judge DeSanto said.

"What other inappropriate gestures did the defendant make toward you?" Bryce asked, looking over at Sean.

"He... he would come into my office and close the door. Then he would begin to massage my shoulders and neck. I told him to stop and that it was not appropriate, but he wouldn't stop," Claudia said, now on the brink of a full-blown meltdown.

"Did he ever rape you?"

"Oh god no. It never got that far. But he wanted to have sex with me. He mentioned it on more than one occasion," Claudia said, getting her bearings.

"I am curious. How does a prominent figure like Sean Lancaster ask one of his employees to have sex with him? Does he send an email?" Bryce said, trying to make a joke.

The courtroom laughed and then stopped as if they suddenly realized they gravity of what was being discussed. I was going to object, but when I saw that the jury seemed disgusted with his joke, I decided to let him dig his own grave.

"He actually came out once and said I was hot, and he wanted to prove it to me."

"What did you say in response?" Bryce asked her, leaning in.

"I reminded him that he was married, and I wasn't going to break up a family."

"And how did he respond to that?"

"He told me not worry about Denise. That she would be taken care of and out of the picture," Claudia said, hanging her head.

"What did that mean to you, Ms. Stetson?" Bryce asked.

"Objection! The witness's opinion on what she felt that statement meant is irrelevant," I said, sitting in my chair.

"Overruled. In fact, Mr. Amici, it is very relevant. Please go on, Ms. Stetson," Judge DeSanto said softly.

"I asked if he was getting a divorce, but he gave me a creepy smile and said, 'Something like that.'"

"No further questions, Your Honor," Bryce concluded.

"Mr. Amici, do you wish to cross?"

"Oh yeah!" I said with enthusiasm.

"Ms. Stetson, you testified earlier that it was Mr. Lancaster who came on to you. Is that correct?" I began.

"Yes, that is correct," Claudia answered.

"You also testified that you felt uncomfortable by Mr. Lancaster's advances. Is *that* correct?"

"Yes."

"Objection, Your Honor. Relevance?" Bryce questioned.

"I am getting there, Your Honor," I replied.

"Overruled! Continue."

"Thank you. Would it surprise you that Mr. Lancaster felt uncomfortable around you?" I asked.

"Yes, it would. I never did anything to make him feel uncomfortable," Claudia said defensively.

"So you never wrote him erotic poems and left them on his desk?" I could see Claudia begin to shift her position in the witness stand, but I was not ready to deliver the knockout punch yet. "You never asked him to leave his wife in an encrypted email?"

"No, never. That's repulsive to even think about."

"Your Honor, if defense has evidence of such events, let him present it now or move on," Bryce argued, clearly getting annoyed because he had no idea these documents existed.

"Very well. I would like to enter defense exhibits alpha and beta," I said as I handed Judge DeSanto photocopies of emails sent by Claudia to Sean, as well as handwritten poems.

"We will get to those documents later. However, since the objection was overruled and you were allowed to proceed with your answer, I would like for you to elaborate on your interpretation of what you think Mr. Lancaster meant by his wife would be taken care of and out of the picture."

"Well, I already answered that," Claudia said, trying to dismiss my question.

"No, you said you asked him if he was getting a divorce, and then he gave you a creepy smile. I want to know more."

"I am not sure I know what you mean?" Claudia answered, acting coy.

"Okay, let me put it like this. What do you think it means when someone says they are so angry they could kill someone?" I asked Claudia.

"Objection, Your Honor!" Bryce interrupted.

"Overruled."

"But judge—" Bryce pleaded.

"Overruled, *Counselor*!" Judge DeSanto screamed back at Bryce.

This was the first time I had Bryce on the ropes and had the judge pulling the strings. I was going to continue to apply pressure until I cracked Claudia Stetson.

"Ms. Stetson?"

"It is just a saying. I have said it a bunch of times also. It is a way to express how angry someone is."

"That's how I look at it as well. In the times you have said or thought it, have you actually carried it out?" I asked her.

"No, of course not."

"Do you know anyone else who has?"

"No," Claudia said, realizing she had taken my bait.

"Then how can you assume what Mr. Lancaster's intentions were toward his wife? He said something even more vague than what you and I just discussed," I said, feeling like Perry Mason.

After a short pause, Claudia answered, "I can't."

"I see," I said with a smirk and a wink back at Sean. "Where are you currently working now?"

"I am currently unemployed."

"I am sorry to hear that. Where was the last place you worked?" I asked, feeling like I was pulling teeth.

"At a PR firm," Claudia answered.

"And how did your employment end with them?"

"I was fired," Claudia said and put her hand on her forehead as she looked down.

"What happened to get you fired, Ms. Stetson?"

"I guess they didn't want my services anymore. You will have to ask them," Claudia said with arrogance.

"Oh, I intend to. I just figured I would save you the embarrassment, that's all," I joked. "Ms. Stetson, I have just one more question. If you claim that Mr. Lancaster fired you because you would not sleep with him, and that he made all of these unwanted, inappropriate advances toward you, why did you not report any of it to the authorities or human resources?”

Claudia Stetson had been waiting for this question. She was prepped for it by Bryce before her testimony, and she was ready to shine. This was going to be her Oscar moment.

“I didn’t have enough evidence. And before you go trying to throw that in my face, let me explain why.” I was curious to hear her obviously rehearsed speech, so I let her continue without interruption. “Mr. Lancaster is a very resourceful, wealthy, and powerful person. He can pay off anyone he wants to and does a damn good job of putting on a hero’s facade. He is manipulative and covers his tracks very well. Every time he made an advance toward me, it was when nobody was around and just out of sight of the surveillance cameras. He never put anything in emails or memos and always made sure he had an alibi, just in case.”

“Just in case of what?” I interrupted her, knowing that I would catch her off guard.

“You know, in case he was accused of something like he is now,” Claudia answered nervously.

“Why would anyone need an alibi in case they were charged with murder if there is no intent?” I questioned.

“Objection, Your Honor. Leading the witness.”

“I don’t see any leading here. Overruled,” Judge DeSanto said calmly.

“Why would Mr. Flores need an alibi if he had no intention of committing murder?”

“Who?” Claudia asked with a puzzled look on her face.

“Who what? Answer the question please?” I said, losing patience.

“Who is Mr. Flores?” Claudia asked.

I suddenly realized I had said the wrong defendant’s name just moments earlier. So much was on my mind that I was losing concentration. Mrs. Castillo was obviously in my head now, and I needed a quick way out.

“Uh, I meant Mr. Lancaster. Question withdrawn. I have no further questions,” I said and returned to my seat both embarrassed and worried.

After the judge excused Claudia from the witness stand, he asked Bryce to call his next witness.

"You Honor, while I reserve the right to recall witnesses for rebuttal purposes, the state rests," Bryce said with a smile on his face.

"Very well. This court will adjourn until nine o'clock tomorrow morning, at which time the defense will call its first witness," Judge DeSanto instructed, then banged his gavel while giving me a death stare.

I was glad that Bryce was not calling additional witnesses because I wasn't sure if I could handle more of the same questioning. I left the courtroom and began finalizing my defense, although I was not sure which defense I needed to focus on more: Sean's or my major blunder in court.

Chapter 41

On my way home, I got a call from Jill telling me that Alan and Steven wanted to see me. They were leaving the office and wanted to meet me at Raines Law Room, which is one of the classiest bars in Manhattan. I was already on the 3 train, coming up to the Forty-Second Street stop, so I would need to travel to the other side of the subway station to take the train downtown to the Fourteenth Street stop and walk the three blocks to the bar. It sounded more daunting than it turned out to be, and once I got there, I was not so eager to go in. I had not talked to Jill in a few days but figured now was as good a time as ever to get some information from her. Rallying my energy, I called her back before entering the bar.

"Hey, Jill. How did they sound? Mad? Angry?" I asked.

"What would they be mad about?" Jill asked as if she had no idea what I was talking about.

"You didn't hear what happened in court today?"

"Oh, when you said Flores instead of Lancaster?" Jill chuckled.

"Yeah, that... smartass."

"Everyone heard about that, but they didn't mention anything to me about it."

"What else did I miss there over the last few days?"

"Nothing much. Everyone is still in shock over Thomas. Evelyn came by today to clean out his office. She barely got through it," Jill told me.

"I can imagine. How did she seem otherwise?"

"As good as she could be, I guess. She was looking for you though. Said she had something important to talk to you about and asked me to tell you to call her when you can."

"Okay, I will. Thank you, Jill. Go home!" I ordered her jokingly.

"I am. I just have a few more things to wrap up here. Have fun at your meeting," Jill said and then hung up.

I entered the Raines Law Bar from the back entrance so nobody would see me. The bar was a very popular gathering site for lawyers, and everyone would have surely heard about what happened in court today. Unfortunately, I was no mood to deal with any crap I would surely get.

I found Alan and Steven in the back corner, where Thomas and I used to meet. I am not sure if they knew that, but it was a nice touch. When I arrived at the table, it looked like the both of them were a few drinks in, which meant I had some catching up to do.

"Sal! Or should I say Flores?" Steven laughed.

"Okay, let's get it out now. Come on, what else you got?" I said, knowing I would have to take whatever they dealt.

"Nah, no more. We can talk about that tomorrow. For now, we are honoring Thomas. Here, have a drink," Steven said as he handed me a glass of Glenfiddich 12. Seeing the bottle of scotch immediately took me back to the time in Thomas's office when he convinced me to stay on for two weeks after I had told him I wanted off the case. I told him then that I would never drink this garbage again, but I had to break my promise. I needed to honor Thomas and provide myself with closure.

"I hate this shit, Steven. But I am going to suck it up for Thomas. I am sure you know this was his favorite drink," I said.

"Yes, we know. You want to lead the toast, Sal?" Alan volunteered me.

"Sure." I raised my glass and asked Alan and Steven to join me.

"Here's to Thomas Greenwood. One of the classiest people I have ever known. He was a mentor, father figure, colleague, but most of all, a friend." I took a moment to gather myself because I knew I would cry and was not going to fight it. "I owe everything I have today to this firm. Thank you to the both of you and to Thomas for taking a chance on me and believing in me. I never got to know Thomas as much as I would have liked to, but I did know him well enough to know that he would have done anything for anyone, no questions asked. He once told me a story about when he was trying to promote the law firm in the early days at local courthouses. He said he would hand cards out and they would get tossed away right in front of him. He was laughed at and sometimes physically assaulted. He didn't care though. He kept persisting and stayed determined. He eventually caught the eye of a hot-shot attorney, who eventually introduced Thomas to the right people. This lawyer took him under his wing and helped Thomas develop a business plan that jump-started the firm. This lawyer was Nicholas DeSanto. Thomas never forgot that and always managed to stop by Judge DeSanto's courtroom to say hi. What a man Thomas was. Our loss was heaven's gain. Here's to you, Thomas Greenwood. I love you and miss you every day. L'chaim."

The three of us touched our glasses, wiped away our tears, and took a big swig of the twelve-year-old scotch. For the next few minutes, nobody said anything. We just sat there in silence and reflected on what Thomas meant to each of us. Who was going to break the silence? I knew it wasn't going to be me. Turned out, it was Alan.

"Ahem... Sal, that was beautiful. So poignant and eloquent. Thomas would have loved to hear that," Alan said, still wiping away tears.

"He did, Alan. He did," I reassured him.

Alan looked over at Steven, and the both of them nodded at each other. I had no idea what that meant, but I was eager to find out.

"Sal, we asked you here tonight to inform you of a decision we have made. It is a decision that does not come lightly and has taken much thought," Alan said, clearly dragging out what he seemed to not want to say. "You know you have been a valued member of this firm and have handled some of our most important cases. This Lancaster case was given to you because we believe in your ability. We believe in your dedication and devotion to your craft. Given all that you have been through lately, we have been utterly impressed with how you have handled your responsibilities."

I felt a knot tighten in my throat. If he was going to fire me, I wished he would just get it out and put me out of my misery. My legs began to get weak. My head felt like it was floating and spinning at the same time. My hands became clammy, and my heart began to beat faster than it ever had. I was having trouble focusing on what Alan was saying, but knew I had to pull it together so that when he told me I was being let go, I could take it with grace and dignity, thank them for all they have done for me, and walk away.

"To that end," Alan continued, "we have decided to make you the next partner of Lowery, Hill, and Greenwood, effective immediately."

I froze. I did not know how to react or what to say. For the first time in my life, I was speechless.

"It's okay, Sal, you can say something," Steven said with a monster grin on his face.

"Are you fucking kidding me? Is this for real?" I said in astonishment.

"Yes, Sal, it is for real. Or should I say, *partner*?" Alan said as he put his arm around me. "You deserve it. Congratulations!"

As soon as Alan wished me congratulations, the entire bar started clapping and chanted, "Partner! Partner! Partner!" It was so overwhelming and unexpected that I burst into tears. I had been through so much emotion during the past few months, and to have this happen, at this time, on the day when I screwed up royally in court... Well, it meant the world to me.

"Wow, Alan, Steven, I don't know what to say. Thanks to both of you for your confidence in me. I will not let you down."

"We know you won't. Now, let's celebrate and have a good time," Alan said as he ordered another round for the three of us.

The rest of the night was filled with stories of Thomas's legacy and how I got to this point. Even Bryce Weatherford stopped by to congratulate me. I was feeling so confident, so free that it overshadowed all the problems I was facing. This moment and this night were the pinnacle of all the hard work I had put in over the years. Nothing could take me down from the cloud I was riding on. This would turn out to be one of the best nights of my life and one that I would never forget.

Chapter 42

Hangovers are a bitch. They have a way of ruining your day when it hasn't even begun. I had the monster headache of all monster headaches, and my stomach felt like it was being ripped out of my body. I knew I needed grease, and lots of it. Fortunately for me, New York City is flooded with food carts on every corner. I would need to make a stop on the way to work.

I stumbled out of bed and was still half sleep while walking to the shower. I was in such a fog and daze, but I didn't care. I was now a partner of Lowery, Hill, and Greenwood. I would be riding this high as long I needed to in order to get me through the rest of this trial. Last night had been such a surprise, I was still in disbelief. The celebration was perfect. There was nothing that could have been done better. Then, I suddenly felt a great sadness come over me.

I realized in an instant that last night was missing someone. Someone who meant the world to me and had been there with me from the very beginning. I was so caught up in the excitement last night that I failed to realize I was not sharing my success with Danielle. I had not even thought to call or text her. What did that mean? Was I moving on from her, or was I too self-consumed? Before I left the house for court, I decided I needed to call her. To my surprise, she picked up on the first ring.

"Hey, you. What's going on?" Danielle said joyfully.

"Uh, hi. You're in a good mood."

"I am. Feeling pretty upbeat. Not sure why though."

"Well, then I am about to make your mood better. Guess who made partner last night?" I said, not sure of what her reaction would be.

"Ahh! That's terrific, Sal! I am so proud of you! You did it!" Danielle screamed in my ear.

I was sort of taken aback by how happy she was for me and the overall mood she was in. It was as if nothing had ever happened to us. I began to wonder if something was up her sleeve or if she had finally calmed down and wanted to get back together.

"Thank you. I got to be honest, I was not expecting this reaction from you," I said cautiously.

"Oh, Sal. We may have had some issues lately, but I am still your wife, and I still love you. I want to see you succeed for yourself and the kids. Tell you what. Let's all go out and celebrate this weekend as a family. What do you say?"

"Sure. Where?"

"How about Carmine's in Times Square," Danielle suggested.

"Sounds great. It will be fun."

"Sure will. See you there, partner!" Danielle said, then hung up.

I stood in my doorway, not sure what had just happened, but it was a great way to begin my day. It seemed things may finally be turning around for me. I decided to take the train to the courthouse that morning, allowing time for the Tylenol and grease to kick in. I was positive that a beef gyro with extra tzatziki sauce and a hot pretzel would do the trick.

When I arrived at the courthouse, I was greeted by Alan and Steven. They wanted to wish me good luck as I began my case and reminded me of the confidence they have in me. I should have felt good going into the courtroom, but I felt a bit off. It was very unusual for Alan and Steven to show up in court, let alone at eight in the morning. I also kept thinking of what Danielle was up to, because she clearly was not acting the way she had this morning.

Realizing I needed to shift gears into work mode, I shrugged off my doubts and entered the courtroom, beaming with confidence. I knew that today was going to be a bad day for the prosecution because my first witness would set the tone for the fireworks that were set to go off.

Chapter 43

"Mr. Amici, are you ready to call your first witness?" Judge DeSanto asked me as he began the morning session at precisely nine o'clock.

"Yes, Your Honor, I am. The defense would like to call Traci Coleman," I said with a smile.

No one knew who Traci was, I had double-checked my sources, so this witness would be to the defense's advantage.

"Good morning, Ms. Coleman. How are you today?" I began softly.

"Fine. Just want to get this over with," Traci responded with an attitude.

"Well, just answer the questions that are asked of you, and you will be out of here in no time. Do you know my client, Sean Lancaster?"

"Yes, I do."

"How do you know him?"

"He is my... client," Traci said with a hint of embarrassment.

"Your client? What line of work are you in?"

"I am in the entertaining industry... I guess you can say."

"Are you in any movies or on TV?" I asked, already knowing the answer.

"I am an escort, okay? Jeez, nothing like getting embarrassed first thing in the morning."

"There is nothing to be embarrassed about, Ms. Coleman. We are all adults here," I reassured Traci. "Does your business have a name?"

"High End Entertainment, Incorporated," Traci answered.

"I like that. So when you say Sean is your client, you mean he has booked your services?"

"Yes, that is correct."

"Did you know Sean was a married man?"

"I didn't know, and I don't care. I get paid five hundred dollars per hour. There is no reason to ask questions," Traci said smugly.

I gave Traci a look that said she was coming on a bit too strong. I had told her to be defensive and to have a slight attitude, but she was offering too much too early. She seemed to recognize the look because she looked away to refocus.

"Ms. Coleman, do you keep records of all of your clients' appointments?"

"Yes, I do. I have to so someone knows where I am at all times. You never know what kind of creeps are out there."

"You can't be too careful, I agree. Do you remember if you were working on the night of July 17, 2021?" I asked, hoping everyone knew where I was going.

"Yes, I work every night. I have a child to look after."

"Do you happen to remember who some of your clients were that night?"

"Objection! How is the witness supposed to remember who her clients were on one particular night last year if she works every night?" Bryce argued.

"Sustained!" Judge DeSanto ruled.

"I'll rephrase. Ms. Coleman, if I looked at your appointment book, whose name would I see from eight o'clock in the evening on July 17 to two o'clock in the morning of July 18?"

"Sean Lancaster," Traci answered.

Even though everyone in the courtroom knew the answer, it was still a shock to hear Sean's name linked to an escort service.

"I see. Is Mr. Lancaster a frequent customer of yours?"

"Not really. He does book me occasionally. Maybe one or twice a month."

"I would say that is a regular customer, wouldn't you?"

"I guess," Traci answered, uninterested.

"What is the usual form of payment you accept?"

"Cash only. It is better for me and the client if there is not a paper trail."

"I see. If you only accept cash, then why does Mr. Lancaster's credit card statement show a $3,000 charge on the night of July 17, 2021, to High End Entertainment, Incorporated?"

"I don't know. I take cash only. All I know is that Sean paid me in cash that night. Maybe when he booked the visit with the office he paid by card over the phone," Traci answered just as instructed.

"I find that very odd that you do not know what goes on in your business. Either way, you are certain that Sean Lancaster was with you and paid you in cash between the hours of eight o'clock the evening of July 17 to two o'clock the morning of July 18?"

"Yes, I am positive."

"Thank you, Ms. Coleman. No further questions."

"Mr. Weatherford?" Judge DeSanto said.

"Thank you. Ms. Coleman, you say that the defendant was with you between eight o'clock the evening of July 17 to two o'clock the morning of July 18, correct?" Bryce questioned.

"Yes, Sean was with me. I already said that," Traci answered, making sure to say Sean's name as she was told to do.

One of the key aspects to successfully defending a client is to humanize the defendant. The prosecution will almost always refer to the defendant as *defendant* and not by name to make it seem to the jury that that person is not of any importance. As a defense attorney, it is my job to use his or her name as much as possible to make sure the jury knows he has a name and, therefore, has significance to someone. We had prepped Traci for this and instructed her to use Sean's name every time she answered a question. To this point, she was doing a masterful job.

"Hmm. That is interesting because I have surveillance footage of the defendant leaving a convenience store directly across from his home at ten minutes after nine the evening of July 17, 2021," Bryce said, then paused for a response.

"Yes, that is probably correct," Traci said as she hunched her shoulders and smiled as if she was about to blush.

"Wait, I am confused. If you are admitting that he was at that convenience store, then how could you be with him at the same time?"

"Because I was in the car with him. He was stopping to get condoms, a lot of condoms," Traci said, laughing. "He wanted to do it where his wife might see him. It excited him to be in that much possible danger. And when my clients are excited, well... I make more money."

"I see. So when you say you were with the defendant from eight p.m. to two a.m., you were not necessarily in the hotel room with him?" Bryce asked, looking annoyed.

"Right you are, Counselor," Traci said.

"No more questions," Bryce concluded before he dug himself another hole.

"Your Honor, the defense would like recall Dr. Randolph Davis," I said, surprising everyone in the courtroom.

"Dr. Davis, you do realize you are still under oath?" Judge DeSanto asked.

"Yes, Your Honor," Dr. Davis replied.

"Dr. Davis, I have only one question for you, so I promise not to keep you long. You testified earlier that you were able to determine the time of death. Can you please remind the court of that time frame and explain your method to determine that time frame?

"Well, determining a time of death is not an exact science. We can, however, generate solid estimates based on body temperature, rigor mortis status, body decomposition, etcetera. Using these techniques, I was able to determine the time of death between was between ten p.m. and one a.m.," Dr. Davis answered.

"Thank you, Doctor. No more questions."

"Mr. Weatherford, do you wish to cross?" Judge DeSanto asked.

"No, Your Honor," Bryce said, twirling his pen.

"Defense would like to recall Detective Anthony Harris."

"Detective, you are still under oath," Judge DeSanto said, clearly tired of repeating himself.

"Detective, like Dr. Harris, I will not keep you long. I have two questions for you. What time did you arrive on the scene?"

"Around three a.m.," Detective Harris answered.

"And was Sean present at that time?"

"No, he was not."

"Thank you, Detective, no further questions."

The rest of the day was spent going over and refuting forensic evidence that potentially tied Sean to the scene of the crime. I am not much of a forensic expert, so I did not go into too much detail on what I was questioning; just enough to make it seem like I was an expert.

Once the trial ended for the day, I wanted to speak to Sean for a quick moment and asked the judge if I could have a moment with him before he was sent back to Rikers. The judge granted my request and instructed me to wait in his chambers while Sean was cuffed.

"You have five minutes, Mr. Amici," said Judge DeSanto.

"More than enough, Your Honor. Thank you."

"Sean, listen carefully, because I am only going to ask this once. I need to know right here, right now, that you will stick by your story no matter what happens the rest of the way. That you will not deviate from what you told me when we first met. That you understand my career is on the line with this case."

"Yeah, I promise. I won't change it because it is the truth. What's going on?" Sean asked, concerned.

"I made partner last night, and the last thing I need is to look like a fool by a client who lied to me," I said with purpose.

"Congrats, Sal! I am genuinely happy for you. You deserve it."

"Thank you. Just remember, no matter what happens, you cannot deviate from anything."

"Sally, baby, I got it. You can trust me."

Chapter 44

That night in his jail cell, Sean wanted to be left alone. He needed as much rest as he could get because he was in for a rough day the following morning. Of course, in jail there is no such thing as rest.

"Yo, Lancaster! Yo, Sean!" Titus Baxter yelled.

"I am trying to rest. What do you want?" Sean asked, annoyed.

"Rumor has it you and that cat Johnny are tight. What's up with that?"

"Why do you care?"

"Cuz we got this thing going, homie, and I don't want nothing messing it up. That's why," Titus said, getting more assertive than usual.

"Yeah, Johnny and I know each other. That's about it. What have you been hearing?"

"Just that the two of you have been sneaking around, talking to each other about something you guys did together a while back," Titus replied.

Sean felt his body get tense. Who the hell could have heard them? They were so careful not to talk with anyone around. All of a sudden, Sean felt a rage go through him like he had not experienced before. Was jail life getting to him, or was he getting tired of suppressing his anger? Whatever it was, Sean needed to get it out before court the next morning.

"Titus, come here. I need to ask you something," Sean said as calmly as he could.

When Titus was within range, Sean reached his arms through the jail bars, grabbed Titus by the neck, and banged his head repeatedly against the bars. Blood began to pour out of Titus's nose and mouth. His skull was making a cracking noise, but Sean did not stop. His rage was out of control, and he kept shouting, "You fuck! You fuck!" over and over again. After a few seconds, Titus went silent. Sean continued to pull Titus into the jail bars until he ran out of energy. Titus was laying on the ground, motionless. His eyes were severely swollen, and blood covered his entire face. There were numerous teeth spread out on the ground as well. Sean stood there for a few seconds, staring at Titus's body. He then went to his sink to wash his hands and face, then lay down on his cot. He did not say a word, nor did he show that cared at all what he had done. Nobody was around to see what had just happened, so he knew he would not get caught. After a few minutes, Sean began to yell for a guard.

Three guards came rushing to help Titus and call for emergency support. One of the guards asked Sean what happened. Sean explained that he was asleep when he was woken up by fighting. He said he did not see the other person but saw him run off to the left. One of the guards went running down the hallway to the left, while the other two attended to Titus until the doctor got there. The doctor quickly took Titus away, not saying if he was alive or dead. The other two guards escorted Sean to an interrogation room where he would be asked what happened. Sean began to panic because he was not sure what had happened. He knew he went into a fit of rage and recalled grabbing Titus, but everything else was a blur. He would have to think quick on his feet because he needed to confront the one person he suddenly realized could have told Titus that he and Johnny were tight. The one person he talked to about his past with Johnny. The one person who had unlimited access to Titus. James "Jimbo" Duncan.

Chapter 45

I had spent much of the evening watching TV and sipping on Kendall Jackson Chardonnay. I am not much of a wine drinker, but this brand of wine is my favorite. I can drink a whole bottle by myself and be ready for more. I was about three glasses in when I got a call on my cell.

"Hey, what's up?" I said.

"Nothing much. Can we talk?" Danielle said.

"Sure. Let's talk," I said with hope.

"No. In person. Can you meet me at Lou's in an hour?"

"Danielle, it is nine p.m. and I am three glasses of wine in. Can you come here?" I said, hoping she would come.

"I have the kids with me tonight. They are about ready for bed now."

"Oh, bring them. I would love to see them."

"Okay. I will be there in fifteen minutes."

"Great, see you then," I said, smiling ear to ear.

The call from Danielle was so unexpected, I did not know what to do next. I went upstairs to change clothes, put on deodorant and cologne, and brush my hair. I felt like I was getting ready for a first date. Based on our last conversation and then this call out of the blue, I was hopeful she wanted to get back together.

The next ten minutes were some of the longest of my life. Not only was I going to get the chance to speak to Danielle, but I was also going to see my kids. I had missed them so much since this thing with Danielle and I began. I found myself pacing in the living room, gulping my wine. I went through another two glasses by the time they arrived, having opened a second bottle.

"Hi, Daddy! I missed you!" Angela screamed and then ran into my arms.

It felt so good to pick her up and give her a hug. I squeezed her with all my might and did not want to let go. I then went to hug Gio, and he began to cry as he hugged me back. I am not sure if it was a combination of the wine and emotion, or just the emotion, but I cried with him. We all had been through so much the past six months and never had the chance to talk about it as a family. I often wondered what Danielle was telling them about what was going on. I had wanted to ask her but never found the right time. Maybe tonight would be that time.

"Hi, Danielle," I said, leaning in to give her an awkward peck on the cheek.

"Hey, Sal," Danielle said, a bit reserved. "Kids, why don't you go upstairs so your daddy and I can talk."

"Okay, Mommy. I love you, Daddy," Angela said as she ran upstairs.

"See ya, Dad," Gio said and slowly paced himself up the stairs.

"Man, they are complete opposites. How are they handling this? What are you telling them?" I asked as my lawyer instincts took over.

"I know. Angela is okay. She doesn't really know what's going on. Gio sort of knows, but I think he is trying to hide it for Angela's sake."

I couldn't help but thinking that is my boy. Not even ten and already he's the man of the house. I had big dreams for Gio, and he was off to a great start fulfilling them.

Once we were alone, my heart began to race a bit faster. I was not sure what to expect, but I knew it was big for Danielle to come here at this hour and talk. I tried to get a read on her before we started our conversation but she was a closed book. She had developed a great poker face over the years and was using it to perfection. After a few minutes of silence, Danielle finally broke the ice.

"Sal, listen. I need to talk to you. What am I saying, of course you know that," Danielle said, putting her head down and her right hand over her forehead. "I know I have been a mess the past few months. On top of that, I've been trying to make it as easy as possible for you and the kids."

"Well, you sure as hell haven't been doing a good job. What did I do, other than the outburst that morning?" I asked, genuinely confused.

"Sal, it wasn't just that. I told you, it was the fact that you were always so consumed in your work and barely recognized us when you *were* home."

"That's who I am, Danielle. That's what you married. I will always be attached to my work, especially now. I know I need to be around more. And now that I'm a partner, I might be able to do that, but I will still always be on call," I explained, not wanting to sugarcoat anything.

"Ugh, this is not what I wanted to talk about. Sal, I wanted to ask you if you are willing to give me another chance. If you are willing to try and put this behind us so we can move on as a family. I know it is what the kids want, and I want it too," Danielle said with a look of hope on her face.

I didn't know how to react. Half of me was expecting this, while the other half had cautioned me not to get my hopes up. I didn't want to look desperate and give in right away, but I also didn't want to blow this opportunity because I wanted her back in the worst way. I decided to play it cool and see what happened from there.

"Wow. I gotta say, that's a surprise. Not that I mind, because I don't, but where is this coming from? Why the sudden change of heart?"

"Well, I realized we have had a great life together, and it was a bit selfish of me to want you to change all of a sudden. I should have told you how I felt a while ago, but I didn't know how to. Please forgive me," Danielle said.

"Of course, I forgive you. I want us to be a family again, and now it seems like we can be," I said as I leaned in and gave Danielle a soft, romantic kiss.

It was the first kiss we had in over six months, and it felt just as electric as our first kiss many years ago. No matter how much she may have angered me, I still loved her more than ever, and it felt incredible to be close to her again.

"I missed that," I said to Danielle as we embraced on the couch.

"Me too. How much wine did you have?" Danielle asked, smiling.

"Five glasses or so. I wasn't expecting company."

"Why stop now? I'll get another bottle," Danielle said and gave me a peck on the cheek.

We downed the bottle in about twenty minutes and soon made our way to the bedroom.

As we headed into the bedroom and began to undress each other, I got a strange thought that crossed my mind. I am not sure why I thought of it in that moment, but I had to know before we moved further.

"Danielle," I said, pushing her away a bit. "Where did you go the night Thomas died?"

"What?" Danielle asked, caught off guard. "I went to the hospital to be with Evelyn. I told you that."

"I know, but I spoke with Evelyn, and she said you weren't there. She said you called her and said there was traffic."

"Yes, that's right. There was a lot of traffic with the construction going on around William Street. Where is this coming from?" Danielle asked.

"I was just curious because I thought it would take you less time to get to the hospital at that time of night. Where was there traffic, exactly?" I asked, knowing I would get pushback.

Danielle sat up and put on her bra and shirt. "What do you mean *where was the traffic*? What is this?"

"Danielle, I looked up the traffic report that night, and there were no reports of delays or construction anywhere near New York Presbyterian that night. So like I asked earlier, where did you go?"

Danielle took a deep breath and stared at the ceiling. It was in that moment I knew my life would change forever. I knew I had just blown any chance I had at reconciling with Danielle, but I was glad I asked. I needed to know what was going on. I was getting nervous because she looked like she wanted to say something but couldn't get it out. Finally, she did.

"Rikers Island," Danielle said with shame in her voice.

"*Rikers Island*? Why the hell would you go to Rik—?" I asked, suddenly realizing who she saw but needed confirmation. "To see who?"

"Sean Lancaster," Danielle said, hanging her head as low as it could go.

"Why? What possible reason do you have to go see Sean Lancaster in jail?" I asked, confused.

"Sal, do I really have to say it? Come on."

"Say what?" I asked, still confused.

"Sean and I are having an affair, Sal. That's why!" Danielle blurted out with anger.

I felt my stomach drop. I have had heartache plenty of times before. Hell, I was still grieving over Thomas. But *this*? This hit me harder than anything else. I had no idea the two of them even knew each other, let alone were having an affair.

I stood in the corner of our bedroom and looked around. All the memories we made here. The family we built here. Everything was now gone forever. I was in utter disbelief and tried to leave but my legs were locked. My mouth was still wide open, and a sudden feeling of nausea came over me. I was able to free myself enough to run to the bathroom and vomit in the sink. I had never felt like this before, so I was confused on what to do. I stared at myself in the mirror for a good two minutes, then I suddenly had an epiphany. At that moment, I was able to calm down and go back into the bedroom to confront Danielle.

"What you have done to this family and to me is unforgivable. I can't even begin to describe how I feel right now, but I have to put that aside for now. My job is to get that scumbag Sean acquitted. So far, I have been doing an okay job, and I think the jury is with me, but I now know a way to get them totally on my side," I said with a stern voice.

"Yeah, how's that?" Danielle said very softly with a broken voice.

"I'm going to put you on the stand."

Chapter 46

After six grueling hours of interrogation, Sean Lancaster was finally able to relax. He had convinced the guards and the warden that he did not see anything and was sleeping when the altercation took place. He was sure his reputation and deep pockets had something to do with being let go, but he didn't care. He needed to find Jimbo before he went back to court later that morning.

Sean was allowed free time because he missed it earlier. He used this time to ask around to see where Jimbo was. Each person he asked he gave a hundred-dollar bill to so they would keep quiet about him questioning them. Five hundred dollars later, the fifth guard finally was able to tell Sean that Jimbo was last seen in the cafeteria grabbing a snack.

Sean hurried to the cafeteria so he would not miss this opportunity to settle the score. The hallways are not that long, so it took Sean no time at all to reach the cafeteria. He was surprised he was not met with any resistance from the guards, but he wasn't upset with that either. He searched the cafeteria from end to end but did not find Jimbo. He went to search the walk-in refrigerator and dishwashing areas as well. No sign of Jimbo at all. Sean then heard a noise coming from the closet attached to the rear of the cafeteria; the same spot he had met Johnny when he first saw him at Rikers.

Sean walked cautiously over to the closet and opened the door to find Jimbo with a gag in his mouth and his arms tied behind his back. Sean lowered the gag and asked what happened, angry that someone had gotten to him first.

"It was that fuck, Johnny. He cold-cocked me and then must have stuffed me in here," Jimbo explained.

"Probably with good reason. You've been a naughty little boy, Jimbo," Sean said, waving his finger at him.

Jimbo's eyes got wide as he suddenly felt a sense of fear course through his body. He realized he had made a mistake by talking, and now Sean knew that. He was much more afraid of Sean than Johnny, which is why he began to pee all over himself.

"You need a urinal? Damn, Jimbo, you are a little bitch, aren't you? What do you think I am going to do to you?" Sean said, faking a punch to scare Jimbo. "You see, Jimbo, I heard that you ran your mouth about my gatherings with Johnny. I also heard that you also mentioned Johnny and I did something together. You see why this can be a problem for you?"

"I'm sorry, Sean. I really am. I don't know what I was thinking. It will never happen again. I swear. Please don't hurt my family," Jimbo pleaded.

"Oh, I know it won't happen again. You know how I know it won't happen again? This is why..." Sean said as he punched Jimbo in the stomach.

Jimbo doubled over in pain and again apologized to Sean. He was preparing himself for a beating but was surprised when Sean pulled up a chair instead.

"See, Jimbo, this is how it's going to go. You are going to tell whomever you told this little secret to that you were looking for attention and made the whole thing up. You are going to give an Oscar-like performance as if your life depended on it, only it isn't your life on the line. If you want that pretty little thing at home to keep breathing and making you pancakes every morning, you will be very convincing. If you don't, well... let's just say different pieces of Hailey will come to see you from time to time."

"I got it, Sean. Trust me, I do," Jimbo said, shaking nervously.

"Good. Make sure you do. Now tell me how you found out, and remember, don't lie to me."

"Not long ago, I was around the corner when you told Johnny that you were the one driving the car that killed Sal's brother. I made sure to be quiet so you didn't know I was there. I waited until you were gone before I left. I swear I didn't mean to hear that. I wasn't eavesdropping. I just happened to be there," Jimbo explained.

"Alright, alright. Calm down. Jeez, you're freaking me out with your coward chicken-shit attitude. So you heard me say that to Johnny, and then you told *who*?"

"Oh please, Sean, don't make me get him in trouble also," Jimbo begged.

"He already is in trouble; he just doesn't know it yet. That's why I need a name."

"Sean, please," Jimbo continued to beg.

"That's okay, Jimbo. You don't have to tell me," Sean said, patting Jimbo on the shoulder. "I will have my guy ask Hailey if she knows, and then cut off a finger if she doesn't."

"Okay, fine. I told Warden Paulson," Jimbo said, finally caving.

"There. See? That wasn't so hard, was it?" Sean said as he hit Jimbo so hard in the temple, it knocked him out.

Sean got up from his chair and slid it back in its place at the nearest table. This was much bigger than he originally thought because now the warden knew that he killed Sal's brother, and Sean wasn't sure what the warden would do with this information. He needed to confront Warden Paulson as soon as possible, but he first needed to take care of some business before he went back to his cell. He needed to find Johnny and warn him before it was too late.

Chapter 47

While searching for Johnny, Sean began to have what felt like a heart attack. He was breathing heavily and sweat poured down the sides of his head. He had a piercing pain in his chest, and his heart was pounding. He had to sit down for a moment so he didn't fall over from the dizziness he was experiencing. What the hell was going on? Was he going to die right there on the jail floor? After a few minutes, he was able to gather himself enough to continue his search, although he was still shaking quite a bit.

Sean searched all the usual places he thought Johnny would be, but he didn't find him anywhere. He began to panic when a second search of the area turned up nothing. Was Johnny hiding, or did something happen to him? The morning session of his trial was beginning in a few hours, and Sean had not slept at all. He decided he needed at least two hours of sleep but wanted to check one more spot where he thought Johnny might be.

Sean went to the laundry room, where Johnny often smoked up. Sean had warned Johnny about the addiction spiral, but he never listened. Johnny was a drug addict and had no desire to get clean. Sean had done his best to scare Johnny off of drugs, sharing horror stories of how they bring one to death's door through violence, murder, or simply from the body's inability to tolerate high dosages, thus eventually shutting down. But Johnny would have none of it. The truth was, Sean's real motive for Johnny getting off drugs was to prevent a confession. He did not want Johnny, in one of his drug-induced highs, to confess what they had done to someone.

As Sean entered the laundry room, he immediately was blown back by the humidity. It felt like the rainforest in the Everglades in the middle of summer. The laundry room was filled with dirty clothes, towels, and other garments that looked like they belonged in a thrift shop. As Sean made his way through the maze of soiled garments, he spotted something in the corner that caught his eye. He wasn't sure what it was and wasn't sure he wanted to investigate it, but he knew this was his last chance to find Johnny before he left for court.

Sean cleared a path for himself and made his way over to the corner, holding his nose, as a foul stench emanated the area. He knew the laundry room had a distinct smell, but this was something different. He had smelled this before, but not in quite some time. When Sean lifted all of the towels and sheets away that were stacked up, he saw the source of the smell. Johnny was sitting up against the corner of the wall, his eyes wide open, with a needle stuck in the crook of his right arm.

Sean was taken aback at first, but then, selfishly, he began to smile as a feeling of relief settled over him. He realized all his problems had just gone away. He liked Johnny but was not going to lose any sleep now that he was gone. All his secrets would die with Johnny. Sean was now free of his past and did not have to worry about anyone finding out what he had done. Then he remembered that Jimbo had told Warden Paulson what he overheard, and panic set back in as quickly as it had escaped. How much did Jimbo actually tell the Warden? And how much did he actually hear? Sean would not need to wonder for long.

"Damn shame, isn't it? So young," a voice said, approaching Sean.

Sean turned around and stumbled backward, a bit in shock.

"Warden Paulson. I didn't know you came to work this early," Sean said.

"Oh, I usually don't, but I had some paperwork to file and... Oh hell, why am I lying to you? I wanted to talk to you before your trial resumed today," Warden Paulson said slowly now only feet away from Sean.

Sean felt his muscles tense as he wondered what the warden was up to. "Yeah, about what?"

"Oh, I think you know, Sean. Don't try and be cute with me."

"There are so many things I know, Warden. Which *thing* are you talking about?" Sean asked, trying not to sound too nervous.

"Something about a car and a certain brother of a certain prominent attorney."

"Right. That. What do you want to talk about? The type of car it was or what was on the radio?"

"Knock off the shit, Lancaster. I know what happened, and now I want you to know what I am going to do about it," Warden Paulson said, leaning toward Sean's ear. Then he whispered, "Nothing. Absolutely nothing."

"Excuse me, sir. I'm free? Just like that?" Sean asked in amazement.

"Oh, I didn't say that. You are going to be my new informant. You are going to let me know whenever you see something going on that should not be going on. In particular, I want you to watch Titus Baxter. He is bad news. But then, I guess you already knew that," Warden Paulson teased. "I wouldn't be here when they come to get the body. You don't want to go through another interrogation."

Warden Paulson turned around and left while lighting a cigarette and whistling. Sean knew he was fucked one way or another. If he didn't report anything, he would be outed about Sal's brother and face another murder charge. If he reported on Titus's actions, he was setting himself up for punishment, possibly even death. There was only one thing Sean knew to do. One thing that would be his best option to get him out of this mess. He needed to talk to Sal.

Chapter 48

I was woken up the next morning at 5:45 a.m. by a series text messages. I am used to getting text messages at all hours, but they are never a welcome sight when they come that early and that frequent. I cleared the crust from my eyes and looked at my phone through blurry eyes. The messages were from a number I recognized but did not have stored in my phone: Jimbo Duncan.

5:42 a.m.: Sal, it's Sean. I need to talk to you right away.
5:43 a.m.: Sal, where the fuck are you? I know you are up.
5:44 a.m.: WTF Sal? Answer me, you prick.
5:45 a.m.: Tell me where I can meet with you prior to the court hearing today. We need to talk ASAP.

I had no desire to talk to Sean after last night, but he was my client, and I had an obligation to represent him to the best of my ability, and that included returning his text messages. I didn't want Jimbo to be the middle person, so I called his phone instead of texting and asked to speak to Sean. I could tell right away something was wrong.

"Sal, I need to talk to you before court today. Can you meet me at eight o'clock this morning in the courthouse? Room 104."

"Slow down, Sean. What happened?" I asked, trying to avoid an unwanted meeting.

"Not on the phone. Meet me it the courthouse at eight o'clock. I'll be in room 104," Sean repeated, then hung up.

I showered, got dressed, and went downstairs to have breakfast. It's usually a calming feeling to sit in the dark at six a.m. all alone. Typically, I reflect on the day before and then focus on what I have to do that day. This morning, however, was a mess. All I could think of was Sean and Danielle together in my bed. The thought made me so sick to my stomach that I couldn't even finish half of my breakfast. How was I supposed to face Sean when all I wanted to do was beat the ever-living shit out of him? I would have no time to worry about that because I wanted to see what he wanted, and the suspense was driving me crazy.

I arrived at the courthouse at 7:55 a.m. and made a beeline toward courtroom 104, where Sean had requested. We would have the room to ourselves for fifteen minutes, which was fifteen minutes too long for me.

"What is so important?" I asked Sean, annoyed.

"Sal, something happened at Rikers last night that sort of speeds up my need to win this case."

"Excuse me? Your need? What happened that is so catastrophic?"

"I can't tell you yet, but just know that I am in a world of shit if this trial doesn't end soon," Sean said, panicking.

I had never seen Sean panic like this. He always acted calm and collected. I knew something big had to have happened, but I really didn't care. I wanted this trial over for different reasons than he did, and I was confident I could make that happen.

"Well, frankly, I don't give a shit what you want. I need this trial to end soon as well, but it is for a very different reason," I said, anger rising in my tone.

"What does that mean?"

"You will see. Just be prepared to be blown away by my first witness," I said, walking away.

"Who is it?" yelled Sean.

I didn't answer him back. I walked out of the courtroom feeling as giddy as I had in a long time. I had Sean's fate in my hands, and I could send him away for life if I wanted. I had the power to help Bryce's case by misfiring on the examinations of my witnesses and laying a guilty verdict on a silver platter for the prosecution. But that is not what I am about. I am about winning at all costs. I am out to prove to Alan and Steven that they made the correct decision in making me partner. I was preparing myself to win this case, not for Sean, but for me. My job came before anything else, even if that meant ruining the good things in my life. In that moment, I knew what I needed to do. I was going to swing for the fences and go for it all at Danielle's expense.

Chapter 49

"All rise!" the bailiff said. With that, my heart once again began pounding because I was about to create the most fireworks I ever had in the courtroom. I wasn't sure if I was mentally prepared for it, but I was about to find out.

"Who is this witness you are bringing in? Will they help me?" Sean asked, obviously scared.

"Oh, they will help you. They will make you look like the scumbag that you are. Enjoy the show, you prick," I said. Moments later, my knees shaking, the judge asked me to call my first witness.

"Your Honor, the defense would like to call Danielle Amici."

The courtroom burst into a state of shock and disbelief. Sean punched me in the leg and asked what was going on. The judge looked at me with confusion. I had created the perfect storm and had not asked one question yet.

"Objection, Your Honor! This witness was not on the list!" Bryce shouted.

"Your Honor, Mrs. Amici is on the witness list previously disclosed at pretrial," I responded.

I had put Danielle's name on the witness list as precaution. I usually include a witness if I feel there is even a slight chance I might need to call that person. Truth is, I always put Danielle's name on the witness list just in case I need her to testify to either my character or the character of my client. She never knew this, which is why it caught her by surprise when I mentioned it to her the previous night.

"Counselors, approach the bench," Judge DeSanto ordered us.

"Gentleman, why the discrepancy on whether a witness was disclosed?" Judge DeSanto asked.

"Your Honor, Mrs. Amici is on the witness list as a precaution on my part. She is the last name listed," I said boldly.

"I have the list right here, Your Honor. Mrs. Amici is not—" Bryce stopped suddenly. "I must have either missed it before or skipped over it because I did not see her being called as a witness. My mistake, Your Honor. Objection withdrawn," Bryce said, cowering back to his table.

"The witness will be allowed. Please continue, Mr. Amici," Judge DeSanto ruled.

I have known Bryce Weatherford for a number of years and have never seen him make a mistake like this. He is very meticulous in everything he does, so it shocked me that he would not focus on Danielle's name on the witness list. I, of course, did not mind the blunder, as it allowed me to accomplish two things. First, it helped paint Sean as a cheating, lowlife asshole. Second, it allowed me to find out more about what went on between the two of them.

"Thank you, Your Honor. Mrs. Amici, I am going to call you Danielle, if that is okay."

"That would be fine. I am your wife, after all," Danielle joked.

"Okay, then. Danielle, can you please tell the court how you know Sean Lancaster."

"Well, he and I met at a fundraiser a number of years ago."

"What fundraiser was that?" I asked with great interest.

"It was to raise money to rebuild some of the parks in the inner-city area," Danielle answered calmly.

"And when was this?" I asked, deliberately wanting to drag this out as long as I could.

"I don't remember. Maybe ten or fifteen years ago."

"So you have known the defendant for ten to fifteen years and never said a word to me when he became my client?"

"Objection! Relevance?" Bryce yelled.

"Withdrawn!" I said immediately, yet still getting my point across.

"Danielle, did you remain in contact with Sean after meeting at the fundraiser?"

"Yes," Danielle answered in a matter-of-fact way.

"For how long?"

"Objection, Your Honor. Where is this going?" Bryce interrupted.

"I am establishing a baseline, Your Honor. I am getting to the relevance soon," I said.

"Overruled. Continue, Mr. Amici," Judge DeSanto ruled.

"Thank you, Your Honor. Danielle?"

"We never lost contact. We always managed to find each other, whether it was on Facebook, Instagram, whatever."

"And in that time, what was your relationship with Sean?"

"It was professional one," Danielle said, annoyed.

I determined it was going to be tougher than I thought to get Danielle to admit to having an affair with Sean. I would have thought she wanted to get it off her chest. Apparently, though, she was fine with playing this game. It worked for me, too, because I was up to the challenge. I also realized that I'd better get to the point quickly because DeSanto's patience looked like it was running out. It was time to go for the jugular.

"Danielle, can you tell the court where you were on the night Thomas Greenwood died?" I asked, staring intently at Danielle.

Danielle gave me a glare that would have been intimidating to anyone else, but it did not faze me. "At what point of the evening? I went multiple places."

"Okay, let me rephrase the question. After you stopped by our house, with our children, where did you go when you left?"

After a few seconds of silence, Danielle said, "I went to Rikers Island to see Sean Lancaster because I wanted to *fuck him*! You happy now, you asshole?" Danielle screamed.

The entire courtroom broke out into a bunch of oohs and aahs. Chaos spread throughout the courtroom, causing Judge DeSanto to have a hard time calming everyone down. Finally, he'd had enough.

"I said quiet! Now!" Judge DeSanto screamed, standing up and banging his gavel with great force.

"Young lady, you will not use that language in this court again. And you, the audience, will listen when I demand quiet, or I will dismiss all of you. Is that understood?" There was no reaction or sound in the courtroom. You could hear a pin drop. "I said *is that understood*?"

In unison, everyone said, "Yes, Your Honor."

"Good. Now, counselors, in my chambers, now!" Judge DeSanto yelled and threw his gavel down.

I was not sure if I was in trouble or if Judge DeSanto just needed to reset the atmosphere in his courtroom. I knew I had struck a nerve with Danielle and Sean, but that was my intention. I wanted the jury to see genuine shock on both of their faces to illustrate that Sean is a bad person who commits adultery, not murder. As soon as the chamber door closed, I knew I was in for a rude awaking.

"Sal, what the hell was that? Are you trying to prove a point other than your client's innocence?" Judge DeSanto asked as he took a swig of whiskey.

"No, Your Honor. I would never dishonor your courtroom. I am trying to establish a pattern with my client that suggests something other than murder. I just found out about their affair last night. I was not hiding this from the prosecution."

"Bullshit, Sal. You expect me to believe that you had no idea your wife was banging Sean?" Bryce said, trying to annoy me.

"Bryce, I swear, I had no idea. My obligation is to my client, not to my family. If my wife can help me with the perception of my client to the jury, then that is what I am going to do," I said, turning to the judge. "Judge DeSanto, I promise, I have no intention of dishonoring your courtroom. I feel this is the best chance to defend my client. That is all this is. I swear," I said, hoping he would buy my lie.

Judge DeSanto stared at me for a minute or two. My heart was pounding so hard it was about to jump out of my chest. At any moment, a number of things could go wrong for me. I could be removed as counsel. Danielle could be disqualified as a witness, and her testimony could be stricken from the record. Anything! As I waited for Judge DeSanto's decision, I glanced over at Bryce. He was sweating profusely and tapping his leg rapidly. The tension was clearly getting to both of us. Finally, we heard a decision.

"I am going to allow the questioning of this witness to continue; however, I want to make something very clear. I will *not* allow personal attacks to be part of this examination. If I hear one more attack or question that has nothing to do with this case, I will not only disqualify the witness, but I will hold you in contempt of court, Sal. Am I clear?"

"Crystal, Your Honor," I said, feeling relief.

"Good. Now let's go back into the courtroom and continue this charade."

After a few minutes of instruction to the jury and audience from Judge DeSanto, I was allowed to continue my questioning of Danielle.

"Danielle, you said earlier that you wanted to go to Rikers to have sex with Sean after leaving our house. Does that mean you were having an affair with him, or was it just a spur-of-the-moment thing?"

"I was having an affair with Sean," Danielle said in a low voice.

"I see. How long has this affair been going on?" I asked, not really wanting to know the answer.

"Eight years," Danielle whispered.

I felt my stomach drop for the second time in less than twenty-four hours. How could I have not known Danielle was having an affair for the last eight years? What does that say about me? I needed to refocus quickly because there was more, and I needed to find out what.

"Eight years. Wow. That must have been a difficult secret to keep," I said.

"Objection! Your Honor, what did we just talk about?" Bryce asked.

"Overruled! Continue."

"How were you able to keep it a secret from me and the kids for so long?" I asked again, not wanting to hear the answer.

"Well, with you so consumed with your job and the kids either at daycare or someone else's house, it was actually pretty easy. Maybe if you paid more attention to me, you would have figured it out," Danielle said, trying to goad me into an outburst. Her tactic didn't get to me.

I ignored Danielle's comment and began the trek toward the intimate details of their affair. "In your eight years with Sean, did he ever display signs he was a violent man?"

"Never. He was always a gentleman. He was compassionate, warm, and caring," Danielle said, almost making me throw up.

"Did he ever talk about his family?"

"All the time. He mentioned how proud he was of his wife and kids. That he was looking forward to turning his business over the to his kids when they got older. He loved his family," Danielle answered with a smile.

"So if Sean loved his family so much, and he was never violent with you, how can he be charged with these horrific crimes?"

"Objection! The witness is not a legal expert," Bryce said.

"Sustained!" Judge DeSanto ruled.

"Danielle, are you aware that adultery is considered a class B misdemeanor in New York State and can carry a jail sentence of three months to one year?" I asked with the intention of scaring her.

"No, I am not," Danielle answered without looking at me.

"Well, it is, so you should be aware of that in the coming weeks."

"Mr. Amici, I warned you. This is your last warning," Judge DeSanto said sternly.

"Yes, Your Honor. I apologize," I said. "Did you ever meet Sean's family?"

"No. I never wanted to take the chance. We did not see each other that often, so there was no point."

"How often did you see each other?" I asked, curious how she could have done this without me getting suspicious.

"Whenever we could. We usually met up on Saturdays... but not always."

At that moment, all I could think about was that for the past eight years, Danielle had told me she went out with a few friends for some drinks, which apparently was not true. I could not grill her about it now because DeSanto would disqualify her as a witness, and my biggest question was still to come. I was thrown off my game a bit by that answer and had to grab a drink of water before continuing. As I did, I shot Sean a look that said, *We will talk about this later* and *You'd better be ready to give me answers.*

"Danielle, I have one last question for you. In all your time with Sean, did you ever once feel your life was in danger?"

"No, not at all."

"Thank you. I have no more questions," I concluded.

"Mr. Weatherford, your cross please," Judge DeSanto said.

"Thank you, Your Honor," Bryce said as he approached the witness stand. "Mrs. Amici, you mentioned you never met the defendant's family because you didn't want to take a chance. Is that correct?"

"Yes," Danielle answered abruptly.

"But you were having an affair with him. Isn't that taking an even bigger chance?"

"I didn't want to make his wife suspicious. Sean and I were very careful," Danielle answered.

"I see. So if you never met his family, is it then fair to say you never experienced his demeanor around his family?"

"I suppose so, yes."

"Did the defendant ever tell you of the numerous domestic dispute calls the police were dispatched to his house for?" Bryce asked calmly.

"He told me his wife hit him and the kids, then he would show me proof with bruises," Danielle answered, tilting her head and squinting her eyes as if she was curious if Sean was telling the truth.

"Of course he did. Would it surprise you that the police were called to the defendant's house eleven times over a seven-year span, and each time he was the suspect?"

At this point in any other trial, I would have objected. This line of questioning was extremely damning to my case and my client, but I wanted Danielle to suffer. I knew all of this information beforehand and knew Bryce would uncover it, but I also knew that based on how naïve Danielle has always been, she'd had no idea. Sean whispered for me to object, but I just turned my chair and let Bryce continue to fire away at Danielle. This was the reason I put Danielle on the stand. I had no intention of getting anything damaging from her with my questioning. I would leave that up to Bryce because I knew he would do his job and do my dirty work for me.

"Yes, it would. I-I did not look at Sean that way," Danielle said, taken back.

"Like what, Mrs. Amici?"

"Like someone who was capable of something like that."

"We all have skeletons, Mrs. Amici. I am sure you have some. But then again, a lot of yours have been exposed here today," Bryce said coldly.

It was after that statement by Bryce I felt a warmness come over my body. I did not think I would feel this satisfied seeing Danielle attacked like this, but I enjoyed it. Maybe a little too much. I tried to hide my grin by covering my mouth and pretending to cough. I could tell Sean was affected as well but remained silent through all of Danielle's testimony.

"Mrs. Amici, two last questions. During your affair with the defendant, was he ever rough with you in bed?"

Danielle hesitated and looked at me before answering. I can tell she was about to say something that I did not want to hear, yet I needed to.

"Yes. I asked him not to, but he did anyway," Danielle answered after a long silence.

"In what ways was he rough against your will?" Bryce asked.

Danielle was clearly uncomfortable with that question and didn't want to answer it. I could have stopped it by objecting, but didn't. I wanted her to talk.

"He would force himself on me sometimes when I wasn't in the mood, or he would try to choke me and ask me to play dead. Things like that."

"And yet you sit here today and call the defendant a caring person. No more questions, Your Honor," Bryce said and sat down.

"Your Honor, if it pleases the court, I would like reexamine this witness," I asked the judge.

"Very well. Go ahead, Mr. Amici"

Now came the final part of my plan. I had been setting up the chance to have Danielle disqualified as a witness the entire day. I wanted the truth out of her and wanted to embarrass her, yet I did not want anything she said to go against Sean. To this point, the plan had worked to perfection.

"Danielle, how do you feel now about your lover, you cheating whore?" I said, delivering the knockout blow.

"That's it! I warned you, Mr. Amici. This witness's testimony is being stricken from the record as she is disqualified as a witness based on the grounds that she provided testimony prejudicial to the client; therefore, the integrity of our judicial system suffered as a result. The jury will disregard everything this witness said. Mr. Amici, I want you in my chambers, Now! Court is adjourned until this afternoon at one o'clock," Judge DeSanto said and stormed off.

I knew I was facing a contempt charge, but I did not care. I had accomplished my goal. It may have been cruel, but Danielle deserved it. She had deceived me for eight years, and now I was getting a small piece of retribution. I was not proud of what I did by any means; however, I did feel satisfied. Whatever punishment the judge was going to hand out to me was well worth it. After today, it would never be the same again between Danielle and me. It was a decision she made when she decided to go outside of our marriage.

Chapter 50

"What is wrong with you, Sal?" Judge DeSanto asked me with as much anger as I have ever seen from him. "I specifically told you not to make this personal, and you went ahead and did it anyway."

"I apologize, Your Honor, but it couldn't be helped."

"Couldn't be helped? What is that?" Judge DeSanto asked, now annoyed even more.

"I know I was out of line and deliberately disobeyed your order, but calling my wife to the stand did have a purpose," I explained.

"And what purpose is that?"

"To establish my client is not a violent person."

"But Sal, her testimony is invalid now. How...? No, you know what? I am not going to discuss this with you anymore. I will not hold you in contempt of court, but this better not happen again. *Ever.* You got that?"

"Yes, Your Honor. Again, I apologize. Is there anything else you need from me?" I asked, wanting to leave.

"No. Get out of here. See you after lunch," Judge DeSanto said as he took his robe off.

I couldn't eat because of all that had just happened, but I was going to have to force myself if I was going finish the day. I went over Danielle's testimony in my head to try and comprehend how I could have missed her affair with Sean. I like to think of myself as a pretty intuitive person, but now I was severely doubting my detective skills. I knew that after the trial I would have to deal with the fallout from court this morning, but for now, I had to decide between tuna or ham.

The afternoon session began with Judge DeSanto providing some instruction to the jury about what happened in the morning. He was throwing a bunch of legal jargon at them, and most of their faces appeared more vacant than a deer in headlights. Once the judge was done with his instructions, he looked at me with evil eyes and asked me to call my next witness.

"Your Honor, the defense rests," I said, knowing I would piss off Sean.

Sean wanted to testify on his behalf, but like I do with all of my clients, I don't recommend it. Some people think that if the defendant does not testify, then he or she has something to hide, which is simply not true. The Fifth Amendment was created to protect individuals from self-incrimination. If a person chooses to exercise that right, that does imply guilt. I explained this to Sean and told him I was not going to call him to the witness stand.

"Very well. Now that the state and defense have had a chance to present their cases, each will now have an opportunity for one final summation of their case. Mr. Weatherford, you are first," Judge DeSanto stated.

Bryce's closing argument lasted fifty-five minutes. He did a masterful job of summarizing his case and pointing out the evidence against Sean. Closing arguments are not short and sweet like in the movies. They take time to reiterate everything that was covered. In some cases, evidence from weeks before needs to be reintroduced because the jury will have most likely forgotten about it. This trial went on for eleven days, which makes the length of Bryce's summation appropriate. I did not need that much time.

"Ladies and Gentlemen of the jury," I began, "I do not intend to bore you for fifty-five minutes like Mr. Weatherford just did. In fact, I will take up only a few minutes of your time. Why is that? Well, because I do not have to prove my case. I do not have to provide you with evidence. I do not have to prove my case to you beyond a reasonable doubt. All I need to do is convince you that there *is* reasonable doubt, which in this case, there is plenty of. As Judge DeSanto will instruct you in a few moments, I do not have to prove my client's innocence. Keep that in mind when you deliberate the case amongst yourselves. Also keep this in mind. Sean Lancaster is not a good person. We all saw how he manipulates people to get what he wants and uses people until he tires of them. He wrecks people's lives and marriages. Look what he did to me. But does being a bad person without a heart make someone a murderer? No. The prosecution did not provide enough evidence to prove any guilt here, nor did they prove beyond a reasonable doubt that the killer of

Denise Lancaster, James Lancaster, Paul Lancaster, and Samantha Lancaster is sitting right over there at that table. This was a terrible tragedy, and somebody needs to pay for it. That someone, however, is not Sean Lancaster. Thank you."

"Mr. Weatherford, do you wish to rebut?" Judge DeSanto asked.

"No, Your Honor."

"Very well. I will now give the jury some instructions before the case is turned over to them," Judge DeSanto said.

Over the next fifteen minutes, Judge DeSanto gave the jury their instructions to follow during their deliberations. One of those instructions was to disregard Danielle's testimony, which brought an involuntary smile to my face. Once the judge was done, he ordered to the jury to begin their deliberations and to come to a fair and just verdict based on the facts presented in the case.

This has always been my least favorite part of a trial. At this point, I had no control over what happened. The tension and anxiety caused by the unknown is palpable. A verdict can come in the next ten minutes or the next ten days. There is no way to tell when it will come, only that it will. The common thought is that a short deliberation usually ends with a guilty verdict, and a longer deliberation tends to lean toward an acquittal. I was hoping we were in this stage for the long haul.

I packed my up stuff and left the courthouse to go home and get some much-needed sleep. I also needed to meet with Sean and eventually deal with Danielle. But all I needed at that moment was sleep. As soon as I got home, I changed into my sweats, put on some music, poured myself a glass of Chardonnay, and lay down on the couch. Within minutes, I was fast asleep, leaving the turmoil in my life behind me for a few hours.

Chapter 51

Sean Lancaster sat on his cot in his jail cell, wondering what fate awaited him. He began to think for the first time about what life in prison would be like and tried to see the positive in it. He would not be doing his time at Rikers Island, so everything he had done to this point would be for naught. He was pretty sure he would do his time at Attica, which was good for him because he knew some inmates who were recently transferred there from Rikers. But he still couldn't get past the idea that he might be locked up for the rest of this life.

His trial went about as good as he had hoped; however, he knew that his reputation was damaged by the testimonies of both Traci and Danielle. He was not expecting either one to be called on to testify because Sal did not warn him. Was that part of Sal's plan? Was he being played by his own lawyer? Sean would have to wait until he spoke with Sal to get those answers. In the meantime, he had some unfinished business to take care of.

During his free time, Sean went to the infirmary to check on Titus. He was hoping that Titus was still in a coma because if he was awake, he was fucked. The warden had ordered Sean to spy on Titus and report back to him, and he was sure Titus would enact revenge on him, especially if his trial was coming to an end.

When Sean got to the infirmary, he was shocked that Titus was not there. He had not heard anything about him getting better or worse, which concerned him even more. Did Titus instruct the infirmary staff to not say anything to anyone about him? Sean began to panic when he finally saw the doctor who had taken Titus away.

"Doc, I wanted to know if you know what happened to Titus Baxter?" Sean asked politely.

"Mr. Baxter passed away last night from a massive hematoma and a fractured skull. Whoever did that to him did not want him alive," the doctor told Sean.

"Oh my god. That's awful," Sean said and smiled. "Thank you, Doc."

One loose end was now tied up. Sean no longer had to worry about retribution by Titus, or anyone else for that matter. Nobody had seen what he had done to Titus, which meant he would not face murder charges. Suddenly, things began to look up for Sean.

Next, Sean wanted to speak to the warden about Titus and what he intended to do with the knowledge he had about Sean. Once he found Jimbo Duncan, Sean told him he wanted to go see the warden. Jimbo was reluctant at first, but when Sean told him he would have matching bandages on his head if he didn't help him, Jimbo complied.

While Sean was waiting for the warden in his office, he began to ponder how he would handle this. Should he come right out and threaten the warden's family, or should he try to play nice and make a deal? He was running out of time at Rikers, so he needed to make an impact right now.

"What do you want, Lancaster?" Warden Paulson asked.

"Well, I am sure you have heard about Titus by now, so I wanted to check in for my next task, sir," Sean said as he saluted the warden like an army officer.

"What do you mean *your next task*?" Warden Paulson asked. "See, Sean, when you have so much power over someone, you can't help but turn it into a game for yourself? That's the position I am in."

"Huh?" Sean said, confused.

"I don't *need* you to do anything for me, Lancaster. I want you to be in constant fear that one day, I might just feel the urge to tell a secret."

"Why are you doing this?" Sean asked.

"Because I can. Because I am sick of people like you always paying their way out of a mess and not suffering any consequences. If you are acquitted, which I highly doubt is possible, you then know what it feels like to be helpless. That reason enough for you?"

"Fine. Just know this. I will never be afraid of you. I will never be intimidated by you. I have powerful friends on the outside who can have you replaced faster than you can say *Sean killed Sal's brother*. You want to play this game, fine. Bring it," Sean said and turned to walk out of the warden's office.

On his way back to his cell, Sean felt a sense of calmness. He had been relieved of both Johnny and Titus and had put a scare into Warden Paulson. The only thing left for him to worry about now was what verdict the jury would return. They had been deliberating for a few hours when they were told to go home by Judge DeSanto and come back in the morning. Not wanting to think too much about what he couldn't control, Sean began to drift off with a smile on his face and a feeling of peace; something he had not experienced in a long time.

Chapter 52

Three days had passed since the jury began their deliberations, which boded well for me. I tried not to get too optimistic, but it is very difficult when the minutes continue to pass by and there is no verdict turned in yet. I tried everything to keep myself busy. I went to see a movie, read a book, and went to the gym, but nothing worked. All I could think about was how this case was going to turn out. I had so much riding on this, more than ever before. It was not only about having a client acquitted; it was also to prove that Alan and Steven had made the right decision to make me partner now instead of waiting until after the trial. It was to honor Thomas by winning the case he called the "crown jewel" for the firm. It was also about winning the case that destroyed my marriage and my life as I knew it.

Danielle had reached out to me several times during the last three days, but I didn't want to talk to her. I was sure she would keep reaching out to me, but I would have to resist giving in to keep my sanity. I had every intention of settling our issues after the trial, if I could make it that long.

The biggest negative about the fallout from my marriage was that I missed my kids. I was used to being with them every day and seeing them grow up. Over the past six months or so, I had missed some important events, like dance recitals, soccer games, and birthday parties. I hoped the kids would understand why, but I doubted it. I would have to explain it to them someday when they were older. Unfortunately, those conversations don't always go well. If I wasn't avoiding Danielle, I would have gone to see them by now, although I might not have been good company because of my mind being preoccupied.

I tried to call Alan to see if he had heard anything from the courthouse yet, but his phone went right to voicemail. Same story with Steven and Jill. It was odd that nobody was answering their phone, especially when we were all waiting for word when the verdict was in. I was about to actually go see Sean to kill some time when I noticed a limousine pull up in front of my house. Alan stepped out of the limo in his best Brooks Brothers navy suit, white Armani dress shirt, blue-and-red stripped Armani tie, and Salvatore Ferragamo alligator skin loafers. He looked very sharp leaning against the limo on one shoulder. I envied him at that moment. To be able to pull off this look at his age was remarkable. Once I got over my awe, I quickly shifted my thoughts to why he was here. Suddenly, my heart went into overdrive.

"Sal, let's go. I got a suit for you in the car," Alan said.

"Where are we going?" I asked.

"The verdict is in."

Chapter 53

I have walked into a courtroom more times than I can remember. I have been present for countless verdict readings as well. I have never felt the level of anxiety I felt walking into the courtroom that afternoon. Once I sat down, I scanned the room and saw more people than there were at any time during the trial. I am not sure how word got out so quickly, but it must have because there was barely any standing room left.

I was sitting at my table, which had become my home away from home the past two weeks, waiting for Sean to be brought in. I was bouncing my leg uncontrollably, and I felt I needed to change my shirt because I was soaking wet with sweat. The waiting was getting to be too much for me already, and the jury still had to be ushered in.

Sean was brought into the courtroom in his usual high-end suit; he looked almost as good as Alan. I didn't want to look at him, but something drew my eyes to him, and we caught glares as soon as he sat down. He leaned over to say something to me, but I turned away. I was so wrapped up in the moment, I didn't want to say anything stupid.

Once Sean was settled in, the judge came in next. This is all standard procedure, but it seemed like it was a bit extra today. Why couldn't everyone just come in together? It was almost as if someone was out to torture me even more than I already had been to this point. Once the judge was seated, he gave the court some general instructions on how to react when the verdict was read. He did not want any outbursts, offensive language, threats—nothing. Anyone who violated this order would be held in contempt of court. He also reminded everyone of the television crews that were in the back of the room and not to pay them any attention. Once his instructions were given, he ordered the jury into the courtroom.

Jurors are among the easiest to read when a verdict is about to be given. Most of the time, they will hang their heads and avoid eye contact with everyone if they are about to deliver a guilty verdict.

The opposite is true if they are about to acquit. This jury, however, was nearly impossible to read. Half the jurors looked away, while the other half of them looked right at me and Sean. My heart started to beat even faster now because I could not get a read on them. I began to get lightheaded, as if I was going to pass out. I took a few sips of water to try and hydrate myself, but that didn't work. After a few deep breaths, I eventually was able to calm down enough to focus on the scene in front of me. The show was about to conclude.

"Ladies and Gentlemen of the jury. I hear you have reached a verdict," Judge DeSanto asked.

"We have, Your Honor," the foreman said.

"Very well. Bailiff, please collect the verdict and present it to me."

I have yet to meet a judge who did not have a great poker face. The judge must review the verdict form before it announced, no exceptions. This is not so he or she knows the verdict ahead of time, like most people think. It is to verify that all the proper signatures have been captured, the verdict is recorded correctly, and there are no mistakes on any other section of the form. If there is an invalid judgement, then jeopardy can be attached to the case, which means a defendant could potentially avoid facing criminal responsibilities for their actions. Judge DeSanto had the best poker face I had ever seen, so there was no use to even try to get a read on him.

Once Judge DeSanto read and approved the form, he handed it back to the bailiff to return to the foreman to read aloud to the court. He ordered Sean and me to rise, then turned his attention to the jury.

"Docket number 21 CR. 7812 (ND), State vs. Sean Lancaster. Mister Foreperson, please rise!" Judge DeSanto ordered. "On the count of first-degree murder of Denise Lancaster, how does the jury find the defendant?"

"Not guilty," the foreman read nervously.

There was a silent buzz in the courtroom, keeping in compliance with the judge's orders. It was so quiet, everyone could probably hear the collective sighs of relief from both Sean and me. I was not sure what I heard, but my body was telling me it was good. I didn't want to get too far ahead of myself because there were five other charges to be read.

"On the count of first-degree murder of James Lancaster, how does the jury find the defendant?"

"Not guilty," the foreman said, a little calmer than the last verdict.

"On the count of first-degree murder of Paul Lancaster, how does the jury find the defendant?"

"Not guilty," the foreman said, as if it was routine now.

"On the count of first-degree murder of Samantha Lancaster, how does the jury find the defendant?"

"Not guilty, Your Honor," the foreperson added.

"On the charge of sexual assault in the first degree of Samantha Lancaster, how does the jury find the defendant?"

"Not guilty."

"On the charge of sexual assault in the third degree of Denise Lancaster, how does the jury find the defendant?"

"Not guilty."

The courtroom erupted. Most of the noise was clapping and cheering, while there a few sobs and cries of "No!" Judge DeSanto banged his gavel to restore order in the courtroom, but it took a good two or three minutes for everyone to hear him. Once everyone quieted, Judge DeSanto gave his final instructions of the trial.

"The clerk will record the verdict as such. I would like to thank the jury for their devotion, time, and dedication to this trial. I know it is not easy to put your lives on hold for two weeks, and for that, this court thanks you again. Your service has now concluded, and you are free to leave. Thank you again," Judge DeSanto said and banged his gavel.

Once the jury left the room, the judge continued giving his final remarks.

"Docket number 21 CR. 7812 (ND), State vs. Sean Lancaster, has now concluded. The verdicts of not guilty on all six counts have been recorded. Mr. Lancaster, you are now a free man. Court is adjourned." Judge DeSanto rose, banged his gavel, and retired to his chambers.

I was floating in the air, unsure if I would ever come down. There was no way I thought the jury would return a not guilty verdict on all six counts. At that moment, I felt like I could accomplish anything, and nothing was going to stand in my way. Then reality hit. I realized I had to congratulate Sean.

"Congratulations, Sean. You know this is not at all what I want to do, but it has to get done." I said as I extended my hand to shake his.

"I gather we will be seeing more of each other sooner than I want to."

"I know you hate me, and I know I am an asshole, but I want to sincerely offer my thanks, Sal. Thank you for your dedication and commitment to me and this case. I know it wasn't easy for you with everything that happened, but I will never forget this," Sean said with deep emotion.

"You're welcome, Sean. Take care," I responded, wanting to be as professional as I could.

The bailiff took Sean away without placing him in cuffs for processing. It would take a while to get all the paperwork done, but Sean Lancaster would be a free man within a matter of hours. I sat back down in my chair and thought about everything I had been through over the last six months. From David Flores to finding out my wife had been having an affair with my client for the past eight years, I sat in the empty courtroom in amazement of myself. I couldn't wait to speak to Alan and Steven about this case and see what their thoughts were. I didn't know what I was going to do next, but I knew one thing for sure: I needed time off. I needed time to recharge and catch my bearings. I also needed time to deal with the mess my family was in. That time would come, but for now, for this moment, I was going to savor every minute I could.

After fifteen minutes of on and off crying and laughing episodes, I finally got up to leave the courtroom. I felt like I was in the closing scene of a movie and the credits we about to roll. Life was going to get harder for me, but I was feeling pretty good about myself in that moment, despite what was to come. As I went to exit the courtroom, my phone rang. There was no caller ID, but I answered anyway.

"Hello?" I answered, smiling from ear to ear.

"Hello, Sal. Congratulations on the big win in court today," a distorted voice said.

"Who is this?" I asked, feeling anxiety all over again.

"We have time for that. For now, you just need to know that Sean Lancaster is a very dangerous man, and I would watch my back if I were you," the voice spoke.

"Yeah, and how do you know he's dangerous?" I asked, getting annoyed.

"Because I am the one who helped him plan the murder of his family."

Part III

Chapter 54
Two Weeks Later

There is nothing like going on a vacation to clear your mind. It is so refreshing to not be on a schedule and to sleep as late as I want. After the trial was over, I told Alan and Steven I was taking two weeks off to clear my head and recharge. I did not have a destination in mind but decided later on Aruba. The crisp eighty-degree sunny weather was just what I needed. I spent many nights walking on the beach, listening to the waves crash against the shoreline and staring at the stars, wondering if my kids were okay. I didn't mingle too much because I didn't want any company or drama while trying to relax. It really was two weeks of paradise.

Another reason I needed to get away was to stay away from Sean. The phone call I received in the courtroom after the verdict was read really rattled me. If Sean did indeed help plot the murder of his family, then he was certainly guilty, just not of first-degree murder. This was another David Flores situation for me, which meant two cases in a row I helped free guilty men. Of course, this person who called me could be lying or could be someone who wants to get Sean in trouble. But judging by the fact they disguised their voice using a voice scrambler, I didn't think that was a real possibility.

When the plane landed at 7:10 p.m. at JFK International Airport, all the anxiety I had suppressed over the past two weeks came roaring back like a tsunami. Suddenly, I began to panic about seeing Danielle again and having to speak with Sean to wrap up his case. A part of me wanted to stay on the plane and return to Aruba, for good this time.

I was hoping for an easy ride home and then have some time to myself to unwind from the travel before dealing with life again, but it was not going to be that easy for me. For starters, my Uber driver got lost at the airport trying to find me. I kept thinking to myself, *How does someone get lost at an airport?* Once I was in the car, the driver was on his phone but not using AirPods. He then took the wrong exit and ended up having to travel an additional ten miles out of the way because of construction. When I finally got home, I was more exhausted from the Uber ride than the plane ride.

After I finished unpacking, I wanted to call Danielle to see if we could meet and go over what happened at the trial. I brought her contact up so many times, yet never actually pressed the green button to make the call. I felt like a middle schooler getting nervous to call a girl for the first time. She was my wife and the mother of my children. Why was I so nervous to call her? I decided to sleep on it and call her in the morning.

In the middle of brushing my teeth, my phone rang. I really wanted to go to bed but was also curious who was calling me after eleven o'clock. When I saw it was Alan, I was relieved.

"Hi, Alan, how are you?" I answered.

"Hey, Sal. Enjoy your trip?"

"Definitely. It was nice to get away and forget about everything for a few weeks. What's up?"

"Nothing really. I know you aren't supposed to come back until Monday, but I was wondering if you could stop by the office tomorrow to complete some paperwork," Alan said in a very soothing voice.

"Sure, no problem. Everything okay?"

"Oh, yeah. It's just that it takes a lot of paperwork to make someone officially a partner."

"Sounds good. Is eleven good?" I asked, hoping to sleep in.

"Sure. I'll see you then. And Sal, great win on the Lancaster case."

"Thank you, Alan. Have a good night," I said and hung up the phone.

Even though I was back home and in my own bed, the peace I felt after my phone call with Alan brought me right back to my bungalow in Aruba. I put on my sound machine to the setting of waves crashing, shut out the lights, snuggled under my blankets, and fell asleep, knowing that everything was going to be okay.

Chapter 55

Sean Lancaster sat in his Realtor's office waiting for confirmation that his bid on a new apartment was going to be accepted. He had decided after the trial that he needed a fresh start, and that began with selling his apartment and moving into a smaller one. He didn't care too much if his offer was accepted because he was still living on cloud nine being a free man. He was now able to go wherever he wanted and do whatever he wanted—luxuries he had been stripped of for the past five months. He knew eventually he would come down from this high, but until then, he was going to enjoy every minute of it.

The Realtor came back in and told him the apartment he wanted had just sold but she would continue to help him look for a suitable place. He smiled, shook her hand, and got up to leave her office. On his way out, he made sure nobody was around when he placed his next call.

"Have you heard anything?" Sean whispered.

"No, not yet. When do you think I should call back?" the voice on the other line said.

"Well, he just got back from vacation, so let him think he is in the clear for a few days. I don't want to rattle him too early," Sean said, laughing.

"Understood. Just tell me when, and I'm game," the voice replied, then hung up.

Sean had been planning his next move for the past two weeks. He didn't want to move too quickly but also knew that he wouldn't have as much time as we wanted. Sal Amici was a busy man, and sooner or later, he would get another case. If he was going to be successful, Sean needed to decide soon when to start the game.

Later that night, Sean returned to his apartment and made himself a pepperoni hot pocket. He liked to have simple meals because he didn't like spending money unnecessarily on food. He felt that it was a waste to have an expensive dinner if it all goes to the same place.

He turned on the TV and immediately was captivated by what was on the news.

"Meanwhile, police are convinced they had the right person and at this time have no other leads," said an attractive anchorwoman. "When asked if the investigation will reopen, Chief of Police Donald Yorkin had this to say, 'At this time, we have no intention of reopening this case. Sean Lancaster was tried among a jury of his peers and was exonerated of all charges. While I disagree with that assessment, I must abide by it.' More on this story a little later."

Sean smiled and thought, *They can look all they want, but it won't be me who's charged again.* As soon as he finished his hot pocket, the doorbell rang. "Right on time," Sean said to himself as he got up to open the door.

"Well, hello there, beautiful," Sean said, grinning.

"Hello there yourself," Traci said. "Ready to have some fun tonight?"

"You know I am. But first, I want to just talk. That okay with you?"

"Hey, it's your money. Whatever you want, baby," Traci said as she took off her coat. "So what do you want to talk about?"

"Has anyone asked you anything since you testified?"

"No. Most people don't even know I did," Traci said, a bit confused.

"That's good. That's good. For you anyway."

"Yeah, why's that?"

"Well, let's just say if people knew what you said in court, I might not be such a happy client," Sean said cryptically.

"Okay, Sean, cut the shit, huh. What the fuck are you talking about?" Traci asked, getting annoyed.

"What am I talking about," Sean whispered to himself. "What am I talking about? Here's what I am talking about..." Sean brought his closed fist out in the open and hit Traci in the eye so hard, it knocked her onto the glass table in the middle of room. Glass shattered everywhere, and Traci ended up on the floor covered in most of it.

"Don't for one second think that because you are my whore, I won't hurt you. You got it? Now you know what I am talking about?" Sean screamed.

Traci had never seen Sean like this before, and she was fearful for her life. Her instincts would need to take over if she wanted to survive.

"Yes, Sean, I got it. Why did you have to hit me? Jesus, now I have to explain this to everyone with a bullshit story that nobody will believe."

"You are a clever girl. You'll think of something. Think of this as a warning because the next time, you won't be walking away. Take your money and get the fuck out of my house," Sean said, throwing a thousand-dollar bill at Traci.

Traci picked up the money and her jacket and got out as fast as she could. Sean could hear her crying all the way down the hallway, which made him feel even better than he already did. There were more loose ends that he would have to tie up if he wanted to live a completely stress-free life, but those would have to wait for another day. Right now, he needed to ice his hand and continue watching the news talk about how he got away with murder.

Chapter 56

The offices of Lowery, Hill, and Greenwood on the weekend is often a ghost town. Mostly everyone in the office works Monday through Friday, which always amazed me. It was almost as if the law stopped on the weekends. I had been here a few times on Saturdays and always found the quiet to be relaxing. I was able to get caught up on a lot of work. Plus, it looked good to the partners.

I got to my office, put my coat down, and called Alan in his office. I knew I would get him because even though he was in on a Saturday, he would not make his assistant come in as well. That's the kind of person Alan is. He likes to give people more time off than anyone I have ever worked for. His philosophy is that his employees work hard during the week and need these two days to unwind and recharge. He picked up after two rings and told me to come on over and to bring a notepad as well.

As I made my way over to Alan's office, I looked around the various empty desks and wondered how many of them knew that I was made partner. I am not sure why that popped into my head because I'm not a material guy. Titles have never been my thing, but for some reason, being a partner made me want people to notice more.

Once I made it to Alan's office, he was typing an email about my promotion to the entire firm. He really was not messing around when he said he wanted this done by Monday.

"What was your GPA at Columbia?" Alan asked as he typed away.

"I graduated with a 4.0," I said with pride.

"Show off," Alan joked.

We spent the next forty minutes or so signing document after document; it was worse than buying a house. Once I was done, Alan and I shook hands and embraced for a few seconds. I was now officially a partner of Lowery, Hill, and Greenwood. I asked Alan to keep the name for two reasons. One was to keep the name recognition of the firm, and the other was to honor Thomas. He had done so much for not only me, but the community as well. It was a great way to keep his legacy alive. Alan happily agreed, and we both shared a tear or two before toasting to my promotion with a morning mimosa.

Over the next two hours, Alan and I reminisced about Thomas, my first case, and the good old days. It was a tranquil time for both of us. We were laughing and smiling like we hadn't done in quite some time. He told me stories of Thomas parading in the subways when the firm was just getting started, most of which would embarrass Thomas if he were here.

It was around one o'clock that I realized I would have to talk to Alan and Steven about what happened after the trial ended. I did not want to ruin this special moment between Alan and me, but I felt if I didn't say anything, I might keep it quiet for the rest of my life.

"Uh, listen, Alan. There is something you need to know about what happened after the verdicts were read," I said shyly.

"Oh, it can wait until Monday. Here, have another one," Alan said as he waved his hand in my direction.

"Are you sure, because it's kind of big."

"Yeah, I'm sure. Saturdays are about having fun, and it sounds like what you have to tell me isn't fun. So unless it's a matter of life and death, it will have to wait."

I didn't react to what Alan said because what I had to tell him sort of did have to do with life and death. I wanted to tell him, but I just couldn't bring myself to ruin the jovial mood that he was in.

"Okay, Alan. Monday it is," I agreed.

We spent the next three hours doing much of the same things as the previous two. By the time four o'clock came around, both of us were in no condition to drive, yet we wanted to continue this party. I knew it would not do us any good to continue drinking and suggested we each take an Uber home. Clicking on my app, I scheduled rides for both Alan and me. They would each be at the office in ten minutes, which was barely enough time to gather our things and make it downstairs.

When we reached the parking lot, Alan's Uber was already there. He waved and said goodbye, got in the Uber, and promptly fell asleep in back seat before the Uber driver left. My Uber arrived two minutes later. It was a smooth ride all the way home, which was made more enjoyable by some great conversation about the Yankees.

When we arrived at my house, I thanked the driver and stumbled to my front door. I fumbled with the keys and eventually dropped them. Bending down to pick them up, I noticed my front door was open. I was positive I didn't leave it that way this morning, so I was curious as to who was in my house. When I regained focus, I saw a figure standing in my foyer, waiting for me to say something. It didn't take me long to realize who it was. I reached out both of my arms and said, "Come here, angel! Daddy has missed you."

"Me too, Daddy! Did Mommy tell you? We are going to be living together again!" Angela said with great excitement.

"That's great, honey. Is she here? Your mommy?" I asked, not wanting to alarm Angela that I was beyond furious.

"Yes, she is upstairs unpacking."

"Thank you, angel."

Before I headed upstairs to confront Danielle, I took a minute to compose myself. I did not want to overreact, especially with my kids here. But I also knew that anything I did from here on would be used against me in a divorce lawsuit, so I wanted to be extra careful. I was also piss-ass drunk, so I was not sure I could hold my own in an argument right now. I calmed myself down, drank a glass of water, and headed upstairs to begin the end of my marriage.

Chapter 57

"So are you going to give me any ideas on how we are going to do this?" Sean asked.

"I thought you were the witty one," his friend on the other end said.

"I am, but I thought I would give you a crack at it as well."

"I have nothing. I will roll with whatever you want to do," the friend said.

"Okay. I will let you know when the time is right. For now, stay low and don't let anyone get suspicious."

"Ten four," said the friend and hung up.

Sean was getting excited knowing that his secret would be revealed to Sal any time now. He wanted to wait for the perfect moment to present his story to him. It had to line up just right. It had to be poetic. It had to be memorable. In time, he would get his satisfaction, he had no doubt of that.

Until then, Sean had some loose ends to tie up, including one major nuisance. It was going to take a lot of meticulous planning to get rid of Warden Paulson, but Sean still had some connections inside Rikers Island to get it done. He knew he couldn't be seen around the jail, so all of his work would need to be done over the phone and through encrypted emails.

Sean made his first call to Jimbo Duncan. He knew that Jimbo was terrified of him, so he could ask him to do pretty much anything he wanted, and Jimbo would do it. He dialed Jimbo's cell phone, making sure to block his number.

"Hey there, Jimbo. It's your old pal, Sean," he said in his best intimidating voice.

"Oh god, what do you want? You ain't an inmate anymore, so I don't gotta listen to you, man," Jimbo said, sounding like he already pissed his pants.

"Calm down there, boy. Damn, you are such a pussy. I just want to know how you are doing after the beating you took at the hands of an unknown assailant," Sean teased Jimbo.

"I'll heal. What do you want, Lancaster?"

"Well, I need some intel. I need you tell me the schedule of Warden Paulson."

"Why?"

"That is not your concern. Just know that I need it, or do I really need to say what will happen?" Sean asked, hoping for full cooperation.

"Yeah, I know you'll hurt Hailey. Blah, blah, blah," Jimbo said, seemingly having had enough of Sean's games. "Problem for you is, I told Hailey about your threats, and she's left to go somewhere safe. So you can stop trying to scare me, cuz it isn't going to work."

"Damn, look at you? Your testicles finally descended, huh? I gotta say I'm proud of you, Jimbo. I didn't think you had it in you."

"Well, I do. So piss off, Sean," Jimbo said and hung up.

Sean couldn't help but laugh at the situation. If only Jimbo knew. He couldn't afford to let more time go by, so he called Jimbo right back.

"What? I said leave me alone," Jimbo answered angrily.

"Jimbo, Jimbo, Jimbo. You still haven't learned anything, have you?"

"What are you talking about?"

"You sure Hailey is safe?" Sean asked, poking a hole in Jimbo's immunity.

"Yeah, I know she is. I just spoke with her."

"Oh yeah, that's right. She was going to the supermarket today to get fresh seafood. Is it going to be lobster or shrimp?" Sean teased.

Once again, Jimbo was scared out of his mind. How the hell did Sean know where he told Hailey to go? He had told her in the waiting area at Rikers after Sean was acquitted.

"You son of a bitch. Don't you hurt her," Jimbo said, anger filling his voice.

"I know, you hate me. But for now, just listen. Now that you know I know where Hailey is, there is no sense in moving her again. It will be for her safety that she stays right where she is. She will have protection around the clock, which in times like these will be a great benefit to her," Sean explained, reestablishing the upper hand with

Jimbo. "I need you to spy on Warden Paulson for a few weeks. I need to know when he gets in, goes to lunch, takes a shit... everything. I need to know where he is at all times during his time there. Is that understood?"

"Why? What for?"

"You really don't learn, do you? You don't need to know that. In fact, the next time you ask me why on something I order you to do, Hailey loses a finger. Got it?"

"Yes. How will I get the info to you?"

"Don't worry about that. For now, just watch him and take the best notes you have ever taken," Sean said and hung up.

After his call with Jimbo, Sean went to get some rest. He was going to need it for what he had planned in the coming days.

Chapter 58

“Just what in the hell do you think you are doing?” I asked Danielle.

“Um, unpacking my stuff. What does it look like?”

“I can see you are doing that, but *why* are you doing that?”

“I decided that since we are still married and not separated, I deserve to be here,” Danielle said, her words irritating me to no end.

“Why the hell do you think you deserve to be here? You are having an affair with Sean Lancaster. In what world do you deserve to be here?”

“Our world. Can you excuse me? I need that drawer,” Danielle said shoving me out of the way.

I stood by and watched Danielle unpack in utter disbelief. I couldn’t quite grasp the idea that she thought she could move back into the house without even talking to me about it first. Did she forget that I am a lawyer and can eat her alive in court if I wanted to?

“Okay, look,” I said as I grabbed her bag and threw it to the ground. “I don’t know what kind of game you are playing here, but this is not happening. If you wanted to move back in, why didn’t you say we needed to talk or something like that? This is so unlike you.”

“Oh, honey. You have no idea who I *really* am,” Danielle said with a squint.

“Fourteen years and I don’t know who you are? Yeah, okay. Did your scumbag boyfriend put you up to this? Why don’t you go live in his world where you can have anything you want?”

“I don’t want to live with Sean. Anyway, it’s over between me and him.”

“*Over*? How can you say it is over when you went to see him in jail the night Thomas died? You know what? You are something else,” I said, angrier than I ever had been.

“Yeah, I know. I am a cheating whore. Thanks to you, that’s what everyone thinks of me now.”

“Good. You deserve it,” I said, storming out of the bedroom.

Downstairs, Gio and Angela were watching TV and snacking on some pretzels. I thought this would be a good time to talk to the both of them about what was going on. I was going to ask Danielle to come downstairs and join me, but then I remembered that we don't discuss anything anymore, so it was okay if I went at this alone.

"Hey, kids," I began timidly. "Dad wants to talk to you about something."

"Is this about you and Mommy?" Angela asked.

"Yeah, and to tell us you two are getting a divorce!" Gio blurted out.

"Gio, we are not getting a divorce, and knock off the attitude, huh?" I responded harshly, wishing I hadn't. "We have been having some disagreements lately, and when adults have disagreements, sometimes it is best for them to be apart for a while. Eventually, they talk those disagreements out and everything goes back to normal. That is why your mother came back."

"The fuck it is!" Danielle screamed as she ran down the stairs. "Don't you go telling our kids lies."

I wasn't going to feed into Danielle's manic state, nor do this in front of my kids. It took every fiber in my body to walk away and go out the front door. I knew she would follow me and cause a scene in the front yard, which is exactly what I wanted her to do.

"Where do you think you are going, asshole?" Danielle yelled as she came outside to greet me.

"Danielle, why are you so mad, and why are you acting like this in front of the kids?" I said as softly as I could.

"Why am I so mad? Really? You don't know why? Well, let's see. I came back the other night to reconcile with you and make me tell you about Sean—"

"Whoa, whoa, whoa! I made you tell me about Sean?" I said, putting up my hand up in front of her. "There should not have been a Sean to tell me about in the first place. Eight fucking years, Danielle? *Really?*"

"Then you embarrass me in court by calling me a whore," Danielle said, ignoring what I said. "And now you want to turn my kids against me."

"Okay, listen, Danielle. I know you don't know much about the law, but you are really not helping yourself here. All those reasons you gave me as to why you are mad at me have nothing to do with me. You instigated all of it. You had the affair, not me."

"Ugh, Sal. I don't want to keep doing this. I am tired of it all," Danielle said as she sat down on the porch.

"I don't either. I never wanted to, but you did what you did and now we have to deal with that. We can either continue to yell and insult each other, or we can talk about how we are going to move forward," I said, hoping to make sense with her.

"Okay. Let's talk about how we are going to handle this, but not now. I am tired, so I'm going upstairs to take a long bath and then take a nap," Danielle said and went inside.

I stood on my front porch, thinking of the time Danielle and I first got together. We told each other that no matter what, we would never stay angry at one another. We would never fight in front of our kids if we had any. We would also talk everything out, no matter how mad one person may be. Our promises lasted a long time, but I felt like a fool not knowing of her infidelity for the last eight years. The more I thought about it, the more I needed to know what else she was hiding from me. For now, I would need to explain to my kids what had just happened and hoped they understood, although I had a feeling this was just the beginning of something bigger about to come.

Chapter 59

My first official day as partner began with a breakfast celebration and gifts from everyone in the office. I was truly caught off guard but was thankful for all the admiration and respect I was receiving. Promotions are a big deal at Lowery, Hill, and Greenwood, but being made partner put those parties to shame.

As much as I liked the congratulations and gifts, I wanted to get to my office and get to work on closing out Sean's case. There was some paperwork I needed to complete for the firm, as well as see Sean one last time. I did not need to see him as part of the process; I wanted to. When I got to my office, I closed the doors, closed the blinds, sat in my chair, and leaned back with my arms high above my head, signaling victory.

"I know you don't want to be bothered, but this just came for you," Jill said as she interrupted my two seconds of peace.

"It's fine. All these gifts, they are nice. But boy, I'm going to be writing a lot of thank-you cards," I responded.

"I can type them for you, if you want?"

"No, Jill. I appreciate that but, it would mean more if they were handwritten from me. How is your studying coming along?" I asked, changing the subject.

"Good. My licensing exam is next month, and I am very confident I will pass. I've been studying so much lately, I've not had any kind of a social life. I don't even know what's going on in your life anymore.

"Oh, there is nothing you need to know other than I am probably getting a divorce, Danielle has been cheating on me the past eight years, and I became partner," I said with a sarcastic smile.

"I knew all that already, you ass. I meant how are you handling it all?"

"I know," I said, laughing. "Eh, I have my moments."

"Well, if you need anything, you know where I am."

"Actually, Jill, there is one thing you might be able to help me with."

"Yeah, what's that, boss?" Jill asked me, intrigued.

"Can you research if Sean Lancaster attended any other school before Boston University? I want to cross-reference something."

"Okay, but isn't the trial over?" Jill questioned.

"Yes, but I have a feeling he is hiding something from me, and I want to double-check something. Thanks," I said, hoping she would get the hint I was not going to discuss it anymore.

"Anything else, Sal?"

"No, thank you. And Jill? Thank you for everything. I mean it," I said, smiling at her.

"You're very welcome. Now open your last gift."

I almost forgot that that is why she came into my office. Before I opened it, I was trying to figure out who it was from. Everyone who knew I was a partner now was either here or at home. The intrigue was certainly exciting, something I was glad to have after the past few weeks.

There was no return address on the package, and the address label was typed. The package was medium-sized and seemed to be hollow inside. There was a single layer of packing tape, which was easy to open with a pair of scissors.

Inside the package sat a ton of Styrofoam peanuts that spilled out onto to the floor and all over my desk. Once I was done digging my way through the rest of the mess, I uncovered a wrapped rectangular package. Whoever sent this to me sure wanted to me to earn what lay inside. As I slowly opened the gift, I flashed back to when I was a child, when my parents would give me prank Christmas gifts to hide the real ones. Could this gift be from them? It would make sense.

Once I got the package open, I was immediately hit with confusion. I stared at what was inside the package for a solid minute or two, trying to figure out what the hell it was. There was a smashed-up matchbox car, a miniature laptop computer that seemed more likely to belong in a dollhouse rather than my office, a picture of an English literature college textbook, and a dismembered action figure. Was someone trying to send me a message, or was someone playing a game with me? All I knew in that moment was that this was not from my parents.

For the next two hours, all I did was answer a few emails, return some phone calls, and stare at the contents spread out on my desk from the package I received.

"Hey, Jill. Can you come in here for a minute, please?" I shouted.

Within a few seconds, Jill came in with a huge smile on her face. Was this from her?

"Was what, Sal?"

"Take a look at this," I said, pointing to the items I had received.

"What is it?" Jill asked.

"I have no idea. This is what was in the package you brought me earlier. I have been racking my brain the last two hours, and I got nothing," I said with frustration.

"Well, it obviously is some sort of puzzle. Like a mystery," Jill said with excitement.

"If you are so excited about this, why don't you help me solve it?"

"Okay, Let's look at the pieces and think of what they can mean. We have a picture of a textbook, which clearly means school or education or learning. We have a matchbox car with a smashed hood, which means it must have been in some kind of accident. We have—"

"Stop." I said suddenly feeling a sense of fear running through me. "It's someone sending me a message. The book and laptop mean college classes, the figure and smashed car signify a hit-and-run incident. I know what this is."

"What?" Jill asked with anxiety.

"It's about Peter. Someone is trying to tell me they know what happened to my brother."

Chapter 60

The next morning, Sean woke up early to get a head start on the busy day he had planned. He didn't want to get too far ahead of himself, but he knew that this day would put into motion the events that would lead to his endgame. First on his agenda was a call to Jimbo.

"Jimbo, my informant, how's it going?" Sean asked with great enthusiasm.

"What do you want, Lancaster?" Jimbo replied with a ho-hum response.

"I want your notes on Warden Paulson. What can you tell me?"

"Over the phone? Really?"

"You watch too many movies. Nobody is interested in you enough to tap your phone," Sean joked. "So, what do you got?"

"He arrives at work around eight forty-five every morning and goes right to his office for the morning briefing with the head guards. That usually lasts around an hour or so. Then he makes his rounds through the jail to make sure everything is running smoothly. He does this in thirty minutes flat. Then he must have an open space in his calendar because he spends the next two hours in his office doing God knows what. Next, he has lunch, most of the time by himself, but sometimes with other guards. He spends his afternoon in meetings with various departments and leaves the jail about five or six o'clock p.m. That good enough for you?"

"That was great. Well done! These meetings he has in the afternoons, are they every day?"

"Yes. I don't know who they are with though. He always has his door closed and does not let anyone interrupt him."

"Interesting. Does he always keep his door closed?" Sean asked.

"No, only in the afternoons," Jimbo replied shortly. "Is there anything else you need me to do, or am I free of this bullshit you keep putting me through?"

"Thank you for your help, Jimbo, you have no idea how much you have helped me. There is one more thing I need you to do though."

"Jesus Christ, Sean, what now?" Jimbo yelled.

"Look out that window across from you and tell me what you see."

Before Jimbo could answer, a quiet, quick piercing sound came from the window. It sounded like a pebble hitting a car windshield on the highway. Jimbo fell to the floor, not sure what had happened. He looked at the window again and saw there was a small hole with spider web cracks around it. He felt a burning sensation in the middle of his chest and looked down to see what had happened. His guard uniform was covered in blood, and there was a hole in his chest, the same size as the one in the window. Once he realized what had happened, Jimbo began to panic and tried to yell for help. Nothing came out of his mouth, and his breathing became labored. Not having much fight left in him, Jimbo closed his eyes as the world around him slowly drifted away.

"Oh, and don't forget to say hi to Sal's brother," Sean said as he broke his burner phone in half.

Sean felt good that he had accomplished one of his tasks so early in the day. He picked up his cell phone and dialed the person who had made the fatal shot.

"Nice shot! Impressive," Sean said with a giant smile.

"Thanks. What next?" the person on the other end asked.

"For you, that is all for today. But I need you to stand by. I may need to call an audible if needed."

"Ten-four," the person on the other end said and hung up.

Next on the agenda for Sean was a visit to the Doubletree Hotel in Fort Lee, New Jersey, which was right over the George Washington Bridge. He had no time frame for the visit because it depended upon how the meeting went.

When he arrived at room 327, Sean knocked on the door while looking both ways to see if anyone was around. The door immediately opened, and Sean went inside.

"Hey, stranger," Danielle said as she began to undress Sean.

"Wait, wait. We need to talk first," Sean said, pushing Danielle away.

"Okay. What's up?" Danielle asked.

"How did it go with Sal?"

"Great. Actually, better than great. It was perfect."

"What was his reaction to you moving back in?"

"Just like I thought it would be. He got pissed and asked me what I was doing, but I did like you told me and just kept moving forward. I didn't answer any of his questions directly, and when I did, it was with a short and simple sarcastic remark," Danielle said waiting for Sean's approval.

"That's my girl," Sean said and gave Danielle a quick kiss on the cheek. "So he didn't suspect anything?"

"I don't think so," Danielle answered.

"Good, because we need him to lower his guard so he doesn't begin to suspect anything."

Danielle moved closer to Sean and wrapped her leg around his and then wrapped her arms around his waist. "So when are you going to tell him?"

"Soon. The time has to be right, and he has to figure it out by himself," Sean answered, trying to control his excitement.

"You know everything is going to change once you tell him, right?"

"I know, but I will be prepared for it," Sean said, losing his battle with self-control as Danielle began lowering her hands from his waist.

Sean and Danielle spent the next few hours in bed, fulfilling each other's desires. When Danielle got up to take a shower, Sean looked at the clock and realized he was way off schedule, but that did not matter to him. He was having a great time, something he needed. While Danielle was in the shower, Sean seized the opportunity to make one more phone call.

"Listen, we are going to have postpone tonight. I got tied up and didn't have time to plan properly," Sean said.

"You sure? I know how important this is to you," a voice said.

"Yeah, I'm sure. Can you be ready in two days?"

"Same time, same plan?" the voice asked.

"Yes. I'll call you if anything changes."

"Sounds good. Have a good night, Sean," the voice said and hung up.

After the phone call, Sean got dressed and packed up his things. Before he left, he said goodbye to Danielle and told her they would do this again in a few days. They shared a passionate kiss, then said goodnight to each other. On the way out, Sean placed an envelope on one of the pillows for Danielle to read. In the letter, Sean explained the next steps for her to take. This time, it would be more difficult than just moving back into her home.

Chapter 61

I arrived at the office at seven-thirty in the morning, which is very early for me. Alan had asked me to stop by his office at eight o'clock so he could brief me on a potential new case. In my line of work, cases come in as quickly as they go out, so it was not unusual to be assigned to another case so soon after Sean's case closed.

To my surprise, Jill was already at her desk, eagerly awaiting my arrival. She usually never comes in this early, so I knew something had to be wrong.

"Sal, when you settle in, I have that report on Sean you asked me for," Jill said anxiously.

"Come on in," I said as I opened my door and took off my coat. "You want a pork roll egg and cheese bagel? I am ordering one now."

"Sure, but you might not have an appetite after you read this," Jill said as she handed me her report.

I sat down at my desk and began to comb through the report. It showed the schools that Sean had graduated from and his brief stint at Boston University in 1999, where he met Joseph Love. This report was nothing out of the normal, which is why I questioned Jill on what would bother me.

"Keep reading," Jill said, biting her fingernails.

I scanned down farther on the page and came across a school Sean attended that stopped me dead in my tracks.

"Utica College in 1998? Are you sure this is correct?" I asked, hoping it was an error.

"Yes, Sal. I checked it three times. He withdrew from Utica College and transferred to Boston University, saying he needed a change of scenery."

I was so shocked, I couldn't move. I even forgot to breathe at one point. Peter was attending Utica College in 1998 when he was killed in a hit-and-run accident. The driver was never caught, and his case remains unsolved to this day. Could this just be a coincidence, or is it possible that Sean had something to do with it?

"Can you reach out to Sean's assistant and set up a meeting with him, please? I need to ask him about this before I go crazy."

"Sure, Sal. You still going to order that breakfast sandwich?"

"Yeah. You want one?" I asked, still staring at the documents Jill had given me.

"Yes, thank you. Anything else?"

"No. Thank you, Jill. This is a huge help."

"No problem," Jill said as she walked away with a puppy-dog look on her face.

I began to connect the dots, and the first thing I figured out was that it must have been Sean who sent me that package the other day. Why was he toying with me *after* the trial? He was free because of me, and this is the thanks I got? Maybe I was overreacting. Maybe this was just a coincidence. Either way, I needed to find out as soon as I could.

Chapter 62

My meeting with Sean was set up for eight o'clock later that night at the 48 Lounge on West Forty-Eighth Street. It was just six blocks from Times Square, so I would be able to pass the time by window shopping. 48 Lounge is one of my favorite places to go in Manhattan because it is a quiet setting with excellent, upscale food and quality mixed drinks. I've even seen a celebrity or two there as well.

Around 7:45, I walked to the lounge and found myself getting nervous. I was not sure why, but it was something I could not control. As I got closer to West Forty-Eighth Street, my heart began to pound a little harder and my legs got a little weaker. There was no way I was going to be able to do this if I didn't get a hold of myself. I double-timed it so I would get there before Sean and still have enough time to down a shot or two to take the edge off.

I got to 48 Lounge at 7:55, and Sean was already there. So much for beating him.

"Sally, baby! Come. Join the party!" Sean yelled, already a few drinks in.

"Sure thing, Sean. What are we drinking?"

"Dealer's choice," Sean said, raising a glass.

"I'll take a vodka tonic with a lime and two shots of Licor 43, please," I told the bartender.

"Not messing around, are you?"

"Not tonight, Sean, not tonight," I said.

The bartender brought me my drinks, and I gave a shot glass to Sean. "Here's to new beginnings," I said, raising the shot glass to tap with Sean's.

We both downed our shots and asked for a table in the corner where we could sit in quiet and discuss business. I was clearly able to tell that Sean was in a great mood, and I didn't really care why. All I knew at that point was that it was going to make my life that night a little easier.

"So, Sal. What did you want to talk about? My assistant said it was about the trial?"

"Well, kind of. Just some routine follow-up questions I need answered to complete the paperwork for my firm," I said, pacing myself.

"Sounds good. What questions?"

"First I want to get your thoughts on the trial. I haven't really had a chance to speak to you about it and wanted to know what you thought," I asked, hoping Sean would not suspect anything.

"Sal, really? What is this? Like... a Gallup poll? Come on. What do you really want to ask me?" Sean said with a smile.

I took a huge sip of my drink and then took a deep breath. Should I go for it now or ease my way into it? Either way, I was going to be a nervous wreck, so I figured it was best to dive right in and not waste my time.

"I got a package the other day. A rather odd package, I should say. It contained a dismembered action figure, a mini laptop like from a doll house, a smashed-up matchbox car, and picture of a college textbook. Do you know anything about that?" I asked, curious as to how Sean would answer me.

"No, but it sounds creepy as hell. Who was it from?"

"Well, if I knew who it was from, I wouldn't be asking you now, would I? Okay, let's pretend for a minute that you don't know anything about this. What do you think it means? Should I be worried?"

"How am I supposed to know. It sounds like someone might be sending you a message," Sean said while finishing his drink and signaling for another.

"I figured you might know about this cryptic stuff because of all your experience sneaking around and hiding secrets," I said, delivering the first blow.

"There it is. The real reason we are here. Okay, Sal. Let's do this. Fact is, I have been waiting for this moment."

"Oh, I am not here for that, but since you brought it up—"

"I brought it up? You are the one who said I have experience hiding things."

"Yeah, you do, but I wasn't thinking of that. So now we are on that topic, how did you two meet?" I asked, not really wanting to know the answer.

"You really want to go down this path, Sal? There is no turning back. You should just lick your wounds and drop it," Sean, trying to sound intimidating.

"You're right. That is for another time. Let's talk about why I really called this meeting. But first, let's get another drink."

I waited in silence for the waiter to bring us our next round of drinks. I was not going to say another word until Sean had a drink and continued to drink himself into a state where he could do little harm to me.

Our drinks finally came after ten minutes of complete silence. Ten minutes might not seem like a long time, but sitting wordless with Sean felt like an eternity. Sean also knew the game I was playing. He was a successful entrepreneur and knew how to complete a sale. The same concept applied to the stand-off the two of us were having. The first person who talked lost their leverage.

"Okay, now we've had our drinks, let's get to it," Sean said, drinking half the glass.

"Utica College. Tell me about it," I said, feeling lightheaded and dizzy. The moment had come, and I was experiencing unparalleled anxiety.

"It's in upstate New York. Nice little place. Friendly people," Sean said, trying to torment me.

"Sean, cut the shit. Tell me about your time there."

"Well, clearly you know something, so why don't you share it with me."

"I want to hear it from you, you prick," I said, gritting my teeth as I spoke.

"Ha-ha. You are getting quite testy, huh? Alright, I'll tell you a little story. I went to Utica College in 1998 but didn't like it there. There were too many parties and not enough studying. I wanted to conquer the world, so I needed an environment I could thrive in academically. After a semester or two, I decided to transfer to Boston University, then ultimately UCLA. Pretty interesting, right?"

I did not respond. Instead, I stared at Sean with the most intense look I could give him. He did not intimidate easily, so I knew I would have to stare, unblinking, to get my point across. After two minutes, he finally gave in.

"Your eyes have so much water in them, I could go swimming. Blink, for Christ's sake," Sean said, joking. "I forgot to tell you about one night at Utica where I decided to join one of those infamous parties instead of studying. I had not been much of a drinker, so it didn't take me long to get drunk. You know how it is. Once you get buzzed you keep going and don't stop till you either pass out or get behind the wheel of a car. Well, I chose the latter because all I had to go was a few blocks. I pulled out of the parking space and knew right away I should not be driving. I went to call my roommate, but my cell phone battery died. You know batteries back then didn't last more than a few hours. Anyway, I said fuck it and decided to just head back to my dorm. Well, when I backed out of the spot, I mistakenly floored the gas pedal instead of applying the brake pedal. My car took off and went over a bump, which I thought was odd because that bump hadn't been there when I arrived. I stumbled out of the car and saw someone on the ground, barely breathing. I knew what I had done but didn't want to face the consequences, so I decided quickly to put the person out of their misery. I grabbed a rag from my trunk and suffocated him until he stopped moving. I then got in my car and sped away."

I was numb. I did not know the details of what happened to Peter, so hearing them from Sean somehow had made everything worse. *He had been alive after Sean ran him over? He could have been saved?* I was trying to bottle my emotions but couldn't. Tears flowed down my face as I looked at my Peter's killer in the eyes, not sure how to react.

"Did you ever find out who it was that you killed that night?" I asked, playing dumb.

"Not right away, but yeah, I found out a few years later. But you? You found out tonight who killed him, didn't you?" Sean said, smirking.

Normally, in this moment I would have jumped the table, grabbed Sean by the neck, and strangled him till his face turned purple, but I couldn't afford to lose my cool. I remained silent while I collected my thoughts and planned my next move. I knew Sean was waiting for me to attack him because he was in a defensive position. Instead, I continued asking questions.

"Why didn't you help him? You could have called 911 anonymously. You didn't have to suffocate him."

"Sal, I was drunk out of my mind. I could barely put one foot in front of the other," Sean said, attempting to explain himself.

I could tell at this point that I was not going to get anything else out of him, so I decided to end the night and get the hell out of there.

"Let me tell you something, *Lancaster*. You may not have told me everything now, but you will. You better be looking behind when you leave your house. When you get out of your car. When you go to fuck my wife. You never know what could be lurking in the shadows," I said, staring into his eyes with a possessed look.

"Is that a threat, Counselor?"

"It is whatever you want it to be. Just know that you have been warned."

I look out five twenty-dollar bills, folded them in half, and threw them on the table like they do in the movies. I have always wanted to do that to see how it feels. If it really makes an impact on the moment. I was surprised at how much of an impact it made because Sean didn't move a muscle as I downed the last of my drink and placed my glass on top of the money. It seems I had finally gotten to him, and he didn't know how to handle it.

I left 48 Lounge and walked the six blocks to Times Square to where I'd parked my car. The whole time I was nervous Sean would come up behind me and attack me. I tried to stay within crowds, occasionally dipping into a store to break up any surveillance Sean may have had on me. I finally got to my car and began to drive home, thinking this wasn't the last I would see of Sean Lancaster.

Chapter 63

I woke up the next morning still feeling the shock from my meeting with the Sean. The idea that Sean was responsible for Peter's death still had not set in. I was not sure what I was more upset at: the fact that Sean hid this from me, or knowing he could have saved my brother. Either way, I was not yet done with Sean.

I was also faced with another dilemma that plagued me. Do I report what Sean told me to the authorities? On one hand, there would be the potential for Sean to go to jail, where he belonged, and I would get justice for Peter. On the other hand, it would make the firm and me look bad because that would make two consecutive acquittals of guilty people.

Another obstacle I would have to overcome was the lack of evidence I would have. Sean confessed to a murder while severely intoxicated, not exactly hard evidence. I also did not have any other witnesses around to support my story, so I would have a hard time finding a DA who would be willing to pursue murder charges. After careful thought, I decided to let this one sit for the time being and keep it to myself.

I went downstairs and saw my kids having breakfast and watching TV. It was as if nothing had changed, and we were the happy neighborhood family again. Angela was brushing her doll's hair while humming something to herself. Gio was on his iPad either playing a game or watching a YouTube video. These are the moments I would miss if Danielle and I got divorced.

"Hey, guys, what's for breakfast?" I asked.

"Mommy made us waffles and cheesy scrambled eggs. Yummy!" Angela said as she rubbed her stomach.

"She did, huh? Wow, that's great. Where is she?" I asked.

"She went out to the car for a minute to get something," Gio answered, not looking up from his iPad.

"So, Gio, spring training is about to start, that right? You excited?"

"Kind of. Who knows what the Yankees will be this year. I still say they need more pitching," Gio said, still staring at his iPad.

"Hey, you want to put that down and talk to me?"

Gio let out a loud grunt and put his iPad on the table. "Fine. What do you want to talk about?"

"Angela, why don't you take your breakfast in the living room and watch TV," I said, needing a minute alone with Gio.

"But Mommy said I'm not allowed to," Angela rebutted.

"I say it's okay."

"Okay, Daddy, but you will get in trouble," Angela said, laughing.

When Angela left the kitchen, I turned my attention to my son. I have not been the best father to him over the past six months or so, but a lot of that had to do with Danielle taking the kids away from the house. I could tell Gio did not want to have this conversation, but it was something we both needed to do.

"Giovanni Antonio Amici, what is going on with you?" I asked, giving Gio my courtroom stare.

"What do you mean? I am fine."

"Gio, I know these last six months have not been easy on you. They have not been easy on anyone. But I cannot help you until you tell me what is on your mind."

"Dad, I really don't want to talk about this now," Gio said, trying to give me a guilty look.

"I know you don't. I don't want to either, but we have to. Now, tell me what's going on."

"I hate how you and Mom are always fighting and aren't living together anymore. I want to stay home and play with my friends. I want to be a family again!" Gio blurted out and began to cry.

I hated seeing my son like this. I knew this was tearing him up inside, and I wished I could just make it go away for him. I needed Danielle to see what her actions were doing to Gio and let her know that only she could fix this.

"I know, son. I am so sorry you have to go through this. I want nothing more than to be a family again as well. But no matter what, just remember that I love you and will always love you. Do you want to be alone now?"

"Yes, please. Can I go to my room?" Gio said, talking through the intermittent sobs.

"Yes, go ahead. I'll be up later to check on you."

Gio went upstairs, hanging his head and wiping the tears from his face. I tried not to look at him because of how much my heart ached for him, but I couldn't help myself. I watched him mope all the way to his room and then went outside to find Danielle.

"You bitch. Do you have any idea how much pain your son is in because of you?" I said to Danielle at the bottom of the front stairs.

"What *I* did to him? What about you?"

"*Me? Me?* You can't be serious. I am not the one who up and left. I am not the one who has had an affair for the past eight years. I am not the one talking shit about you to our kids. You have some nerve."

"Oh, calm down. I talked to Gio last night and he seemed fine."

"Yeah, well he is upstairs in his room crying because he thinks we are not a family anymore," I said quietly.

"That's ridiculous. How can he think that?"

"Maybe because he is eleven years old. Hell, I am thirty-five and I don't even understand it."

"Don't be so dramatic," Danielle said, waving her hand at me.

"All right, Danielle. I have had enough of your shit. You need to decide right here, right now. How are we moving forward? No more games, okay."

"Why is it up to me? What do you want to do?"

"I want to bash your skull in. That's what I want to do. But I can't do that now, can I?" I said, trying to control my anger.

"Wow, I never knew you could be so violent. I don't know what I want to do."

"I'll tell you what. Pack your shit back up and get the hell out of my house. There, I made your mind up for you. You are leaving the kids though. They do not deserve to go through this."

"Oh, I don't think so. They are coming with me," Danielle said.

"I am not playing this game with you. Fine. Take the kids for now, but we will see what family court says. I am meeting with a divorce attorney later today; someone I know very well. I am done with you."

After my encounter with Danielle, I went back inside the house to take a shower and get ready for work. I stood under the steaming hot water, wondering to myself how things got so bad, so quickly. Was Danielle ever happy with me? Was our marriage a complete lie? The more I thought about it, the more upset I got. I couldn't let Danielle do this to me, not when I was going to be depended on more at the office. No matter how hard I tried, I could not get over the fact that the last fourteen years with Danielle meant nothing to her.

As soon as I got out of the shower, my phone rang. There was no caller ID, so I let it go to voicemail. Five seconds later, my phone rang again. Still, no caller ID. This time, I picked up.

"What?" I answered with an attitude.

"You might want to tone down the fighting in public, Sal. Especially if it is on your front steps," a scrambled voice told me.

I ran to the window to see if anyone was outside because clearly this person knew what had just happened with Danielle in front of my house. There was nobody there, but the person on the line was laughing.

"Looking for me, are you? You should get dressed; you are getting the floor wet."

"Who the hell are you and what do you want?" I said, running out of patience.

"Patience, Sal. You wouldn't want anything unfortunate to happen, would you?" the voice asked me, then hung up.

I hated being toyed with by someone who clearly enjoyed tormenting me. I mentally ran through the list of people who I have either wronged or would want revenge on me. That list was pretty long, so I finished getting dressed and headed to the office in record time. I had a lot of research ahead of me and not a lot of time to do it.

Chapter 64

"How did it go?" Sean asked anxiously.

"As planned, Sean. You really know Sal well," a voice on the other end said.

"He is so predictable. It wasn't hard. I have gotten under his skin so deeply, I don't know if I can find my way out," Sean said, laughing hysterically.

"Yes, you have. So when do we make our final move?" the voice asked.

"Very, very soon. I just have one more thing to wrap up to protect myself. I will let you know when the time is right, but be prepared at any moment," Sean said and hung up.

Sean was beginning to feel excitement for the days ahead, but first he needed to address a lingering problem. He knew that it would be a challenge because Warden Paulson was such a meticulous man. But Sean was up to disrupting his routine and rattling his cage. Using the information he received from Jimbo Duncan, Sean waited in the employee parking lot at Rikers Island for Warden Paulson to pull into his reserved, front-row parking spot. Sean did not care that there may have been surveillance cameras covering the parking lot or other patrol cars; he needed to get this done. Once the Warden arrived, Sean would have to act quickly in order to accomplish his goal.

At precisely 8:45 a.m., just as Jimbo had said, Warden Paulson pulled up in his Mercedes S500. Sean put on his ski mask, exited his car, and snuck up behind the warden, surprising him.

"What the hell?" Warden Paulson yelled out.

"Don't make a sound or you're gonna regret it. Got it?" Sean whispered.

"Yeah, yeah. I got it."

"We are going for a little drive. Get back in the car," Sean ordered the warden.

"Where are going?"

"Just get in the car, shithead."

"Alright, just take it easy," Warden Paulson said, getting back into his car.

Sean entered the Mercedes from the passenger side and quickly closed the door so no one would see him. The windows were tinted with 5 percent shade, blocking out intrusive eyes. Once inside, Sean took off his mask to let the warden see who he was.

"Lancaster! Are you out of your frigging mind? Just what in the hell do you think you are doing?" Warden Paulson yelled.

"Greg. Can I call you Greg? I'm going to call you Greg. We are going to have a little chat. How that chat goes is entirely up to you. Think of it as a sort of 'choose your own adventure,'" Sean said, pressing a hunting knife up against the warden's side near his liver. "Now, tell me everything you learned about me from Jimbo, and don't leave out any details."

"He told me you killed Sal's brother in a hit-and-run accident in college. He didn't tell me the details, I swear. He also said that you were close with another inmate named Johnny."

"That's it? Are you sure? Think before you answer now."

"Yes, yes. I am sure. What are going to do with me?" Warden Paulson asked nervously.

"Well, that depends on you, Greg. See, I would like to go on living a free life, because that is what I am now—free. But I also can't have the warden of Rikers Island walking around with my little secret. You see my dilemma here, Greg?" Sean asked.

"Sean, listen. I know how the game works, okay? I have been the warden for six years and have tons of inmates on my payroll. I have kept juicy secrets on mostly all of them. So let's make a deal and make sure both of us are happy," Warden Paulson said calmly.

"Oh yeah. What secrets?"

"Secrets I'm not telling you, no matter what you do to me."

"Very good, Greg. Very good. Alright. You know what I want, now give me a reason why I should trust you to keep my secret. See, you have the upper hand on the inmates because they aren't going anywhere, and you can manipulate them into giving you information. As I said earlier, I am a free man and don't need anything from you," Sean explained.

"That's true. You don't need anything from me, but that doesn't mean I can't help you."

"And how exactly are you able to help me?" Sean asked, intrigued.

"I have connections all over the city. I know you do too, but I have different kinds of connections. I can introduce you to those connections, and they can help you with protection," Warden Paulson offered.

"Does it look I need protection, Greg? You are talking to the man who overtook Titus Baxter and ran Rikers Island. What kind of protection do you think I need?" Sean said, becoming irritated at the insult.

"In here, it's different. Guys are limited to what they can do. Out there, there is no limit as to what can happen to you."

"Is that a threat, Greg?"

"No, no. Not at all. I'm just saying that it is different than what it is in here."

"Greg, you are really starting to piss me off. Not to mention you are running out of time. I will give you one more shot. How do I know you will keep my secret?" Sean asked, gritting his teeth.

"Sean, you aren't going to do anything. I know that, and you know that. I am the warden of Rikers Island. If anything happens to me, they will come after you with more force than you could ever dream of," Warden Paulson said, suddenly getting a burst of confidence.

"Who said I was going to do anything to you? All I want to know is how do I know you will keep a secret?"

"You don't, so you'd better behave yourself out there. It can get rough, especially when you least expect it."

"Yeah, tell me about it," Sean said as he plunged his knife into Warden Paulson's liver.

"You shouldn't be such a pompous asshole, Greg. It gets you into trouble." Sean twisted the knife upward. "You think I am worried about the police coming after me? I am untouchable, Greg. Nobody can touch me. I got away with murder once, and I will do it again. If you see my wife, tell her I said she's a bitch."

Sean continued to twist the knife farther into Warden Paulson's side until it would not go any deeper. Sean had never actually killed someone up close like this. Sure, he'd killed Titus in jail, but that was in a fit of rage, not planned like this. This was up close and personal. He began to wipe down the inside of the Mercedes in every spot he had touched, which, to his surprise, was not much. When he finished cleaning the inside of the car, he checked the mirrors to make sure no one was looking. Once the coast was clear, he calmly opened the door with the cloth he used to wipe down the inside of the car and then closed it the same way.

Sean walked away smiling, knowing all the loose ends from the murders of his family and Sal's brother were now tied up and dealt with. There was nothing left for Sean to worry about, and he could now live a worry-free life. The only thing left for him to do was to clue Sal in on everything and see him go down in flames.

Chapter 65

Once back in the office, I asked Jill to help me pull files on every case I have defended since I arrived at Lowery, Hill, and Greenwood. This was a daunting task, to say the least, but it needed to get done if I was going to find out who was on the other end of that phone.

After two hours of digging in the computer and retrieving files from the file room, Jill and I had over three hundred case files to sift through. We both knew we would have a long day ahead of us, so we ordered Chinese food for both lunch and dinner and planned to work deep into the night.

I have had to go through enormous amounts of files for cases in the past, so I was used to it. On the other hand, Jill was used to leaving between six and seven every night. I felt bad asking her to stay late and help me, but I didn't trust anyone else with this information. I also told her that if she was going to be a paralegal, then she would need to get used to the long hours, so this was good practice.

Jill and I had been reviewing files for almost ten hours and were beyond exhausted. I had told her to look for cases that were high profile, as well as any cases that I lost, which was not many. We were not sure exactly what we were looking for but would know it when we found it. Finally, around seven o'clock, Jill found something.

"Sal, does the name Roland Crenshaw mean anything to you?" Jill asked.

"*Roland Crenshaw*? Now there is a name I have not heard in a while. What does the file say about him?"

"Assault and battery back in 2016, was released about eight months ago on good behavior," Jill said, scanning the document.

"Roland Crenshaw was a low-level thug who thought he was bigger than he was. He's too stupid to put anything elaborate like this together. Let's keep looking."

I was disheartened that the file Jill found did not turn out to be anything of interest, but I continued to dig. I knew there were violent criminals in the stacks of files we had in front of us, but I also knew I could not chase down everyone. There had to be a specific pattern or behavior that would make me want to pursue someone.

After another few hours, we were getting nowhere. I had heated up some of the cold Chinese food from earlier, even though the MSG made my stomach feel like mush. We were almost done with the files when Jill spotted something I had missed earlier.

"Hey, Sal. You reviewed this file, right?" Jill asked as she handed me a file that had been laying on top of an old pile.

"Yeah, why?"

"The name sounds familiar to me, like it should mean something," Jill said, intrigued.

"Samuel Porter," I said as I read the name while leaning over Jill's shoulder. "Sam was charged with raping his girlfriend's best friend back in 2015. He was one of my first cases at Lowery, Hill, and Greenwood and my first win. What made you look at his file?"

"This," Jill said, handing me a photo.

I stared at the photo and took a few moments to focus on what I was looking at. In the photo, Samuel Porter was holding one end of what looked to be a twelve-pound bass. Holding the other end of the fish was Sean Lancaster.

"Interesting photo, huh? How did I miss that? What else is in the file?" I said with a sudden burst of excitement.

"Nothing of significance, just facts about the case. Has Sean ever mentioned Samuel Porter to you?"

"No, not that I remember," I answered, staring intensely at the photo.

"Well, I think you and Sean have something to talk about," Jill said and continued going through the rest of the files.

"Jill, I think we've covered enough ground for this evening. Go home. You need to get some rest. Thank you for all your hard work today. You have no idea how much I appreciate it."

"No problem. You sure you don't need help cleaning up?"

"I'm sure. Good night, Jill."

"Good night, Sal. I hope you find the answers you are looking for."

"Me too. Me too," I said to myself.

I was packing up the files Jill and I had examined but stopped about a quarter of the way through. I was troubled by the fact that I had missed this huge detail in one of the files that *I* reviewed. If I was going to get answers, I would have to have laser focus the rest of the way and block everything else out. That laser focus would begin with an interrogation of Sean about how he knew Samuel Porter.

Chapter 66

When I am overtired, I can sleep through anything. A truck can drive through my bedroom, and I wouldn't move. Such was the case when I got home from a long day of research with Jill. I slept through my alarm clock, my cell phone ringing three times, and the kids running around getting ready for school. I had told Danielle I wanted her to officially move out, which she was fine with, but she was taking the kids with her. I wanted to spend time with my kids, so I told her to stay until we sorted our mess of a marriage out.

I went to the kitchen to make myself something to eat while I continued to look over Samuel Porter's file. Something was not adding up, and it was really eating at me. *How is Samuel Porter connected, and what motive could he possibly have if he is involved?* There were so many questions I had for Sean, yet I was not sure I wanted to hear all of the answers.

I brought my lunch to the kitchen table, turned on the TV, and set the file next to my plate. The news on the TV was talking about Sean's case, something that was nonstop since the trial ended. I changed the channel and the next station had on the same news. I could not escape Sean no matter what I did, and now I would have to see him again to get the answers I desperately needed. The only way to avoid him for now was to turn off the TV. As soon as I turned off the TV, the doorbell rang.

I slowly walked to the door because of how tired I was, which must have pissed off whoever was ringing because they kept doing it over and over. I finally made it to the door and, when I opened it, I thought I was dreaming.

"Sean, what are you doing here?" I asked, not wanting to talk to him.

"I need to talk to you about something. Can I come in, please?" Sean asked.

"No, I'm tired and about to eat lunch. What do you want?"

"Sal, please. It's important," Sean said with a serious face.

Something about his tone told me whatever he had to say, I needed to hear.

"Fine, come in," I said and closed the door behind him. "Now, what do you want?"

"Is that any way to treat a guest?"

"You are no guest. A guest is welcomed. I have a lot of work to do, so get on with it," I said, losing my patience quickly.

"Well then, I guess I ought to be quick. May I?" Sean asked, pointing to the couch.

"Why not. You want a drink while you are at it?"

"Scotch on the rocks would be nice," Sean said with a smile.

"Sorry, I don't drink scotch. Now tell me what's going on."

"You ever get the feeling that something isn't quite right, but you can't put your finger on it?" Sean asked, tilting his head.

"Yeah, all the time. I am a defense attorney. I get paid to feel that way." I had no idea where Sean was going with this, but I knew he'd better get there fast before I lost my cool. "Can you stop with the games, please, and tell me what's going on?

"I will, just have patience, my friend. We have nothing but time. The family isn't here. You took the morning off of work because you were at the office late last night. Things are okay. Just relax."

"How do you know where I was last night? Were you spying on me?" I asked, getting more and more angry.

"Me? Ha-ha. No, no. I don't spy," Sean said as he burst into laughter. "I have people who spy for me. That is the beauty of having more money than you know what to do with."

"But why spy on me? Shouldn't you be kissing my feet after what I did for you?"

"That's true, but then again, you are the one standing in the way of... Well, you know."

I could tell Sean was trying to goad me into hitting him, but I wasn't going for it. Instead, I spent the next few seconds thinking of two things: Why was he doing this? And what was he hoping to accomplish? I gave up trying to figure out my questions and went with my instincts to react to his taunting.

"Sean, I don't know what you are trying to do here, but it isn't going to work. Now, if there is nothing else, I would like you to leave so I can get back to doing nothing."

"I'm not done yet," Sean said as he grabbed my arm.

"Whoa, easy there, cowboy. No need for that," I said feeling a little pain.

Sean released my arm but still had a look in his eyes that made me feel uncomfortable.

"Now that I have your attention, we can get down to business. I understand you have been receiving some rather obscure phone calls about me. Is that true?"

"Am I supposed to ask how you know about this? Is that how this game is played?"

"You can if you want, but I would rather you just answer my questions to save time," Sean said.

"Yes, I have been. The voice on the other end has a voice scrambler and seems to be watching me because they are able to always describe what I am doing or what I just did. Since you told me earlier that you don't spy, I going to assume that the caller is not you and that you have an accomplice. Am I correct?"

"Boy, nothing gets by you, huh? I guess that's why I picked you to represent me."

"You picked me because you killed Peter and thought it would be ironic if I defended you in a murder trial. Come on, Sean, I know how you think."

"Oh, there's much more to it than that, Sally baby. If you only knew," Sean said with a hint of mystery.

"What do you mean, *more to it than that*?" I asked not sure of what he was talking about.

Sean began smile ever so slightly and then burst into an evil laugh that I thought only existed in movies. I was genuinely terrified at this point because I did not know what Sean was going to do or what he was referring to, but I knew it was not good. I also knew that I could not let him see my fear because then he would have the upper hand and I would have no shot at getting him to leave peacefully.

"Sal, I have been playing you since day one. From the first moment you stepped into Rikers Island until right now, you have been my puppet. You think I got to this point in my life without knowing how to manipulate and control people? You honestly think that I chose you to represent me on a whim? Or because I killed your brother by accident? Sal, I chose you to defend me before my family was murdered. But I had help. I wish I could take credit for it all, but I can't."

"What do you mean before your family was murdered? Did someone help you murder your family?"

"I need to make a quick phone call. Please hold," Sean said as he opened his burner phone and dialed a number. "It's me. I am ready for you."

"Sean, whatever you are thinking of doing, don't. I promise I won't say a word about my brother or your family or anything. I just want to move on with my life," I said with as much fear as I have ever had.

"I know you won't, Sal. But I am not here to hurt you."

I was scared out of mind and must have jumped back ten feet when the doorbell rang.

"You want to know why I am here? You want to know what this whole thing is about? You want to know who was on the phone making those calls to you? The answer is on the other side of the door," Sean said as he motioned his arm toward the door. "Go get it."

My legs were shaking, and my hands were trembling as I walked toward the door. I had so many thoughts going through my mind that I didn't know how to control them. For the first time in my life, I did not have control of a situation. I felt like I was having an out-of-body experience and didn't know when it would end. As I approached the door, I wondered if this was it. If this was how I was going to die. If it was, what a shitty way to go. When I finally worked up enough courage to open the door, I saw someone I never in my wildest dreams thought I would see in this situation. Someone who had not even been on my radar. Someone who I had a hard time processing in that moment. I was in such a state of shock that I couldn't move or hear anything. I stood in the doorway and had to rub my eyes and pinch myself to make sure I wasn't in a nightmare because the person I was staring at was... *David Flores!*

Chapter 67

"Surprised, Sal?" David Flores asked me, using the voice scrambler I had grown accustomed to hearing.

I was numb all over and couldn't answer David. My body felt lighter than hydrogen, as if it would float away at any moment. Every time I tried to open my mouth, nothing would come out. All I could process in that moment was Sean's evil laugh and David's sinister grin.

"How's that for a shock, huh?" Sean asked as he crept up behind me. "Earth to Sal? Are you in there?"

"We did it, Sean. We finally did it. We silenced the great Sal Amici!" David said as he made his way into my living room.

Both Sean and David left me standing by my front door and went to sit on my couch. I turned around to look at them both, still feeling numb all over. I was able to move my feet now, and the feeling of being outside my body was beginning to subside. After a few more minutes of staring at Sean and David together, I finally was able to talk.

"What in the actual fuck is going here?" I said, throwing my arms up in the air. "How do you two know each other? And again, what the actual fuck?"

"Sal, first you need to relax. You are not going to comprehend anything in your state," Sean said calmly. "Come, sit down with us and we can talk about this."

I didn't want to play Sean's games, but I knew I had no other choice. I had to comply with his demands in order to get the answers I was looking for, although I knew I wasn't going to like any of them.

"Okay, I am sitting down, now talk. No! Wait. First, I want to know why you are not in prison," I said, pointing at David.

"Oh, that's easy. I escaped with help of my buddy Sean here."

"How? And why hasn't it been on the news?"

"I paid off several people at Rikers to keep their mouths closed about it. Money talks every time," Sean bragged.

"Okay, but how did you get him out? That place is near impossible to escape."

"*Near impossible* is key there, Sal. Anyway, how he got out is not your concern," Sean told me.

"Fine, you want to know how I escaped? We have some time. I guess I can enlighten you. It was really pretty easy. See, Sean was able to secure me a repairman outfit to make it look like I was working on the power lines in the yard. Now, not all of the guards got a chance to know me, especially the ones in the yard; therefore, it was easy for me move around undetected. I was also able to stay in the yard long after the inmates were called back to their cells," David explained.

"Didn't the actual repairmen recognize you are not on their team?" I asked.

"No, because Sean paid a lot of money to have an ID printed. I was able to use that to fool the workers. Once the job ended for the day, I left with the team and got into the car Sean had left for me three blocks away," David concluded.

"Wow, that is quite a story. I'm amazed it didn't reach the papers," I said, stunned.

"Like I said, money is everything," Sean said.

"David, I get why Sean is doing this, but for the life of me, I cannot figure out why you are," I said, hoping to get an answer and not another smart-ass comment. "I mean, when I was defending you, we got along great. There was no animosity at all. Please, tell me why you are here."

"Sal, you always were a bit overdramatic. Just because you were my lawyer doesn't mean that I liked you. I mean, I had to put up with you so you would continue to defend me, but all along, I knew it would come to this."

"Come to what?" Can you guys just please tell me what is going on and stop fucking around?" I said, raising my voice.

"Okay, Sal. You want answers? You have to ask the right questions," David said.

"How do you two know each other?" I asked both of them.

"Well, it really is not that complicated; in fact, the answer to that has been staring you right in the face. You just were too consumed in yourself to see it. If you were half as good as you think you were, you would know to do a little research on your clients before investing your time and effort in them," Sean explained.

"Meaning what? I don't know who you are?"

"Oh, you know who I am, just not who *he* is," Sean said, patting David on the shoulder.

"Then why don't you tell me who he is, Sean, and stop playing these mind games. They are getting really old."

There was a sudden silence in room after my latest outburst. I was on the very edge of my patience with both Sean and David, but I had to compose myself if I wanted answers. I kept reminding myself that I was close to finding out what was going on, and if I went berserk on them, I would never get the answers I needed. To break the silence, I tried a different tactic.

"Look, I know both of you are enjoying this, maybe a little too much. I just want to know what is going and how you two are connected so I can figure out what it is you both really want," I said as calmly as I could.

Sean turned toward David and gave him a look that said it was time to move forward. I tried not to look at how David reacted, but I couldn't help myself. David nodded his head in agreement and began to rub his chin with his left hand. Instantly, my anxiety kicked up another notch; I knew I was going to receive life-changing news or more intense torture.

"Sal, if you had done your research on me, you would have discovered that my dead ex-wife, Denise, was born Denise Santiago," Sean explained.

"Okay? I'm confused. What does that mean?"

"David, tell the poor, lost soul your mother's name," Sean teased.

"Sure thing. Her name was Pamela Santiago," David answered.

"And who was she married to when she died?"

"My father, Guillermo Flores."

Suddenly, I felt the same way as I did when I first saw David Flores at my door earlier. How could I have missed this? I normally do extensive background checks on everyone involved in my cases, yet somehow, I missed this. *David Flores is Sean Lancaster's half brother-in-law.*

"You mean to tell me that the two of you are half brothers-in-law?" I yelled at both Sean and David.

"Ding, ding, ding! What do we have for our winner today, Johnny?" Sean said, clapping slowly.

I was not sure I could handle more shock and surprise, so I was careful with my follow-up questions. I wanted to know the whole truth, but this was too overwhelming, I felt like I was going to vomit all over my living room rug.

"Okay, help me out here, Sean. Was David involved in your family's murder?"

"What do you think, Sal? You are the star defense attorney," Sean said with an evil smile.

"He couldn't have killed them because he was on trial when they were murdered, and I am pretty sure he was in lockup," I said sarcastically. "And you insist you didn't do it. Hey, you were even acquitted of those charges, so in the court's eyes, you didn't kill them. I am going to say David was not directly involved but rather had an indirect hand in the massacre of your family."

"Wow, you should have been a detective, Counselor," Sean joked.

"So who actually killed your family if it wasn't David or you? Let me guess, another surprise, right?"

I could tell I was on to something because I wasn't getting the same sarcastic answers and body language as I had before. All I had to do was keep poking, and eventually their bubble would burst.

"Listen, Sal, we will keep you in the game, but we aren't going to turn all our cards over. If you want to know who killed my family, you will just have to figure it out on your own," Sean said, standing up to leave.

"Where are you going? I'm not done yet!" I demanded.

"Whoa, someone grew a pair of cojones," David said in surprise.

Sean sat back down, seemingly anxious as to what I had to say. I wanted to address the elephant in room of why they were telling me all of this, but I was afraid to find out the answer. As I struggled to think of a way to continue, suddenly the previous night crept back into my mind. I now had the answer and needed to confirm it with Sean.

"Hey, Sean. Caught any fish lately?" I asked. Now it was my turn to smile.

"Uh, it's winter, Sal. We don't go ice fishing in New York City."

"I know that, but I still am curious to know when the last time you caught a fish was."

Sean had a curious look on his face; one I had not seen from him before. He was genuinely confused as to what I meant, which is exactly the reaction I was hoping for.

"I have no idea. Why are you asking?"

"Oh, I don't know. I was thinking that if it has been a while, we could go once spring comes around. Maybe catch some bass together," I said, looking at the floor.

When I looked up at Sean, panic was written all over his face. He seemed to know now what I was talking about and wasn't doing a very good job of hiding his fear. I wasn't sure how he would react, but I knew at that moment I had a stranglehold on him.

"You think you have it all figured out, don't you?" Sean said with a slight laugh. "I was beginning to wonder if you would be able to piece it all together. You really are good, Sal."

"What is he talking about Sean?" David asked.

"See, Sal here has figured out who we got to kill my family, and now he is going to explain what he is going to do with that information."

"What do you mean he knows? How does he know? You said he would never find out," David, panic rising in his voice.

"Well, I guess I underestimated him, David. No worries though. It is nothing we can't work out together," Sean said.

"So tell me if I am right here. You and David decide to kill your family for whatever reason, and you get Samuel Porter to do the job for you. That about right?" I asked, feeling like Perry Mason.

"Almost. You left a few things out. See, I didn't know Sam until David introduced us a little over a decade ago. Sam was a hothead and loved to get into trouble. He didn't care if he got caught or not. He actually liked causing havoc," Sean answered. "When you defended him, he couldn't stop talking about how gullible you were and that he had you eating out of his hand. I almost fell over when he told me about your brother. Apparently, you had told him about what happened to explain why you became a lawyer. Little word of advice, Sal, nobody gives a shit. Anyway, once he told me that story, I did a little research and found out that I was the one who killed your brother. You couple that with the fact that David and I are family, and you have your answer as to why I chose you to defend me. Like I said before, I chose you to defend me before my family was murdered, but your masterful job of defending David sealed the deal for me."

"You are crazy, Sean, you know that. Certifiable!" I screamed. "Where is Samuel now?"

"Don't know, don't care. We paid him his money and he took off," Sean said.

"There is still one thing that doesn't make sense to me. Why?"

"Why have my family killed?" Sean asked. "Again, if you had done your research, you would have found my motive. Then again, that joke of a DA didn't uncover it either, so I guess it's not totally on you."

"What didn't we find out, Sean?" I asked derisively.

"I have been in negotiations to sell my company for a while now. That is not news, it's public knowledge. What is not known to the public is who I am selling the company to. See, I figured that if I had public sympathy, you know my family being murdered and all, the sale would go under the radar. Oh, and the two-million-dollar life insurance policies I have on each family member didn't hurt either. Four million goes to David, and four million goes to Sam. Nothing comes out of my pocket, and I keep all the profits from selling my company."

"You did all this for money when you are already rich?" I asked, not believing what I was hearing.

"What have I been telling you, Sal. Money is everything. Oh, and you can never have too much money. Shame on you for thinking otherwise."

"So I guess I have the whole picture now, huh? I gotta hand it to you, Sean, you fooled a lot of smart people, especially me. But I do have one more question for you," I said as I geared up to deliver my knockout punch. "What's going to stop me from going to the police to report all of this?"

Sean and David both began to laugh. It was as if they were waiting for me to ask this question the whole afternoon.

"Sal, you really think we would be telling you all of this if we weren't sure you wouldn't go to the police?" Sean said, laughing in between words.

"What makes you think you know me that well?"

"It has nothing to do with knowing you at all. See, you don't have all of the information, which is why you haven't pieced it all together yet."

"Sal, I'm getting really tired over here. Can you just figure this out so we all can go our own way and I can collect my four million dollars?" David said to me, annoyed.

"Well, David, if you help me out a little bit, maybe I can get there quicker."

"Sal, let me ask you this," Sean said as he sat up to the edge of the couch. "If I told you who I was selling my company to, do you think you would be able to finally put this all together?"

"I have no idea. Tell me and I will let you know," I said, having lost my patience.

"Sal, are you sure you want to know? There is no going back from this. Once you know, you know." Sean asked in a calm tone as if he had all afternoon.

"Yeah, I want to know."

Sean hesitated a bit and looked upward to think about whether he should reveal who he was selling his company to or not. Finally, he gave in. "Okay, it's Danielle."

Chapter 68

For the third time that afternoon, my body went numb. This time, it was a combination of shock and confusion. Sean's company was worth over $75 million, how in the world could Danielle afford to buy it? I began to think Sean was messing with my head, but then I realized he had been truthful with me to this point, so why start lying now? If Danielle really was the buyer, then where was the money coming from, and how had she kept it from me?

"Excuse me, Danielle? You're messing with me," I said timidly.

"No, Sal, I'm not. I actually feel bad for you. I really do. You have been played so hard by that woman; you wouldn't believe me if I told you," Sean said with a hint of sorrow.

"Enlighten me," I said, suddenly feeling bold.

"Danielle is very, very wealthy, my friend. She has been hiding money from you the whole time you have been married. In fact, her net worth is almost twice what mine is."

"You're lying. That's not true," I said, feeling anger begin to build inside of me.

"You can deny it all you want, Sal, but the truth is, she has the money to buy me out. When we started our affair eight years ago, she told me she wanted to leave you, but she was afraid you would find out about her money, so she stayed. As the years went on, she got more and more disgusted by the thought of being married to you. She felt you were holding her back from where she really wanted to live and that I could give her the life she so desperately wanted."

"I don't believe you, Sean. I don't. There is no way she can hide that much money from me. David, did you know about this?"

"Oh yeah. Why do you think I got involved? Sean is a man of his word and with $75 to $100 million coming his way, he doesn't need the life insurance money," David said with pride.

I was beginning to think Sean was telling the truth. Why would he lie about this now? I also was beginning to see how he was going to ensure that I kept my mouth shut. If I told the police about what Sean and David did, then Danielle would be outed, and my family would be exposed. I would be the laughingstock of New York City. I would certainly be fired from Lowery, Hill, and Greenwood. As a result, I would probably never practice law again. I had no choice but to go along with Sean's plan.

"Okay, let's say this is true. What's to stop me from confronting Danielle about the money she's been allegedly hiding from me?"

"Nothing," Sean said matter-of-factly. "You can ask her all you want. She has gotten pretty good at hiding it."

"So she buys your company, then what? She tells me, 'Oh by the way, Sal, I bought a $75 million company'?"

"Sal, you still don't get it, do you? She is much too smart for that. She has it all set up to be a silent owner. She will not be visible to the public, so there would be no reason for her to have to tell you," Sean assured me.

"Sean, I am starving. Can we please wrap this up?" David began to whine.

"In a minute. There is one more thing I need to tell Sal," Sean said, turning to me. "If you think you will get any of that money in a divorce settlement, you can forget it. See, Danielle is using her own money to buy my company; money she had before you married her, and as you well know, you are not entitled to that money. There is a paper trail going all the way back to when she was a teenager that shows it belongs to her and it was not comingled with your marital assets."

"I still don't get why you planned to kill you family if you are selling off your company anyway. Why not just sell the company and take your profits? Why murder your family?" I asked, confused.

"I told you already. Public sympathy. I also wanted to take care of David and not have to use any of my money, which is why I am using the life insurance money to pay him and Sam. Plus, with my family out of the way, I can live my life with Danielle once she leaves you."

I have never wanted to hit someone so badly in my life. I wanted to, but with David there, I did not stand a chance against the two of them. It was better for me to take my internal beatings and not receive bodily harm.

"So Danielle knew about your plan to have your family murdered and was okay with it?" I asked, not believing what I was asking.

"Did Danielle know about it? Sal, the whole thing was her idea."

For a fourth time that afternoon, I went completely numb. At this point, I was not sure how much more my body could take.

"Now that's a lie and I know it is. Danielle would never do that!" I screamed.

"Sal, she was the one who came up with getting David involved and then hiring Sam as the murderer. She was the one who thought to use the life insurance money to pay them, so *we* didn't have to use *our* own money. She wanted to get filthy rich. Richer than she already was. She thought if she could buy my company, we would have more money than we ever dreamed of. Face it, Sal, you never knew who your wife really was."

"How would you both make money if she bought your company with her money? Wouldn't that simply be changing owners? The money would be the same," I asked, once again confused.

"Is that the question you have after what I just told you? "Sean laughed. "Okay then. If she buys my company, she can then turn around and sell it at a profit in a year or two; after the value goes up by the projected 20 to 25 percent. It would be much easier for her to sell the company than it would be for me because, let's face it, who wants to buy a company from someone who was accused of murdering his family, even if he was found not guilty?"

I was not sure how to react to everything I was told, but it seemed to be the truth because Sean had an answer and explanation for everything. My life had just been turned upside down, and all I could think about was how disappointed Thomas would be in me if he was still alive to hear this. I couldn't take much more of this and I certainly could not handle any more surprises, so I decided to end things that afternoon and think of how I would proceed.

"Alright, guys. You made your points. You got your thrills. Now I want you to leave so I can be alone," I said, lowering my head in shame.

"Sal, look at the bright side. At least you will get to keep everything when Danielle divorces you unless she wants half of that too," Sean said, adding salt to my wounds for the last time.

Sean and David both got their coats and left my house laughing and whistling. I have never felt so low before; not even after Peter died. I had no idea what to do next or who to talk to next. Should I go to Alan and Steven and tell them? If I did, I would surely be suspended pending an investigation. Should I go to the police and risk my family being humiliated? I wasn't sure I could handle that, not now anyway. I couldn't do that to my kids. Should I keep my mouth shut and forget about what just happened over the past hour? I could see myself doing that initially;

eventually, though, I would crack. I decided the best action for me was to call Jill and tell her I was not coming in the office today and then go home to sleep it off. I was emotionally drained, so I would be able to fall asleep with no problem. Just to make sure I would fall asleep quickly, I took two Ambiens. As I drifted off to sleep, the last thing I remember thinking was how I could have been fooled so badly by Danielle for all these years. What did that say about me? Those questions would have to wait for an answer because I fell asleep in record time, hoping I would wake up and find out this was all a crazy nightmare.

Chapter 69

I woke up the next morning, having slept through the night without waking up once. Even though I got over twelve hours of uninterrupted sleep, I was still exhausted. I kept asking myself how Danielle was able to hide her money from me and why I didn't suspect anything. Part of me still wanted to think Sean was messing me with me, but he knew I would do my own research, so there would be no reason to lie to me. I needed to get a handle on what I was going to look into first, but I couldn't concentrate because my mind was jumping all over the place.

I took a few deep breaths and then realized that before I could research any of the statements Sean made, I needed to confront Danielle. I had no idea how or when I was going to do it, but I knew it had to be quick. If everything Sean said was true, I assumed Danielle was making final preparations to buy his company and then file divorce papers. Since New York State law only requires a relationship be broken for six months, Danielle would be able to file for divorce without any issues.

The other aspect of this whole ordeal was my children. How much would this affect them? How would they cope with it all, and would they blame me for everything? Part of me wanted to tell them right now what was going on to beat Danielle to the punch, but I knew I couldn't do that if I wanted any chance for sole custody.

I went downstairs to make myself breakfast and was surprised by how quiet the house was. It looked like nobody had woken up yet because nothing was out of place. Usually, when the kids wake up, the kitchen and living room look like someone set off a bomb. If everyone was asleep still, I was going to enjoy my time alone while it lasted.

I finished making my pancakes and eggs and sat down at the kitchen table. As soon as I took my first bite, Danielle came downstairs.

"Hey, honey. How are you?" Danielle asked as if nothing was wrong.

I completely ignored her and continued eating my breakfast while checking the sports news on my phone. I still had not decided how I was going to approach Danielle, so I figured it was better to stay quiet than to say something I was going to regret. After a few minutes, I didn't need to worry about how I would handle this situation; Danielle did it for me.

"So I heard you found out something yesterday, huh?" Danielle asked as she sat down at the table with her coffee.

Again, I remained silent. I wasn't going to give in to her and let her think she had the upper hand. I knew she would test my patience, but all I had to do was remind myself to keep quiet and I would be able to last long enough to develop a plan.

"Alright, you don't want to talk? Fine. That is better for me," Danielle began. "I know you have a lot of questions, I would too. But the fact of the matter is, I don't have to answer any of them because I don't owe you anything. Maybe if you weren't always consumed in yourself and your work, you would have been able to see things a little differently. You would have seen the things I was buying and would begin to question me on where I got the money from. Truth is, I wanted to tell you. I wanted to tell you from the beginning, but my trust lawyer told me not to. He never gave me a good reason, but I figured he would know better than me, so I went along with it."

"You went along with it? What the hell does that mean?" I said, staring at the table. "Who does that? Who hides money from their spouse? For fourteen years? Danielle, I am your husband. We have two children together. How in the world can you justify keeping this from me? Did you think all I would care about was your money?"

"Sal, you never know what someone is like when money is involved, especially the kind of money I have."

"That's ridiculous. This whole time, I have done nothing but devote myself to you and this family. For you to even think that I would care about money is absurd. What did I do to you to deserve this? *What?*" I asked as my voice began to crack.

"Sal, you still don't get it, do you? I love you, I really do, but Sean has said to you a million times that money is everything. It's all about the money, honey," Danielle said coldly.

I didn't know whether she was trying to let me down easy or if she was enjoying tormenting me. Either way, I had a hard time believing what she was telling me. This was the same woman I saved from a screaming line drive at Yankee Stadium. She was the one I consoled when her parents died. She was the one who held our children so lovingly and then told me I was the best father in the world. How could all of that been a lie?

"Danielle, I am not buying it. I don't care how good someone is, you can't keep up this charade for fourteen years. It is not possible to sustain," I said, hoping to get more information out of her.

"Sal, I don't know what you want me to say. This is who I am. I know you don't believe me, and frankly, I don't care. All I know is that I don't want this anymore."

I had been waiting for the right moment to confront Danielle about her involvement in the murder of Sean's family, but nothing had presented itself—until now. Danielle always had a way of making my job easier when I didn't know what to say. She always had the innate ability to point me in the right direction without even knowing she had done so. My opportunity had presented itself, and just like I would have done if I was in a courtroom, I jumped all over it.

"Okay, let's put the idea that you are a different person than I thought you were aside. I would like to talk about something else that I need you to help me understand," I said, easing my way into coaxing a confession.

"Ugh, really, Sal? Why can't you just accept that we are over and move on?"

"Oh, I have. I just want to clear something up first."

"What?" Danielle said impatiently.

My heart began to pound for reasons unknown to me; something that had been happening to me a lot over the past six months. I didn't do anything wrong, so there was no reason for me to be this nervous. Maybe it was because I was about to ask my wife if she was a cold-blooded killer, or I was beginning to realize that my marriage of fourteen years was really over. Whatever the reason was, I knew I had to press on.

"I want to know when exactly you began to put your plan in motion?"

"What plan?" Danielle asked, trying to play dumb.

"Danielle, knock it off. I am not playing this game. Sean told me everything, okay? I want to hear it from you. When did you begin to plan the murder of his family?" I said, growing impatient.

"Sal, I honestly have no idea what you are talking about or why Sean would tell you lies like that. You honestly think I would plot to kill an entire family?"

"Before yesterday, not in a million years. But Sean was pretty convincing and provided some facts that I would have a hard time disputing in court, so it makes me believe he is telling the truth. So again, when did you begin planning the murder of his family, and don't make me ask again."

Danielle began to chuckle a bit under her breath. She seemed to be amused at how confused I was and wanted to savor the moment. For the next few seconds, she looked at me with a look I had not seen from her in the whole time we had been together. She had an evil smirk and slightly nodded of her head. I stared back, not saying a word, hoping the silence would eventually get to her.

"You think you have me figured out, huh? You think you know everything about what happened to Sean's family? Well let me tell you something, Counselor, you have no idea who I am or what I did," Danielle said in deeper voice than I have ever heard from her.

"Then why don't you tell me," I said, knowing she was itching to tell her story.

"You want to know where I got my money from and what my intentions were when we murdered Sean's family huh? Okay, I will tell you. Not because you asked me to, but because you are weak, and I know you won't do anything to ruin your perfect reputation," Danielle said arrogantly. "When my parents were in that car accident and died, they left me their entire fortune, well over $100 million. I went to a trust lawyer, who advised me to on what to do with it. But he said not to tell you if I was unsure about our future. Well, I didn't tell you about the money not because I wasn't sure about our future; it was the fact that if you knew about my money, you would eventually find out my secret."

I felt a large lump in my throat growing at the idea of what I thought her secret might be. "What secret?"

"I know you know, but I will tell you anyway because I want to see the look on your face. My parents' accident wasn't an accident at all. I knew they had money, and... Well, I wanted it. So I cut the brake line in my father's car, knowing they had an appointment early the following morning. You know how easy it was to get away with that? If getting away with murder was that easy, why not give it a second go? So I came up with a way to get even richer and do it again. Sean was hesitant at first, but once I told him the plan, he climbed aboard. I mean he *literally climbed aboard*."

"You're good. You are *really* good. You had me and everyone who knows us fooled. I have to hand it to you, Danielle. It almost makes me question how good I really am." I could see the arrogant smile on her face from ear to ear was something she was holding in all morning and was now happy to let it out. "There is just one more request I have for you, then we can discuss what to do moving forward."

"Sal, this is getting really ridiculous. What now?"

"Can you look at the end table in the corner over there and tell me what you see?" I instructed.

Confused, Danielle looked at the end table that Sal pointed at and saw nothing out of the ordinary. There was a tissue box, an empty soda can, a picture frame with their wedding photo in it, and a lamp.

"I don't get it. What am I looking at?"

"Would you grab that picture frame for me, please? I want to remember the happy times between us and show you what we could still be again," I said, hoping that would soften Danielle up.

"Sal, you really are a romantic, but give it up," Danielle said as she handed the picture frame to me.

"Tell me, Danielle, what do you see in this picture? Look closely now. I really want you to feel it."

"Our wedding photo. I was happy then, Sal, I really was. I am sor—" Danielle suddenly stopped. "Where is the engraving of our wedding date on the frame?"

"It's not there?" I asked, holding back a smile.

"No, it's not. What is going on here, Sal?" Danielle asked angrily.

"It's not there because that is not the original frame. Inside that border is a tiny microphone, invisible to the naked eye. Our entire conversation was being broadcast to the fellows outside as we spoke."

As soon as I finished my statement, the doorbell rang. Danielle looked at me with a look of horror and confusion. She knew what was happening yet was too shocked to move.

"I wonder who that is?" I said as I went to open the door. "Come on in, Detective Marino. Was that enough for you?"

"Oh, that was plenty. Worked like a charm, Sal. Thank you," Detective Marino replied.

"She's all yours, Detective."

"Danielle Amici, you have the right to remain silent," Detective Marino said as he read her the Miranda rights.

"You son of a bitch. You think you won? You think this is the last you've heard from me?" Danielle screamed as she was taken away in matching silver bracelets.

"That must have been tough, Sal. What made you decide to turn her in?" Detective Marino asked.

"You know, I'm not sure. All I know is that last night when I called you, I kind of did it involuntarily. Does that make sense?" I asked, feeling confused.

"Yes, Sal, it does. I have seen it before, but how did you know she would confess this morning while we were outside?"

"I have come to see over the past few weeks that Danielle is as self-centered as they come. She wants to brag about how she gets away with things yet doesn't pay attention to her surroundings. A classic narcissist. If I pushed her enough, eventually she would give in to her desires."

"So where do you go from here?" Detective Marino asked.

"I don't know, Detective. I don't know. What I do know is that I have to explain to my children why their mother is likely to spend the rest of her life in jail."

Chapter 70

Three days had gone by since Danielle's arrest, and I had not yet told my children what happened. I had not really thought about how to do that because there was an even bigger problem I was dealing with. Sean Lancaster had not been seen in almost four days, and detectives had not found any evidence of where he might be. His apartment was cleaned out, his bank accounts emptied, and his business was signed over by one of his partners. For all intents and purposes, Sean Lancaster was a ghost.

I am not sure why, but I was really bothered by the fact that he turned into a coward and ran away. He always struck me as the type of person who was so arrogant that he thought he was immune to any type of prosecution. Maybe he was that vain. Maybe he'd turn up soon, but for now he was considered a wanted man.

After I received my daily update call from Detective Marino on Sean, I finally turned my attention to facing the two things I was postponing for the past three days: my partners and my children.

Gio and Angela had just returned from staying with their grandparents the past three days. I needed that time to think, so I asked my mom and dad to take them. I knew that would be an easy ask because what grandparent would say no to spending three days with their grandchildren? I had briefed my parents on what was going on, and they respected my privacy and didn't ask to many questions.

Once the kids were dropped off and my parents left, the questions began.

"Where's Mommy? I made something for her!" Angela said.

"Yeah, she promised to take me to the park when I got back," Gio added.

"Kids, listen. I need you both to follow me and sit down on the couch. We need to talk," I said as my anxiety once again kicked up another notch.

"What's going on, Dad? Is everything okay?" Gio asked.

For an eleven-year-old, Gio was very intuitive. Not much escaped him, and he never shied away from asking what was on his mind. That was a quality I admired in him, just not in this instance.

"Well, Gio, no everything is not okay. See, your mother is not coming home for a very long time. She did something bad, and nobody knew about it until recently," I told my children, not knowing if I should elaborate.

"What did she do, Daddy? Did she yell at someone?" Angela asked.

The innocence of a six-year-old was really difficult to handle at that moment. Angela didn't have a negative bone in her body. She was always smiling and laughing. She never thought about anything bad, let alone something bad her mother could have done.

"Well, yes she did, but she did more than that. I can't tell you what exactly. Not yet anyway. Just know that it is going to be just the three of us for a while."

"Why can't you tell us?" Gio asked.

"I just can't, Gio. Trust me," I said firmly.

"That's bullshit, Dad!" Gio yelled.

"Hey! Watch your mouth, young man!" I screamed.

"Sorry, Dad, but it is. If Mom did something wrong, we deserve to know about it."

"No, you don't. I am the parent, and I will decide what you will and will not know. End of story. Got it?" I yelled again.

"Yes," Gio said, hanging his head.

"Now, I know this is difficult for both of you, so if you want to go to your rooms, I will understand," I said, hoping to get some time alone to think.

While Gio stormed up to his room and slammed the door, Angela sat on the couch, staring at me.

"What's on your mind, angel?"

"I trust you, Daddy. I know you will tell us when the time is right," Angela said as she gave me the biggest hug she had ever given me. "Can I go watch TV?"

"Sure, angel. Go ahead," I told her as a few tears ran down the side of my face.

I knew that was not the best way handle to the situation, but I did the best I could. When the kids were settled, I decided I needed to focus on what I would say to Alan and Steven when I met with them the following morning. How much did they know, and how much would I tell them? I would continue to ponder these questions and more as I slowly drifted off into a twilight sleep. My career-defining moment was hours away, and I needed as much rest as I could get, even if that was only for a few hours during the day.

Chapter 71

I decided to go back to my normal routine and take public transportation to work. It allowed me the time to prepare for my meeting with Alan and Steven without having to concentrate on driving. I had a plan in my head on how I would approach the meeting, but given the recent history of our meetings, I was also prepared for the unexpected.

I arrived at the office a little after eight in the morning, and Jill was already there with my coffee in hand.

"How are you doing, Sal?" Jill asked with a concerned look on her face.

"I am okay. How are you?" I asked, trying to deflect.

"I'm a little worried because of the tension in here. Everyone knows about Danielle, yet nobody knows how to react to it."

"Good. The less people have to talk to about it, the better. Any word on Sean's whereabouts?" I asked again, trying to change the topic.

"Nothing. From what I heard last, the detectives think he left the country."

"I am sure he has. That's what cowards do, and Sean Lancaster is the biggest coward of them all," I said, disappointed.

"I am sure he will be caught, Sal. You just need to have patience."

"Jill, how long have you known me?" I said, laughing for the first time in a while. "Are Alan and Steven ready for me?"

"Yup, they told me to send you up when you arrived."

"Okay, wish me luck."

"Good luck. And Sal, remember how you got here and what it takes to stay here," Jill said, giving me much needed confidence.

"Thanks, Jill."

I made my way up to Alan's office, where he and Steven were waiting for me. Even though I knew it wasn't the case, it felt like I was making my way to an execution. Both Alan and Steven were sitting at the round table in the corner of the office with folders in front of them. Did those folders contain my walking papers? Or did they hold new evidence on

Sean's current location? I slowly made my way to the vacant seat, took off my suit jacket, and settled in as best I could, not knowing what the next hour or so would bring.

"Hi, Sal. How are you holding up?" Alan asked.

"It's tough, but I am managing," I answered, wanting to keep my answers brief.

"I understand. Hang in there and know we are all here for you," Steven said.

"I appreciate that, Steven. Thank you."

"Sal, we need to discuss a few things so we can finally put this fiasco behind us. First, let's talk about Sean. He gave you no indication at all what he was up to?" Alan asked.

"With all due respect, Alan, I need to know what you know first before I can answer."

"Fair enough. Detective Marino filled us in on the whole situation with Sean, Danielle, and David. He told us everything you told him about the plot to murder Sean's family, what everyone's involvement was, and what Danielle confessed to," Alan answered.

"No, he didn't give me any indication of anything. He played me. My wife played me. David Flores played me. I know how this looks, and I understand if you question my abilities, but let me say this: it will never happen again. Ever!"

"Sal, we are not doubting your abilities. You are a partner at the firm for a reason. They all fooled everyone. There is not one person who suspected any of this, so you need to stop beating yourself up. You did the same thing with David Flores when we told you not to. It's okay. We just want to hear everything from you," Alan said reassuringly.

"I know, but I keep thinking about what Thomas would think about all of this. I mean, he saw through everyone. Do you think he would have seen Sean for who he really was?" I asked both Alan and Steven.

"Sal, how many times did we get together with you and Danielle? Did Thomas ever say anything to you that she might not be who she said she was?" Steven asked.

He made a good point. I revered Thomas so much that I sometimes act as I think he would have instead of how I should act. I know Thomas would have been proud of me for turning Danielle in and handling the kids the way I am, but I still felt like I owed more to him.

"No, he didn't. I am just upset with myself for not seeing it at all."

Steven's phone began to ring but he declined the call. It rang again and he declined it again. After that, my phone and Alan's phone received text messages at the same time. When I looked at the message from Detective Marino, my mouth hit the floor.

David Flores was found shot to death in his apartment this morning.

There was stunned silence in the room. All three of us knew what had happened but didn't want to be the first one to say it. Finally, I broke the silence.

"So Sean killed David Flores and then left the country? Why?" I asked both Alan and Steven.

"Obviously tying up loose ends. It is a good thing you had Danielle arrested. In an ironic way, you saved her life without even knowing it," Alan offered.

That made me shiver all over because not only was it true, but it also meant that my children and I could be potential targets. With all the money Sean had and all the damage he was able to do inside Rikers Island, what's to say he couldn't do the same thing to me and my family from another country?

"Alan, Steven, can we finish this up another time? I feel I need to be home with my children for a while to protect them?"

"Absolutely. This can be done anytime. Nobody is going anywhere. Sal, remember we are here for you if you need anything," Alan said as he patted me on the shoulder.

"Thank you, Alan, I really appreciate it. I will keep you updated if I hear anything."

I left the office in such a hurry, I didn't say goodbye to Jill. The ride home felt like an eternity because all I wanted to do was get home to my kids. I knew my neighbors were watching them while I was at work, but I felt I needed to be the one with them. When I finally arrived home, the kids were playing in their rooms, and there was no sign of any disturbances anywhere. I thanked my neighbors for watching them, let my kids know I was home, and sat down at the kitchen table with my laptop to research where Sean Lancaster may have disappeared to.

Chapter 72

The next morning, I received a visit from Detective Marino. I was surprised to see him, especially at seven o'clock. I figured he had some news for me, which could either be good or bad. Either way, I let him in and gave him a cup of coffee to prepare for what I was sure to be a lengthy discussion.

"How are you doing, Sal?" Detective Marino asked.

"I am managing, Joe. It is tough, but I am still here. So what brings you here at this early hour?"

"I have some information on David Flores," Detective Marino said, catching me off guard.

"Oh? What sort of information?" I asked nervously.

"Well, we investigated the scene and determined he was killed execution style with a .44 Magnum Revolver."

"Isn't that a bit of overkill?" I asked.

"Yes, yes, it is. Whoever did this wanted him dead in a bad way."

"Come on, Joe, we both know it was Sean. Who else had motive to kill David?"

"Danielle did, but she's in jail. Do you think she could have hired a hit man?"

"Joe, at this point, anything is possible with her," I answered, shrugging my shoulders.

"Did she or Sean ever talk about guns?"

"Danielle never did, but Sean bragged about his collection all the time. Said he bought expensive guns just because he could."

"Did he ever tell you where he kept them?" Detective Marino asked while take copious notes.

"Yeah. He said he kept them in a hidden room behind his bedroom closet. He felt they would be safe there and wouldn't be tempted to use them. It felt strange at the time, but now it makes sense why he said that."

Even though I knew what was happening was real, everything still seemed surreal. Winning both the David Flores and Sean Lancaster cases should have been the highlights of my career. Something I looked back on with fond memories and inspiration when I needed a pick-me-up. Instead, they both have become nightmares.

"Before I go, can you think of anyone else who would want David Flores dead?" Detective Marino asked.

"Not off the top of my head. Everyone he was enemies with is either locked up or dead. If I think of anyone else, I will call you."

"Thank you, Sal," Detective Marino said as he stood up to leave. "I am sorry you have to go through this. Please, let me know if I can help you out with anything. I mean that, Sal. Anything."

"Thank you, Joe. I appreciate. Take care now."

"You as well."

Once Detective Marino left, I was too wound up to go back to sleep so I decided to make breakfast and catch up on some sports news. Opening day for the Yankees was around the corner, and the excitement for the upcoming season was building. I decided in that moment that I would take Gio to opening day, in hopes it will help him deal with what was going on. The smell from the bacon must have wafted upstairs because both Gio and Angela came running down the stairs.

"Daddy, that smells so good. Did you make some for us?" Angela asked.

"I sure did. You can have mine. I'll make more," I said as I kissed her head.

"Hey, Dad, I'm sorry about yesterday. I know I was wrong," Gio said, hoping for forgiveness.

"It's alright, son. I know we are all dealing with this in our own ways. Tell you what. How would you like to go to opening day at the Stadium?"

"Really? I would love that!" Gio said, bursting with excitement.

"What about me? What do I get?" Angela asked, annoyed.

"Well, I was thinking we can build that playroom you wanted."

"Yay! You are the best, Daddy! I am going to get started on drawing the plans right now," Angela said as she ran into the living room, forgetting about her breakfast.

As I sat there watching my two kids with smiles on their faces, I was brought back to my wedding day. When Danielle and I made a promise to be faithful to each other and be there for each other through sickness and health. Well, vows may not mean much to her, but they do to me. And I vowed that I would do whatever it took to make my kids happy. Seeing them on that morning without a care in the world made me feel like a proud father. The road ahead may be a long for all of us, but as long as I have Gio and Angela, I know that in the end, I will be alright.

Epilogue

"Can I put the final nail in, Daddy?" Angela asked me.

"Sure, just be careful. Don't hurt yourself," I said as I watched nervously.

Angela was a natural. She hit the last nail in place to complete her new playroom, which expanded the house another twenty feet. She had already begun to move her stuff from her bedroom into the new area before we finished. Now that we were done, she was excited to move the rest of her toys in there.

"Can I move my bed in here as well, Daddy?"

"No, angel," I said, laughing. "Your bed needs to stay in your room. This room is for your toys."

"Okay," Angela said, disappointed.

"Dad, hurry up. The game is about to begin!" Gio yelled.

Gio was always into watching the Yankees with me, but ever since we went to opening day and he got to meet Aaron Judge, he has become a fanatic.

"Be right there, Gio!" I yelled back.

"Angela, make sure to clean up after yourself every night, or I will put a lock on this door and you won't be able to use the room."

"Okay, Daddy. Thank you again for this. I am the happiest girl ever!" Angela said as she ran up to her room to grab her toys.

"Who is pitching for us again?" I asked.

"Gerrit Cole. He was awesome his last time out, so hopefully he continues it," Gio responded.

I was glad that Gio was handling the situation with Danielle better than I thought he would. It had been a few months since she was formally charged with the first-degree murders of Sean's family and her parents. I had told Gio a small portion of the truth but not everything. There were some details he did not need to know about. In time, he would be old enough to learn the full truth.

"Shall we order the usual?" I asked.

"You know it," Gio responded with a smile and rubbing his stomach.

I called the local pizzeria and ordered our usual Yankee Friday night meal: two large pepperoni pizzas with twelve buffalo wings. When I got off the phone with the pizzeria, I went to sit down next to Gio to watch the game. As soon as I sat down, my phone rang.

Without looking at the caller ID, I picked it up, trying to talk through my smile that was ear to ear.

"Hello? Sal, here."

"Hello, Sally baby! How are you?"

I got up immediately and went into the garage where nobody could hear me.

"What do you want, you asshole?" I said with rage.

"Temper, temper, Sal. That will get you nowhere," Sean replied.

"You have some nerve calling me. Where are you?" I asked, knowing Sean wasn't going to tell me.

"Sal, you know better than that. Just know that I am safe and doing well. Say, how is Danielle doing in jail?" Sean asked, teasing me.

"What do you want, Sean?"

"I just wanted to see how my buddy was doing and to say I'm sorry for everything I put you through."

"*No! No!* You don't get to apologize to me. You hear me? You do not get to apologize for ruining my life!" I screamed, suddenly afraid Gio would hear me.

"You really are a piece of work, Sal," Sean said, laughing. "I don't care a wit if you accept my apology. At least I know I tried. I know you have your phone tapped, at least I hope you do, for your sake, so I am getting off now and won't let you trace this call. I'll leave you with this. Know that wherever you go and whatever you do, someone might be watching you. Until next time, *ciao*," Sean said, then hung up the phone.

In that moment, I was so angry and frustrated I almost threw my phone against the wall. Just when I had been able to begin to move on with my life, Sean found a way to drag me back down. I had to calm down before I went back into the room with Gio, so I went to get a breath of fresh air. As soon as I hit the air outside, I stopped dead in my tracks and thought, *Did Sean just give me a hint as to where he is?*

I immediately called Detective Marino to tell him about my conversation with Sean. Most importantly, how he ended the call. *Ciao!* That is how they say goodbye in Italy. I thought to myself that it couldn't be that easy. Sean does not make mistakes like that. Detective Marino agreed with me and said he would alert the authorities in Italy right away.

I knew it was a long shot, and I was no detective, so there was nothing else I could do in that moment. I decided it was best to go back to Gio and watch the ballgame to take my mind off of Sean. When I got back in the house, I received a text message. One that literally brought me to my knees.

Tell Detective Marino you were right about where I am. Happy hunting, Sal!

About the Author

dam Klein can usually be found reading several suspense thrillers per month. Writing a novel has been a dream of his since he was twelve, and, eventually, with *Unlawful Games*, that dream became a reality. Adam holds a master's degree in Higher Education Leadership and earned a perfect score on his thesis paper. When not reading the latest thriller, Adam enjoys cooking and watching TV. He lives in New Jersey with his wife, son, and Chihuahua.

www.ingramcontent.com/pod-product-compliance
Lightning Source LLC
Chambersburg PA
CBHW030805180726
47991CB00024B/214